RIDING GAIN

***Also by Joyce Krieg
in Large Print:***

Murder Off Mike
Slip Cue

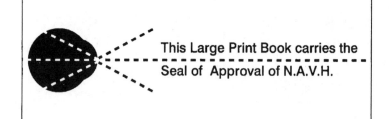

This Large Print Book carries the
Seal of Approval of N.A.V.H.

RIDING GAIN

A Talk Radio Mystery

Joyce Krieg

Published in 2006 by arrangement with St. Martin's Press, LLC.

Wheeler Large Print Hardcover.

The text of this Large Print edition is unabridged.
Other aspects of the book may vary from the original edition.

Set in 16 pt. Plantin by Christina S. Huff.

Printed in the United States on permanent paper.

Library of Congress Cataloging-in-Publication Data

Krieg, Joyce.
   Riding gain : a talk radio mystery / by Joyce Krieg.
     p.   cm. — (Wheeler Publishing large print hardcover)
   ISBN 1-59722-183-X (lg. print : hc : alk. paper)
   1. Bogart, Shauna J. (Fictitious character) — Fiction.
2. Women in radio broadcasting — Fiction.   3. Radio
broadcasters — Fiction.   4. Sacramento (Calif.) — Fiction.
5. Talk shows — Fiction.   I. Title.   II. Wheeler large print
hardcover series.
PS3611.R54R53 2006
                                              2005033292

To
Steve Krieg and Nikki Ausschnitt,
Proprietors of the
Original Wertheim's Pine Rest

As the Founder/CEO of NAVH, the only national health agency solely devoted to those who, although not totally blind, have an eye disease which could lead to serious visual impairment, I am pleased to recognize Thorndike Press* as one of the leading publishers in the large print field.

Founded in 1954 in San Francisco to prepare large print textbooks for partially seeing children, NAVH became the pioneer and standard setting agency in the preparation of large type.

Today, those publishers who meet our standards carry the prestigious "Seal of Approval" indicating high quality large print. We are delighted that Thorndike Press is one of the publishers whose titles meet these standards. We are also pleased to recognize the significant contribution Thorndike Press is making in this important and growing field.

Lorraine H. Marchi, L.H.D.
Founder/CEO
NAVH

* Thorndike Press encompasses the following imprints: Thorndike, Wheeler, Walker and Large Print Press.

Acknowledgments

Talk about life imitating art! Just as I was putting the finishing touches on the manuscript of *Riding Gain*, the news flashed over the well-oiled radio industry gossip grapevine that the station in Sacramento upon which this series is based had decided to cut costs by permanently grounding its airborne traffic reporters. It's a scenario being played out at stations across the country, as well as in the pages of this novel. The thinking seems to be that with Web cams on every freeway overpass and sensors embedded in the roadways, who needs the expense of the "eye in the sky"? The new technology may be more efficient, but it will never deliver warmth, personality, trust, and friendship — the intangibles that make radio great. To "Commander" Bill Eveland and Joe Miano, the real-life inspirations for the "Captain Mikey" character on these pages, I salute you.

Writing is a solitary occupation, but no book is produced in a vacuum. Editor Ruth

Cavin's comments are always helpful and right on the mark. It's obvious why she's referred to as "The Legendary Ruth Cavin" in the mystery community. Grateful thanks also go to editorial assistant Toni Plummer at St. Martin's Minotaur and agent extraordinaire Jimmy Vines. I appreciate Tom Burns for helping me get all the "airplane stuff" right. A special thanks to Hugo Gerstl for his friendship and support.

My depiction of the recovery industry is admittedly biased, and is based on my observation of one friend's experience. It is often said that no treatment program will succeed unless the individual truly wants to change, and I suppose that's true. All I know is, no one cried out for help more than he did, but there was no help to be found — at least not in this world.

"Riding gain" is a way of controlling the volume — and other characteristics — of a radio program as it goes on the air. (This explains why commercials sometimes seem louder than the program itself. They haven't necessarily been that way originally.) At big stations the engineer handles the control board, but in one like Shauna J. Bogart's, the program host does it during the broadcast.

1

The Datsun 240Z swerved off the frontage road and scudded into the parking lot. The pilot's logbook launched off the dashboard, somersaulted past the radio, and made a three-point landing on the passenger seat.

At eight minutes after the hour, you're tuned in to Shauna J. Bogart on Sacramento Talk Radio.

Late. Two minutes and thirty seconds, but still late.

Who could have predicted a police action on Business 80 heading out of downtown, grinding all three eastbound lanes of traffic to a standstill as the freeway crossed the American River? And I, trapped in a tiny sports car in the fast left lane, guardrail and then sheer drop to the river to the left, big rig loaded with gravel on the right, VW bus spewing fumes to the front, and red pickup truck breathing down my neck from the rear. Nowhere to go, nothing to do but wait it out.

Caller, what's your point?

My point? If you're such a big star, when are you going to play a request for the A.V. Club?

I parked the Z-car in an unmarked spot that captured a few square yards of crisp shadow cast by a massive valley oak. It was January, with temperatures peaking in the upper forties, which meant I really didn't need to find a shady parking spot. But after I had survived the searing heat of three Sacramento summers, the reflex to always leave the car in the shade had become permanently imprinted.

You're listening to Shauna J. Bogart on Sacramento Talk Radio. We'll be back right after this.

I shut off the engine, flipped up the hood of my down jacket against the brisk winter wind, trotted across the asphalt, and pushed open a heavy glass door.

The first commercial in the stop-set blared from a speaker mounted in the corner of the lobby. I ignored the receptionist's outstretched handful of phone messages and jammed through the door to the on-air studio. A vinyl banner stretched over the top of the door proclaimed in black and red letters, "Family-owned and independent since 1957."

I'm Shauna J. Bogart, host of the afternoon chat fest on Sacramento Talk Radio, and no, I don't normally make it a habit to bop into the studio at the last minute. But this day was turning out to be anything but normal.

My producer looked up from the broadcast console, where he'd been airing canned, generic bits from previous shows. *Caller, what's your point? We'll be right back after this message. At eight minutes past the hour . . .* Pre-recorded one-liners burned onto a CD for emergency situations just like this.

"You're late," Josh Friedman said.

"Tell me something I don't already know." I ignored his unspoken plea for an explanation.

"Almost ten minutes." Josh tapped his finger against a button to activate the CD with my theme music.

"Three minutes. Four, tops. The network newscast doesn't count." An unwritten rule of radio has it that the host is considered to be on time as long as she's in front of the microphone ready to talk when the top-of-the-hour network newscast ends. At my station, the network signs off at five minutes and thirty seconds past the hour. Ten minutes late? I think not.

"My lunch ran long," I said to Josh. "Captain Mikey didn't get me back to Executive Airport until almost two-thirty, and then I got caught in this huge traffic tie-up on Biz 80 going over the American River. Thanks for covering." I placed the headphones over my ears, adjusted the mike upward, and gave the chair just vacated by my producer a gentle kick into the corner. I like to stand when I'm on the air. Keeps the energy level high, lets me pace. Some people jog, some folks take spinning classes, some strange souls even engage in hot yoga. I pace.

The theme music faded and I could hear the roar of afternoon traffic on Highway 160 through the bulletproof glass. I took a deep breath and flicked the switch controlling the microphone. "You're back with Shauna J. Bogart on Sacramento Talk Radio. Caller, you were saying?"

"Haven't you been paying attention? You know, playing a request for Mr. Halstead and the guys in the A.V. Club?"

The voice was male, slow and deliberate, as if he were pondering each word choice, slight lilt of sarcasm. Could it be . . . ?

"Who's this, and where are you calling from?"

"You can call me Reg. Reg on a cell phone."

"Welcome to the show, Reg."

12

"Next time you're hanging out with your important friends in the news media, think about the guys back in the A.V. Club. Think about your pals in the Reginald Fessenden Royal Riding Gain Academy."

The academy? I don't think I'd heard anyone mention that in at least twenty years. "This better not be a joke," I said.

"Chill out." A chuckle sent another punch of recognition to my gut. "We won't get suspended this time."

I couldn't stand it any longer. "Richie, is that you?"

But the line was dead.

During the next break, Josh handed me the wad of phone messages that he'd rescued from the receptionist.

Doyle Bollinger from RadioLand, wanting to know if I'd take a meeting with him.

The public relations director of the Footprints Institute, hoping to land some airtime for the executive director.

Three messages from Fred Buchanan, program director of one of the major news and talk stations in San Francisco, requesting that I call back ASAP.

"One more thing," Josh said as I scanned the flimsy pink message slips. "O'Brien wants to see you in his office before you go home."

I returned the call from San Francisco the first chance I had, during the local news break at the bottom of the hour. From the in-studio speaker, I could hear Captain Mikey reporting from his eye in the sky. "It continues to be slow and go on Business 80 as both right lanes of the eastbound freeway have been closed by police."

My stomach clenched in anticipation as the receptionist in San Francisco punched me through to Fred Buchanan. I knew they'd narrowed it down to me and one other person to co-host the morning show. I'd been waiting for almost a week now for a decision.

"Sorry to be the bearer of bad news," Buchanan said after I'd identified myself.

Oh.

"I wanted to give you the gig, I really did," Buchanan continued.

I remained silent, trying to digest what I was hearing. So much for moving back to the city by the bay.

"Hey, I grew up listening to you." Buchanan sounded uncomfortable. "But the consultant said we need a younger sound. You know how it goes."

Did I really want to work for someone who would let a consultant convince him the station needed a "younger sound," whatever that might be? For the chance to go back to a major market — and for the kind of dough they were offering — damn right.

I told Buchanan sure, I know how it goes.

I crumpled all three of Buchanan's message slips, chucked them into the trash can, and willed myself to wipe the just-concluded phone call from my mind as easily as I'd destroyed the tangible evidence. As I opened the microphone, I forced a smile back into my voice and steeled myself to project an image of upbeat confidence with my listeners.

The police action on Business 80 and the resulting traffic jam continued to unfold during my show, dominating the local headlines. I was glad to keep busy juggling the reports from Captain Mikey in the traffic plane, dispatches from our reporter on the ground, and calls from listeners who saw — or thought they saw — the whole thing happen. It kept me from obsessing about the lost opportunity in San Francisco, and the reason behind it. "Younger sound" indeed! You're looking at someone who has at least another decade to go before they start bombarding me with applications to join AARP.

"Sources with the Sacramento Police Department tell us the incident began with a shooting in McKinley Park at around two this afternoon," Gloria Louise Montalvo reported via two-way radio from the field. "One of the suspects fled by car onto Business 80, where he was overtaken by police on the American River Bridge."

"McKinley Park?" I interrupted Glory Lou's report. "Can you confirm that?"

"I'm stationed at the command post on the jogging path at Alhambra Boulevard at H Street. I'm looking at the police tape strung out between the trees behind the swimming pool."

McKinley Park for certain. Now that was a surprise. McKinley Park, its swimming pool, tennis courts, branch library, rose garden, and duck pond, stood at the entrance of one of the capital city's most desirable neighborhoods, a community of well-tended homes from before the Second World War, quiet, tree-lined streets, good public schools. No urban area can claim to be completely crime-free these days, but a shooting on the sedate, manicured lawns of McKinley Park would still be a major local story.

"The suspect appears to have been driving a small foreign car, a Toyota, possibly, or a Honda, orange in color," Captain

16

Mikey reported from the traffic plane. "I can see a small foreign car surrounded by at least five Sacramento police cruisers and two vehicles from the CHP in the far right lane on Business 80. Traffic on the eastbound lanes of the freeway is backed up all the way to Fruitridge Road."

I put Glory Lou back on the air for an extended Q-and-A from the command post. "What can you tell us about the victim?"

"Little is known at this time." Glory Lou's voice crackled through the two-way. "Male, late teens or early twenties. He's been taken to the Med Center. Authorities are releasing no information about his identity or his condition."

Now, this is going to sound cold, but the fact is the real story was unfolding not on the blood-soaked grass of McKinley Park but a few miles away on the freeway, where hundreds of late afternoon commuters were stranded. I wrapped up the interview with Glory Lou and directed my attention back to the airborne traffic reporter.

"Captain Mikey, can you recommend any alternate routes out of the downtown area?"

"There's always Highway 160, but a lot of folks have the same idea and it's backed up almost — wait! The suspect just tossed

17

something over the bridge —" the traffic pilot's voice accelerated its staccato pace — "It looks like — yes!"

I flinched as the control room door opened and a woman strode in. Dorinda Delgado, the station's sales manager. She held a compact disc jewel case in her right hand and began jabbering at me about making a substitution for one of her client's commercials. "They're one of our biggest sponsors, so don't screw up," she added.

"Can't you tell we're in the middle of a breaking news story?" I snatched the CD case and forced my concentration back on the drama unfolding on Business 80. What was it with radio salespeople, barging into a live studio just because one of their precious clients broke a nail? If Dorinda Delgado thought I was going to pause for a commercial break while thousands of our listeners waited to find out what would happen next out there on the American River Bridge, she was even more clueless than I'd suspected.

"He's climbed over the guardrail," Captain Mikey said over the two-way. "The police are starting to advance — he's falling! The suspect's either been shot or he jumped. It's hard to tell from up here —"

My right hand gripped the slider on the broadcast console that controlled the volume, riding gain on the sound coming from the airplane. "We're staying right with you, Captain."

They finally fished the suspect out of the river at around five-fifteen and rushed him to the Med Center. Whoever he was, he was lucky it had been a relatively dry winter, meaning the Bureau of Reclamation was hoarding water upstream in Nimbus Dam. During periods of heavy rain, the waters of the American River surged swiftly, and the suspect — or what was left of him — would have been halfway to San Francisco by now.

Just after the five o'clock newscast, Glory Lou called in with a bulletin. The still-unnamed victim had been dead on arrival at the Med Center.

"That caller acted like he knew you," Josh said just after I'd finished the show. "Personally, I mean."

I looked up from the program log, where I'd been scrawling my legal name onto the bottom of the three pages representing the three hours of airtime for which I was responsible. "Who's that?"

"That guy right at the start of the show. Reg on a cell phone."

"Oh, him."

"Yeah. So you do know him, then."

"You might say that." I gathered up my headphones, file folder of news clippings and show notes, and feigned disinterest.

Richie Snelling from the Audio-Visual Club. The kid who stood up for the only girl in the geekiest club in high school.

"He sounded familiar there for a minute, but I must have been mistaken," I told Josh.

Richie Snelling. My junior prom date.

Last I heard, he was serving eighteen months in the federal pen in Lompoc.

2

"I'm really, really sorry I was late." I strode into the boss's office and seated myself in the centermost of the half-dozen guest chairs arranged in a semicircle around the front of his executive throne. I hoped by starting with an apology I might deflate his upcoming lecture.

"I know I let you down, and the entire station," I continued. "But Captain Mikey invited me to come with him to the Airborne Traffic Reporters' quarterly lunch meeting, remember?" I had a momentary vision of riding shotgun in the four-seater Bonanza for the short flight from Sacramento to the Nut Tree Airport, brilliant blue sky washed clean by a storm the previous day, the checkerboard fields and swollen rivers of the Sacramento Valley giving way to the hills of Vacaville, green from the recent rain.

"The meeting ran late, and we didn't get back to Executive Airport until around two-thirty. And then I got caught in that big traffic jam on Business 80. It won't happen again, I promise."

T. R. O'Brien looked up from the stack of paperwork on his desk, where he'd been scratching his name on what looked to me like a backlog of network clearance affidavits. "Now Missy, what have I always told you?" He stabbed the index finger of his good right hand in my direction. His left hand consisted of a silver prosthesis, souvenir of a land mine in Korea.

I responded with a puzzled look.

"Never complain, never explain. Shoot, I never even noticed you were late. So stop digging yourself into a hole."

I sagged back in the chair, momentarily relieved to have escaped a scolding but still anxious over the reason for the summons to the executive suite. Had O'Brien gotten wind that I was sending out audition tapes and résumés to larger-market stations? Jeez, everyone in the business does that. It's not that I was unhappy at Sacramento Talk Radio. T. R. O'Brien was a good guy, a scrappy independent holdout among all the corporate clones. He'd rescued me from the creative desert of commercial music radio three years ago and given me free reign to do and say anything I wanted on my show, as long as I brought in the ratings and didn't scare away too many advertisers. But I felt as if I'd earned my chops in medium-market talk radio and felt I was ready to move on to the big time. As that program director in San Francisco had reminded me, my old age was rapidly approaching. I couldn't afford to wait much longer to make my move.

"Does the name Clarissa St. Cyr ring any bells with you?" O'Brien said.

"Possibly." I searched my memory bank. Stripper? Soap star? "Doesn't she write a column for the *Sacramento News and Review*? Some woo-woo New Age stuff?"

"A psychic, or so she claims. Talks to dead people and all that."

"What about her?"

"That little lady is going to be doing a show for our station. Isn't that jim-dandy?" O'Brien's weather-beaten face creased in a wide grin.

I choked back several replies, none of them polite. Finally I said, "You mean like a special? Something for Valentine's Day maybe?"

"Every night." O'Brien's voice cackled with enthusiasm. "Monday through Friday, nine to midnight."

"Interesting idea," I said slowly, picking my words with great care. "But do you think it's right for our image?"

"Let's go outside."

O'Brien led me through a side door to a patio that consisted of a cement picnic table and benches, a patch of dirt with three camellia bushes in full, glorious bloom, and a circular, galvanized steel receptacle with a long neck. "Park your butts here" was painted on one side. Class, real class. I folded my arms against my chest and leaned against the door, hoping to soak up some warmth from inside the building.

I waited for O'Brien to light up a cigarette and exhale. "When you're fighting a one-man battle against major corporate broadcasters like Federated Communications, you can't afford to be picky about things like image," he said.

"But a psychic? What, is she going to start predicting the news for us?"

O'Brien allowed himself a snort of laughter. "We tried her out on the overnight show last weekend and the phone lines lit up like Christmas in Tijuana."

"I just wonder what this will do to our credibility as a news and information source." I also wondered what Clarissa St. Cyr had to do with me.

"It's like I'm tryin' to tell you, that's a luxury this station can't afford right about now." Even after almost seventy years in

California, O'Brien's voice still clung to traces of his Dust Bowl origins.

"But that's not why we're having this conversation." I strained to read the expression on O'Brien's face in the dim light, but all I could make out was the red glow from the tip of the cigarette.

"She's going to be doing a regular guest appearance on your show. Monday, Wednesday, and Friday from five-thirty to six. Starting this Friday."

"No way!" This time, I didn't bother to edit my comments.

"I was afraid that's how you'd take it."

"C'mon, you can't be serious!" A wingnut like Clarissa St. Cyr would drive away all my regular listeners and tear down everything I'd done to present myself as the voice of reason and authority.

"It's not permanent, just until she gets her show up and running."

I drew my arms closer to my chest. "You sold the airtime to her, didn't you?" There's nothing illegal about a radio station brokering its airtime to anyone who wants to buy a show. But like accepting payment for playing a pop star's new release, it raises a host of sticky ethical issues. "What was I, some sort of bonus you threw in to seal the deal? A gift with purchase?"

"I'm going to announce it at a staff meeting tomorrow." O'Brien stuffed the remains of his cigarette into the long neck of the "park your butt" container, opened the door, and motioned me inside. "At least give me credit for tellin' you before everyone else found out."

I scrolled through the *Sacramento Bee*'s Internet archives until I found the correct date from this past June and clicked on the headline.

"High-tech Exec Begins Prison Term"

The story hadn't been quite big enough to rate the front page. But Richard Snelling was a big name in electronics, prominent enough to earn the number one page of the business section, above the fold.

"Snelling was one of several executives and board members involved in and convicted of securities fraud. In return for cooperating with the SEC, Snelling was allowed to plead to a lesser charge and serve his term at the minimum security federal prison in Lompoc."

Richard Snelling. Sweet Richie, the only boy in the Audio-Visual Club who didn't think it was odd that a girl — a freshman girl at that — wanted to join. He was the first member to support me in petitioning our faculty adviser to allow us to start a noon-hour radio station on the campus public address system. And the co-conspirator who joined me in concocting the Reginald Fessenden Royal Riding Gain Academy.

Our paths diverged after high school, but I kept up with Richie's career via the business pages of the local papers. In classic revenge-of-the-nerds–style, he amassed millions by inventing a library automation software system, then spent several of those millions on big boy toys like a private plane and pilot's license. If you're old enough to remember thumbing through thousands of index cards to search the library catalog, you can thank Richard Snelling for inventing Ref-X and putting all that data onto a hard drive.

If Richie read the same newspapers as I did, and happened to glance at the entertainment pages or the local celebrity gossip columns, he could have stayed current with his old pal from high school. Perhaps Richie smiled to himself as he ran across my name, secretly pleased that I, too, had managed to transcend the A.V. Club and score a victory for geek girls everywhere.

I pressed CONTROL-P to make a hard copy of Richie's latest foray into the headlines, checking in to the "Club Fed" in

Lompoc, the same joint where the Watergate conspirators had served out their terms.

The printer spat out two sheets of paper. I folded the *Bee* article and placed it in my backpack. That caller had sounded like Richie, or what I imagined a forty-year-old Richie might sound like. And who else would remember the Reginald Fessenden Riding Gain Academy?

Since when does a federal prison, no matter how cushy, allow its inmates to make calls to radio talk shows?

The door slammed open and Glory Lou strode into the newsroom with a blast of arctic air and a flurry of gloves, CD recorder, notebook, and sack from her favorite Mexican take-out place. She pulled up a chair next to mine, settled herself in, and kicked off her pumps.

"Long day," I said by way of greeting.

"Yeah." Gone was her usual zest for chasing after a breaking story, and her melodious Southern charm.

"Hey, I'm really sorry I was late today. It won't happen again, I promise." As news director, Glory Lou was technically my immediate boss. But the line separating friendship and work had grown fuzzy between us. She wouldn't turn chilly over my being three minutes late, would she?

"You know that story I was working this afternoon? The shooting in McKinley Park?"

"Of course." My show had been filled with little else.

"They just released the identity of the victim."

"Go on."

"It was Travis."

"Travis the intern?"

"Unbelievable, isn't it, hon?"

Unbelievable, for sure.

No big surprise either.

3

The scent of men's cologne fought to gain control over the reek of sweat, and lost. An aroma of breath mints almost, but not quite, masked various digestive ailments of twenty-five anxious bodies, packed around a table that seated twelve. I'd arrived early and managed to secure a seat at the conference room table. The stragglers leaned against beige plaster walls or hunkered down on the floor.

Nervous conversation hushed as T. R. O'Brien entered, followed by Dorinda Delgado. She wore black wool slacks and an oversize yellow mohair sweater, making her look like a creature hatched by Big Bird.

"I know you're itchin' to know why I called you in here this morning." O'Brien tucked the legal pad he'd been carrying into his artificial hand and jabbed the air with his right forefinger, JFK-style.

"I don't need to tell you how competitive this business has become, what with all the consolidations and mergers."

"T.R.'s right," Delgado said. "We are engaged in a struggle that will require nothing less than a paradigm shift in our core values, a cross-pollination of our commitment to our mission statement."

Enough with the management psychobabble. Just get on with it. I knew O'Brien had called the mandatory-attendance staff meeting to drop the news about Clarissa St. Cyr. But what else was happening? I could sense the anxiety churning through the collective souls crammed in the conference room. Are we changing format? All sports? Do we still have jobs?

T.R. consulted the legal pad. "Effective immediately, we're outsourcing airborne traffic. We'll be getting traffic reports from City Scope from now on."

Murmurs of shock and disapproval filled the conference room.

"Now just hold your horses," O'Brien said. "Nothin' bad's happening to Captain Mikey. He'll be on our air, same's always. His check will come from City Scope Media Services 'stead of us, that's all."

Yeah, right. Nothing's going to change. How many times had I been fed that not-so-little white lie by radio station management types over the years?

"Now here's some news I think you'll all

31

be tickled to hear." O'Brien flipped a sheet on the legal pad with the hook. "How many of you have heard of a little lady named Clarissa St. Cyr?"

You can't outsource someone like Captain Mikey! He'd been a fixture on the Sacramento airwaves for more than two decades. If a legend like Captain Mikey wasn't invulnerable, then what did it portend for the rest of us?

O'Brien and Delgado concluded the meeting with the usual platitudes about maintaining a positive attitude when the news hit the streets. I don't think any of us paid much attention. We shuffled silently out of the conference room, relieved we weren't holding severance checks or signing up for Spanish lessons.

I felt around the front pocket of my jeans for the business card I'd been carrying around for almost a month now. Doyle Bollinger at RadioLand. I supposed I'd better take that meeting with him, assuming he was still interested.

After all, if they can outsource Captain Mikey, they could certainly do the same to Shauna J. Bogart.

A gentle tap on my shoulder. Glory Lou, motioning me back into the now-deserted conference room.

"Just wondering if you'd heard from Travis's family yet."

I leaned against the curved edge of the table and shook my head. "I know I should call his mom, but I just can't. Not yet, anyway."

"I hear you, hon. I swear, I picked up that phone at least three times this morning and started dialing, and then stopped halfway through."

I stared at the gray industrial carpeting, rubbed smooth by years of rolling pressure from the wheels of the conference room chairs. "I thought he was doing so well. Stopped partying, was really concentrating on his studies."

"I know, I know."

"I didn't even realize Travis was back in Sacramento. Last I heard, he was still down at UCLA. Should have been in his senior year by now."

"You did everything you could for that young man." Glory Lou gave my shoulder a squeeze.

"We all did."

"They can't outsource Captain Mikey!" Josh Friedman balanced two clear plastic bags on my desk in the newsroom.

"They can and they did." I pushed a pile

33

of newspapers and press releases to one side of the desk and motioned to Josh and Glory Lou to pull up chairs.

"Welcome to radio, hon," Glory Lou said. She undid the knots in the plastic handles, removed one of the take-out containers, and pried open the lid. "Yum, who wants spring rolls?"

"But I don't get it," Josh said. "Everyone in Sacramento listens to his traffic reports. You can't just outsource a legend."

"How long have you been hanging around here?" I stabbed at a mound of rice with a plastic fork. "Almost a year now? Haven't you figured it out by now?"

"It's the money, honey," Glory Lou said. "It costs this station around a quarter-million dollars a year to keep Captain Mikey in the air every day. That'll cover the salaries of quite a few college student producers like you."

"But the station is going to have to pay City Scope to get Captain Mikey's services. So what's the difference?"

Glory Lou and I exchanged slow shakes of head. Had we ever been that naïve?

"We're not going to give City Scope a penny," Glory Lou said.

"Heard about a thing called barter?" I said.

"Kind of." Josh looked doubtful.

"City Scope will sell commercials inside Captain Mikey's traffic reports. We air the commercials, City Scope keeps the money. More than likely, they'll expect him to do a live read."

"I can just imagine how excited he's going to be about that," Glory Lou put in. "As I live and breathe."

"It gets even worse," I said between bites of kung pao chicken. "Now that he's under contract to City Scope instead of us, they'll expect Captain Mikey to do traffic reports for more than one station. I'll bet he'll be flying for at least two other radio outlets and maybe a TV station as well."

"Your average listener will never notice," Glory Lou said. "But just to make sure, they'll give him a new name for those other stations. Say hello to Snoop Dog Michael in the 'hood."

"Sacramento Police say the man arrested after a stand-off on Business 80 yesterday afternoon is the prime suspect in the death of Travis Ikeda-Nyland." Glory Lou's eyes followed the copy on a computer monitor as she spoke into the guest microphone in the on-air studio. The shooting in McKinley Park the previous afternoon led the 3:30 pm local newscast. "The suspect, identified as nineteen-year-old Markitus Wilson of Rancho Cordova, remains in critical condition at the Med Center. The twenty-one-year-old victim is the son of Sacramento television personality Sapphire Ikeda and local car dealer Ray Nyland. Authorities say they found a small amount of the street drug crystal meth in the victim's clothing, and they believe the shooting may have been the result of a dispute over a drug deal."

I peered through the window separating the talk studio from the call screener booth where Josh Friedman had a telephone receiver tucked between his neck and shoulder, one finger on the hold button, and one hand scribbling notes.

Eighteen months ago, Travis Ikeda-Nyland had occupied that same booth.

I'd resisted taking Travis on as a summer intern at first. *I've got more important things to do than babysit a poor little rich kid with a substance abuse problem,* I remembered telling T. R. O'Brien. *You just want me to do this because the Nyland Automotive Group is a major advertiser.* But the kid turned out to be brighter than I'd expected, quick with the witty one-liners, and I gradually warmed to him. Not that there weren't problems. His attendance was spotty, and there'd be days when he showed up stinking like the morning after an all-night kegger at the frat house. But even at his worst moments, Travis Ikeda-Nyland exhibited an underlying layer of kindness and generosity of spirit that I found endearing in someone so young.

I decided to employ the tactic of assuming the best of him, treating him as just another member of the team instead of a charity case. Damned if he didn't rise to the occasion, or so I thought. By the end of the summer, he was almost always on time, showered, shaved, and clothed in clean cargo pants and T-shirt. We exchanged regular e-mails when he returned to UCLA that fall, and a year later, I received a photograph of him standing in front of the BBC during a semester spent in London.

The e-mails had tapered off in recent months; in fact, I couldn't recall when I'd heard from him last or what he had to say. That realization filled me with guilt and regret. How could I have grown so complacent about someone I cared about?

Easy. Life happens. Kids grow up, friends move on.

I still felt guilty as hell.

 * * *

I hadn't kept up with anyone from high school other than Richie, never attended a reunion. Those carefree days of youth had, for me, consisted of one continuous bout of adolescent angst, the only respite those few hours with the A.V. Club.

No school chums to call, no yearbooks to browse. So I took the easy way out and did a Google search. After a couple of false hits, up popped one Halstead, Eugene, member of the board of something called the Silicon Valley Historic Computer Preservation Society. A phone number in the 408 area code followed. I recognized the exchange as one of several in the immediate neighborhood of the old high school.

I punched in the number and sank back on the couch in my downtown apartment. Through the sliding glass door leading to the balcony, I could see the high-rise corporate headquarters and government office buildings one street over on Capitol Mall. On winter evenings like this, when it was too cold to sit out on the balcony and gaze down at the traffic on I-5, I amused myself by watching the lights wink on and off in the monoliths as the cleaning crews made their rounds.

A woman's voice answered on the fourth

38

ring. Her voice was abrupt and out of breath, as if she'd bolted out of bed expecting bad news. I glanced at my watch. Sheesh, only a little after nine. That's not too late for a social call, is it?

"Eugene, it's for you," she hollered before I had the chance to verify that I had reached the home of the onetime A.V. Club faculty adviser. I could hear the sound of a television in the background and figured I must have interrupted a rerun of *Stargate* on the SciFi channel.

"Of course I remember you," he gushed as soon as I gave him my real name. "The first girl in the Audio-Visual Club, how could I forget?"

"For real. Listen, just wondered —" I glanced down at my notepad, where I had jotted a few reminders.

"I was just thinking about getting in touch with you. This is really most extraordinary."

"How's that?" Out my window, the fifteenth-floor lights of the Wells Fargo building blinked off and the sixteenth floor blazed on.

"Extraordinary, just extraordinary." He sounded like a kid who'd just figured out how to blow up the chemistry lab.

"So you've heard from him too, then."

4

"You ever think about getting in touch with the kids you used to hang around with in high school?" I bobbled a teabag in a cardboard cup of steaming water and watched the liquid turn from tan to brown. "I mean, like the girl you took to the prom?"

"The one that got away." Michael Giordano — Captain Mikey to the listeners — took a tentative sip of coffee, then placed the cup on a Formica-topped table to let it cool. "Sure. We all do, don't we?"

We were the only customers in the pilots' lounge at Executive Airport, home base to Captain Mikey and most of the other airborne traffic reporters in the Sacramento area. With its Art Moderne terminal and tower, Executive Airport could have stood in for the airfield in any number of classic films. Rick and Ilse, saying good-bye on the rain-slicked runway before he puts her on the last flight to Lisbon. The commercial airlines abandoned Executive Airport in favor of Sacramento International thirty-plus years ago, but Sacramento's original airport, only a fifteen-minute drive from downtown, still did a brisk business in private aviation.

A couple of months ago, I finally accepted Captain Mikey's repeated invitation to join him for a spin in the traffic plane. Was I nervous when I clambered into the passenger seat of the Beechcraft Bonanza and strapped myself in? More like terrified. But something in Captain Mikey's calm, confident manner coaxed me into opening my eyes and relaxing my death grip on the armrests as we zoomed off the runway and soared into the skies above Sacramento. As we circled over the rivers and freeways of the capital city, I began to appreciate the beauty, challenge, and sheer adventure of flight.

Since that day, I've started dropping by Executive Airport every chance I get at eleven-thirty, when Captain Mikey takes to the air for his traffic reports in the noon newscast, and hopping on board. He's let me take the stick a few times, even guided me through a landing and takeoff. At the Airborne Traffic Reporters' lunch the other day, he presented me with my very own pilot's logbook to record my flights. I'm not sure if I actually want to go for a pilot's license, or if I'll ever work up the courage to solo, but in the meantime I'm having one thrilling time.

Not today, though. All air traffic had once again been grounded, victims of a dense layer of fog that radiated from marshy areas on cold mornings and evenings in the winter months. The locals call it tule fog, a reference to the reeds and cattails that flourish in the damp. Since California's great Central Valley is basically one big swamp, despite more than a century of efforts to drain it and tame it, Sacramento is usually enshrouded in bone-chilling gray mist from late November until the first of February, the occasional rainstorm providing the only respite. Commercial flights are routinely delayed or rerouted, and you can count on at least one horrendous, multi-vehicle crash on I-5 every season, drivers literally blinded by the nasty stuff. When Carl Sandburg wrote about the fog coming on little cat feet, he obviously had never spent a winter in Sacramento. Fog coming in like Sasquatch is more like it.

"Thinking about it is one thing," I said. "But have you ever done a Google search on one of the girls you dated in high school? Actually tracked her down and called her?"

Michael took another test sip of coffee.

Even after twenty years of retirement, he still bore himself like an Air Force man, steel crew cut, taut posture, leather windbreaker.

"Another chance at love," he said. "Sounds like you've been reading too many romance novels."

"I know this is going to sound crazy." I told him about the listener who'd dialed in to the show yesterday, Reg on a cell phone, who reminded me of the closest thing I had to a high school boyfriend. "Turns out, one of our teachers back in high school got a strange e-mail a few days ago, asking questions about the A.V. Club and the campus radio station. Whoever sent the e-mail wanted information about the kids we went to school with. The class president, cheerleaders, kids like that."

"Seems to me that e-mail could have come from anyone from your high school during the years you were a student there."

"Mr. Halstead told me there was a lot of specific detail that not many people would know or remember. He mentioned this little secret society we formed. Basically, we were the only two members."

"Seems like any or all of your other classmates might remember that. Did you ask your teacher if he might be able to trace the origin of the e-mail?"

"It came from a Hotmail account, so I doubt it."

"Well there you go, then."

"There is this other consideration."

"Really?" Michael leaned forward. "He's got a wife and kids stashed away in Fiji? He's had a sex change operation? He suffers from amnesia?"

"Now who's been reading too many romance novels. He's had a little trouble with the law." I resumed dunking the tea bag, too fast this time, sending droplets of brown liquid over the Formica. "He's serving time in federal prison, if you must know."

Michael whistled and shook his head. "No one can say you don't lead an interesting life, Bogart."

"Yeah, well, what I want to know is, if he's behind bars, what the hell is he doing calling radio talk shows and sending e-mails?"

Michael pulled a PalmPilot from the inside pocket of his windbreaker and punched instructions with a stylus. "Looks like I'll be flying a desk at City Scope for the rest of the day," he said after scanning the latest weather conditions.

"So you're okay with this outsourcing deal?"

"As long as someone's willing to pay my

talent fee and the checks don't bounce, I'm happy. I just wonder how long I'm going to be able to keep flying."

"Everything's okay, isn't it?" I gave Michael the once-over as he unfolded himself from the molded plastic and aluminum chair. He exuded the robust energy of a man in his prime, but I knew he was close to the big six-oh.

"Everything's fine. I have to wonder, though, how much longer the radio industry is going to need people like me."

"You must be kidding. Traffic is one of the biggest draws commercial radio has. People like you keep all of us in business."

"Thanks, but you can get plenty of traffic information on the Internet now. Unless the fog lifts, that's what I'll be doing this afternoon down at City Scope, logging onto the CalTrans Web site. They've got cameras up now on almost every overpass. All you need to do is click on a specific section of freeway on your monitor, and you'll see the same thing the Web cam sees. They have sensors imbedded in the roadway to tell you how fast the traffic is moving. Anyone with a computer can get access."

I put a lid on the cup of tea. "Yuck, I hate those Web cams. Too much like Big Brother."

"Welcome to the brave new world of traffic reporting."

I waited until Michael had left the terminal, watched as his sturdy frame faded into a blur of fog in the parking lot. I placed the cardboard cup on top of a newspaper vending rack, retrieved a well-thumbed card from my pocket, and began tapping numbers into my cell phone. It was one of those new area codes, either San Fernando Valley or Hollywood. I'd given up trying to keep track of them all.

Doyle Bollinger's assistant put me through as soon as I gave my name. "We met at the Broadcast Legends dinner last fall, remember?" I said. "You suggested I get in touch if I were ever interested in exploring career opportunities with RadioLand."

"I've been trying to call you the last few days. Didn't you get my messages?"

"I've been busy," I fibbed.

"So you're interested?"

I gazed out at the white scrim of mist outside the glass door of the deserted airport. Thought about Sacramento Talk Radio, Josh, Glory Lou, and T. R. O'Brien, about being part of the team of one of the few independent, family-run stations left in the country, and felt something tighten deep in my heart. Then I reminded myself about outsourcing, and the program director in San Francisco with his "younger sound," and that psychic with the regular guest appearance on my show.

"Yeah," I said. "I'm interested."

Old Sacramento turned out to be almost as desolate as Executive Airport on this Thursday morning in January, the holiday shoppers long gone and the tourist- and school-field-trip season months in the future. I sometimes wondered why Pete Kovacs didn't just close up Retro Alley until around the first of March and spend the winter in Puerto Vallarta.

A familiar laugh greeted me when I pushed open the door to the cluttered antiques and collectibles store, and I felt a warm glow against the chill of the fog. Just hearing Pete's laugh, so full of joy with only a touch of sarcasm, could bring a tiny smile to my face.

"You've definitely got the wrong customer for your new gadget," I heard him say. "My inventory consists of used, one-of-a-kind items. I don't need to increase my through-put, whatever that might be."

A young woman wearing a floor-length navy blue wool overcoat and black leather boots stood next to the glass display case that served as a sales counter. She had smooth, shoulder-length fawn-colored hair and sported a pair of narrow, black-rimmed glasses that would have qualified her for automatic nerd status when I was a teenager, but were now considered the height of hip trendiness. She had what I assumed were her wares — several black-and-white tags that reminded me of the labels they stick around luggage handles at the airport, a box around the size of a deck of cards, and a full-color brochure — spread over the counter.

"But surely you have a system for inventory control," she said to Pete.

He reached inside the display case and removed a metal Flintstones lunch box. "Here's the only inventory control system I'll ever need." He gestured toward a white oval sticker on the bottom of the lunch box. "The number of the sticker matches the file number in my computer."

She all but recoiled when she spotted the handwritten numbers on the sticker. "But this is so primitive, so time-consuming. And just think of the chances for error."

"Look, you've got an interesting product there, but like I said, I'm just not the right customer. My business is so small I can practically keep track of my inventory up here." Pete tapped his right index finger against his forehead.

"Wal-Mart is already requiring their suppliers in certain markets to use smart-label technology. By the end of the decade, this is going to be the industry standard. Probably sooner."

"When Retro Alley gets as big as Wal-Mart, give me a call and we'll talk."

I waved a hello to Pete and picked up one of the tags from the counter.

The young woman turned in my direction and gave me a smile, apparently sizing me up as a potential customer. "Are you familiar with something called R-F-I-D?"

"I don't think so."

"Radio frequency identification. Take that label you're holding. There's a tiny transponder and antenna imbedded inside."

"What, this?" I turned the label over slowly. It bore the logo of something called Smart Tag, but other than that, it looked and felt like an ordinary airline luggage ticket.

"The transponder is dormant until the user energizes it with a reader device." She picked up the card deck–size box I'd noticed and aimed it toward the tag. "This reader collects data stored in the tag and transmits that information to a host computer."

I dropped the ticket onto the counter as if it were radioactive. "What kind of data?"

"For example, inventory information. Size, style, and color. One of these readers can retrieve data from an entire pallet of goods within seconds. With bar codes, you'd have to unload the pallet and scan each item."

The young saleswoman glanced down at my Australian sheepskin feet warmers. "Your boots probably have an RFID device imbedded in them somewhere."

"No way!" I practically jumped backward.

"I know. I felt the same way when I first heard about this. But don't forget, the device is dormant unless it comes in contact with one of these readers. And even then, the only data being sent is the size, color, and model. I could get the same information just by looking at you."

But-but-but! What happens when those readers are everywhere, as ubiquitous as the Web cams on the freeway overpasses? What happens when the information being gathered and transmitted is a lot more personal than just size, color, and model? If they can plant these microscopic radio transmitters inside a pair of boots, or embed them in the paper of an airline luggage tag, what next?

"Just think of the possibilities," she said. "Tickets for rides in amusement parks or passes for ski lifts, for example. Or identifying a real Louis Vuitton bag versus a counterfeit. Keeping track of files in paper-intensive offices, like insurance companies and lawyers. Or library books."

"Library books!" Kovacs and I spoke in unison, my voice rising to a screech.

The saleswoman took our collective reaction as her cue to gather her samples into a black canvas messenger bag and depart, leaving a brochure behind.

Pete and I exchanged glances as soon as the door closed behind her. "And I thought bar codes were bad." He tossed the brochure into the recycle bin.

Pete Kovacs and I had been what the local celebrity gossip-mongers like to refer to as an "item" for around nine months now. We'd managed to navigate the treacherous waters of the holiday season with only minor emotional trauma. Now there was just Valentine's Day to get through and who knows, we just might make it as a couple.

I just wondered whether he'd be up for moving to L.A.

Two elderly African-American women sat in the Sacramento Talk Radio lobby and

51

looked up in anticipation when I breezed through the door. "They've been waiting for you for almost an hour," Mrs. Yanamoto whispered as I passed the reception desk.

"They asked for me specifically?"

"I tried to suggest that they call to make an appointment, or send a press release, but they insisted on waiting. I'm sorry." T. R. O'Brien's secretary knew I don't like face-to-face confrontations with listeners. It has nothing to do with race, religion, or sexual persuasion, just the inevitable letdown when the listener realizes I look nothing like the way they picture me. Most radio personalities feel the same.

Still, I couldn't just ignore them without appearing rude. I made a one-eighty, retreated to the lobby, and stuck out my hand. "Hi, I'm Shauna J. Bogart. What can I do for you?"

"I am Mrs. Iris Fontaine, and this is my sister Mrs. Leota Swanson." Both women rose to return my handshake.

I felt as if I towered over Iris, and I'm only five-two. Leota had maybe an inch or two of height on me. The sisters had short, fluffy hair the same color as the fog, and each wore a bulky sweater, wool skirt, and thick stockings. The sweaters bore evidence of numerous launderings and several lumpy attempts at darning, and Leota's skirt was a houndstooth check pattern I hadn't seen since around 1972. They both wafted a faint aroma of Jean Naté bath powder, which brought back childhood memories of raiding my mother's makeup kit to play dress-up.

"Markitus Wilson is my grandson," Iris said.

The main, and so far only, suspect in the shooting death of Travis Ikeda-Nyland, the young man who had created a one-man traffic blockade on Business 80 two days previously.

"I'm sorry." I tried to look sympathetic while my mind raced with possibilities.

"My grandson couldn't have done this. He doesn't mess around with drugs, and he never touched a gun in his life."

Yeah, yeah, yeah. He was such a nice young man, quiet, never created any trouble. Goes to church every Sunday. It's always those nice, quiet ones who end up on *America's Most Wanted.*

"The police won't listen to us," Leota said. "We're counting on you to help."

I motioned for the two ladies to seat themselves on the vinyl-covered couch. I pulled up a chair opposite them. "I appreciate your confidence in me, but I'm going

53

to have to back off of this one. There's this slight problem . . ."

"See?" Iris turned to her sister. "I told you this would be a big waste of time."

"All you media people circling around to protect Sapphire Ikeda just because she's been on TV all these years," Leota said to me. "And none of you willing to stick up for Markitus Wilson."

"I'm sorry, I really am. But Travis Ikeda-Nyland used to work for this station. He was my summer intern a year and a half ago. I'm too close to the story. Why don't you approach one of the TV stations?"

"Don't you think we've already done that?" Leota said. "They gave us all the same excuses we're getting from you. Meanwhile, poor Markitus is in a coma over at the Med Center."

"So I'm your last chance."

"Please, you've got to help us," Iris said.

I clasped my hands behind my head and studied the water stains on the ceiling tiles. Lost causes and last chances. Why me, why always me?

"I assume you've got evidence to support your contention that Markitus was set up," I said. "Something you can share with my listeners beyond just the fact that he was a nice boy who never caused any trouble."

"We do." Iris gave Leota a look as if searching for reassurance. "We most certainly do."

No question, the shooting in McKinley Park had the potential to be a hot local story, pitting as it did the classic elements of wealth versus poverty, race against race, status opposite obscurity. The rest of Sacramento's media outlets were doing nothing but spewing an endless volley of police department press releases and photos of the victim.

Why me? Why *not* me!

I leaned forward and placed my hands on my hips. "Ladies, you've just earned yourself some airtime."

5

I settled Iris in front of the guest microphone, while Leota arranged herself on a stool next to her sister. "Just pretend you're having a conversation with me, like when we were out in the lobby," I said while Iris adjusted the headphones over her gray curls. "And be sure to speak directly into the microphone."

As soon as Captain Mikey finished with his traffic report, I introduced Iris Fontaine to my listeners and reviewed the facts of the story: the shooting death of Travis Ikeda-Nyland in McKinley Park two afternoons previous, the stand-off on Business 80, the arrest of Markitus Wilson.

"Your grandson is nineteen years old and still living at home," I said. "What was he doing with himself besides just hanging around the house?"

Iris and Leota exchanged glances. "He talked about maybe joining the army," Iris said. "Or possibly going to trade school to learn how to repair air conditioners. Then last fall, he signed up over at American River College and started taking classes in Web site design."

In a climate like Sacramento, air-conditioner repair promised to be a much more marketable job skill than Web site design, but I kept that opinion to myself. "So he's taking classes at community college. Did he have a job, a girlfriend, anything else going on in his life?"

"He had a steady all through his last year of high school, but she went away to college in Los Angeles and they drifted apart. As far as jobs go, there were a few fast-food restaurants and pizza places, and the past year now he's been working for Ruehl Janitorial Services. Never missed a day of work."

"He never mentioned being acquainted with someone named Travis Ikeda-Nyland?"

"Never. Why would Sapphire Ikeda's son have anything to do with my Markitus?"

"You're talking totally different worlds," I agreed. "But let's talk about the one thing that a young man from one of Sacramento's most prominent families and a nobody from Rancho Cordova might have in common. Something that might have drawn them together. Something like drugs."

Leota leaped from the stool, grabbed the guest microphone, and swiveled it in her direction. "Markitus did not do drugs and did not have anything to do with drugs! That boy was clean. Clean, do you get me?"

"You told me before the show you think Markitus was set up. What evidence do you have to support that?"

Iris snapped open a scuffed handbag made of a brown leatherlike substance, removed a business card, and flicked it onto the broadcast console with a little tap of her fingers. "There's my evidence."

I picked up the card, scanned the front, and felt my enthusiasm vanish like a pair of taillights disappearing in the fog. "Ladies and gentlemen," I said into the microphone. "What I hold before me is a piece of paper, roughly the size of a business card, green ink, offering me a free aerobics class at a dance studio in the South Hills Shopping Center."

"Look on the back," Iris said, while Leota lunged toward the card as if she were going to turn it over for me.

"I see a name handwritten with a charcoal pencil. Brenda. No last name."

"Markitus got a phone call just as he was getting ready to leave to go to class," Iris said. "He jotted that name down on the back of one of these cards. Five minutes later, he just bolts out of the house, leaves all his books behind. Three hours later, he's in intensive care."

"You think this Brenda, if that's who the call was from, might have been the one setting him up?"

"Or she might have been the bait."

"Why haven't you shared this with the police?"

"Don't you think I haven't? I told them everything, turned the card over to the police first thing."

"If you turned it over to the police, then what's this?" I pinched the card between the thumb and index finger of my right hand and waved, even though the listeners couldn't see.

"Just as perfect a copy as I could make. I imitated Markitus's handwriting to the letter. I found at least a dozen of those coupons from the dance studio in his room."

"Really. What do you suppose he might be doing with a bunch of passes for free aerobics classes?"

"He wasn't doing anything wrong, I know that much," Iris said. "Maybe he was passing them out at school and getting a little payback for every coupon that got redeemed."

A possibility, but a slim one. American River College and the South Hills Shopping Center were on opposite ends of Sacramento's suburban sprawl. Potential customers of the dance studio would more likely attend City College than ARC. "Did Markitus ever mention to you about being involved in a scheme like that?"

"No."

"And did he ever mention knowing anyone named Brenda?"

"No again."

"And that's all you've got? Before he left the house the day of the shooting, Markitus Wilson gets a phone call, scribbles a name on the back of a coupon for a free aerobics class, and leaves it behind."

"My grandson is innocent!" Iris sat up straighter and shot me a defiant glare. "He never messed around with drugs, he never owned no gun, and he never shot no rich white boy in McKinley Park."

"Then answer me this, Mrs. Fontaine. Why did he run? Why did he refuse to surrender to the police for almost two hours?"

"Put yourself in his place. If you was young and black and found yourself in the middle of something bad going down, maybe you hear sirens, what would you do?"

Three men and one woman hovered in ambush in the hallway after I signed off the log, gathered up my gear, and prepared to leave for the day. I recognized the wiry figure of T. R. O'Brien and the Big Bird getup worn by Dorinda Delgado. I didn't place the other two at first, although the older man struck a vague memory chord.

The younger of the two men burst forward and planted himself directly in my path. "What the hell was that all about?"

I made eye contact with O'Brien and tried to raise my palms in a clueless shrug, a difficult move when laden with headphones, notepad, and file folder of newspaper clippings.

The older man moved forward and placed a hand on the younger man's shoulder in a calming gesture. I gave the elder of the two a closer look and homed in on a grinning mug and two-thumbs-up sign that greeted Sacramento every week in a full-page ad in the automotive section of the Bee, and on dozens of billboards throughout the region. Save With Ray! Sapphire Ikeda's husband. Travis's dad.

The smile was nowhere to be seen today. He spoke in a dull monotone and his face was ashen, mottled with red. "I believe we met at the Ad Club Christmas party."

I nodded, sure that whatever I uttered would just make the situation worse.

He jerked his head toward the younger man. "Gareth Nyland, vice president for marketing."

Both men had dark blond hair parted on the left and swooped over the forehead to the right, and both wore wire-rimmed glasses. But while the elder Nyland, mid-fifties at the minimum, maintained flat abs and solid jaw, Gareth — who I placed at thirty, tops — was already starting to run to fat, a soft belly spilling over the belt that held up the pants of his designer suit, jowls sinking into a white dress shirt.

"Don't you think this family has suffered enough already?" Gareth placed both hands on his hips and dared me to slink around him in the narrow corridor.

Dorinda Delgado boiled into action at his side. "Do you have any idea how much advertising Nyland Automotive places with this station every year?"

So the truth comes out. Advertising, that's the real reason every other media outlet in town was giving the story the velvet glove treatment. Deference to the feelings of Sapphire Ikeda played only a small part, if at all. The only thing that surprised me was how long it had taken me to get it.

"It's bad enough just trying to cope with all of this, without turning on the radio and hearing some sleazy talk show host giving support to the drug dealer who killed my son," Ray Nyland said.

"I'm sorry about your loss, I truly am. Travis was a great kid. I'm just sick about what happened."

"My wife is at home crying her eyes out, thanks to you and your damn show."

"Saying you're sorry won't cut it," Gareth added. "Not after what you did this afternoon."

"The last thing I would ever want to do is hurt Travis or his mother," I said. "But I thought Ms. Ikeda would understand about presenting all sides of the story, being in the news business and all."

"You thought wrong. Way wrong," Gareth said.

"Now, now," T.R. broke in. "There's no need to raise our voices. The point now is, what can this radio station do to make it up to Travis and his family?"

Four pairs of eyes stared me down. Jeez, what was I supposed to do? I'd already said I was sorry, sincerely sorry.

"May I offer a suggestion?" Dorinda Delgado showed her best deal-closing smile, all maroon lip liner and sharp incisors. "In the future, if Shauna J. decides to air anything about this story beyond the official statements from law enforcement, she clears the content with me first. Me or T. R. O'Brien."

I gave O'Brien an imploring look. There's no way he would go along with this scheme, would he? Censor his most popular on-air personality? Put a muzzle on Shauna J. Bogart?

O'Brien returned the look with his lips pressed in a firm line and an icy stare.

I opened my mouth and in a voice I didn't recognize, I told them the plan was fine by me.

"I didn't want to do it to you, I swear."

I turned and peered through the early evening midwinter gloom of the station parking lot, and made out the figure of T. R. O'Brien in the dark mist.

"Then why'd you do it?" I stood next to the open door of the Z-car, the overhead light casting a feeble shaft of illumination.

"I had no choice. This station can't afford to lose the Nyland account. You know how slow the first quarter is when it comes to ad sales."

"How about my integrity and credibility? Doesn't that count for anything?"

"Shoot, you know it does. But without the dough from sponsors like Ray Nyland, this station doesn't even stay on the air."

"Spare me." I lowered myself into the driver's seat and made a grab at the door.

O'Brien was too fast for me. He parked himself in the doorway, the hook of his left hand and his right forearm planted on the roof of the low-slung sports car. He stuck his head through the doorway. "Just lay low on the story for a few days, that's all I ask."

"Forget it. Either let me do the show you hired me to do, or . . ." I let my voice trail off, unwilling to utter an ultimatum from which there would be no retreat.

"You're the one who wants to consider all sides of the story. Well, how about my side?" O'Brien said.

I turned the key in the ignition and tromped on the gas pedal. "Maybe some other time. Right now, I'm late for my aerobics class."

6

Fifteen minutes into Benji's cardio kick-start class at the Jazz'n Motion studio and I knew I had been deluding myself into believing that pacing in the control room provided the equivalent of an aerobics workout. Sticky liquid seeped from sections of my body that I didn't even realize contained sweat glands. I flailed about on the wooden dance floor to the thumping disco-techno beat and struggled to follow Benji's chirpy commands from the stage. "Kick-ball-change, step, step, chassé cross-over, kick-turn step!"

Around twenty-five women followed Benji in unison. My fellow exercisers wore variations of the spandex tights and leotard uniform, like it was still 1983 and *Flashdance* was breaking box office records. How shlumpy did I feel in floppy sweatpants and a stretched-out sweatshirt from Pete Kovacs's collection of Boston Celtics logo wear? Don't even ask.

The class mercifully over, Benji bounded

in my direction just as I draped a hand towel around my neck. The sleekly toned women gathered up their gym bags and began filing out the door. Now that I had a chance to study Benji up close, I put him at around my age, that is, closer to forty than thirty. Tiny, butt-hugging shorts and a skimpy tank top displayed a body buffed and chiseled to perfection. Too tall and too short of hair to be taken for a Richard Simmons clone, he still exuded the frenetic perkiness that must be an essential part of the job description for aerobics instructors worldwide.

"I hope we'll be seeing you here again," Benji said.

"I'll see if I can fit it into my schedule," I said between gasps for air.

"You might consider buying a monthly punch card, ten classes for forty dollars. That's only four dollars a class, a savings of fifty percent."

Gosh, he's cute *and* does math in his head.

"Just wondering, do you happen to have an instructor named Brenda?"

"Brenda Driscoll." Benji led me to the reception counter and pressed a brochure into my hand. "She teaches Funk-ercise on Monday, Wednesday, and Friday nights."

Benji pointed a beefy arm in the direction

of a line of framed, eight-by-ten color head shots on the wall above the wooden counter. I found Brenda Driscoll third from the left: kohl-lined eyes, gleaming smile, cropped geometric 'do, and hoop earrings the size of compact discs that, I feared, might cause lethal injury during a Funk-ercise session.

"What's she do besides lead aerobics classes?"

"Trying to break into show business, just like the rest of us. Modeling and TV."

"Any luck?"

"She was in the chorus at the Solstice Revels and she just landed a gig at the auto show this weekend. Oh, yeah — she's supposed to be up for a part in an independent film that's going to be shot here in Sacramento. Still, it's a tough business to break into."

Tell me about it. Almost as difficult as surviving in today's corporate radio scene.

I tried to think of how to best word my next question so as not to spook Benji. So far, he knew me only as piece of flab waiting to be sculpted, a potential purchaser of a punch card. What would happen to his willingness to talk when he discovered I was a media snoop?

"You really should think about signing up for an unlimited monthly pass," Benji said.

"That way you can hit my class on Tuesdays and Thursdays and do Brenda's class at the same time on Monday, Wednesday, and Friday. We'll have you in shape in plenty of time for swimsuit season."

"Sounds like a terrific idea. Say, just thinking," I ad-libbed. "There's a guy I work with who might be a good match for Brenda. Or does she already have a boyfriend?"

"She was dating some fellow in the community relations department at the Almond Growers Exchange, but I don't know if anything ever came of it. I haven't heard her talk much about him lately."

"How about a young man named Markitus Wilson? Ever hear Brenda mention him?" I tried to sound offhand.

A frown dampened Benji's peppy façade. "The guy they think killed Sapphire Ikeda's son?"

"Yeah."

"What's he have to do with Brenda Driscoll?"

"That's what I'm hoping to find out."

"Who are you really? A cop?"

According to what Iris Fontaine had said on my radio program this afternoon, she'd turned over the original aerobics class coupon, the one with Brenda's name hand lettered on the back, to the police. I was surprised investigators hadn't already paid a call to Jazz'n Motion. Then again, they might already have done so when Benji wasn't around.

"I'm an acquaintance of Markitus Wilson's grandmother. She found one of your coupons with Brenda's name written on the back. She asked me to check it out and see if Brenda might be able to shed some light on what really happened on Tuesday."

"Sorry. I don't think I can help you." Benji began shuffling and stacking the brochures, the neatness of the reception area taking sudden precedence over the possibility of luring in a new student.

"Thanks anyway." I stuffed a hand into the pocket of my sweatpants and fished around for the car keys. The front door burst open and a young man wearing gray janitor's overalls and hoisting a vacuum cleaner entered in a rush of "Excusa, excusa."

"Sure thing," Benji called after me. "And hey, think about that unlimited pass. Your gluts and abs will thank you, I promise."

"Bogart's house of pleasure," I cooed into the telephone receiver. "How may we be of service?"

70

"Shauna J.?" I recognized Glory Lou's voice on the other end of the line.

Oops. Pete Kovacs almost always calls me at this time of the morning just to check in and plan how we're going to spend the day. Except, of course, on mornings in which such a call would be superfluous.

"Sorry, I thought it was someone else."

"Lordy, I should hope so. Listen, hon, you are not going to believe who wants to meet with us."

Which is how I found myself a half hour later seated next to Glory Lou in News Unit Five heading east on Fair Oaks Boulevard on our way to the suburban ranch house shared by Sapphire Ikeda and Ray Nyland.

"You're sure, you're absolutely sure, she wants you to bring me along," I asked for probably the half-dozenth time.

"Absolutely positively." Glory Lou floored it to beat a yellow light across the busy intersection with Watt Avenue. I stared out the window at the hedges and shrubs sheltering the low-slung estates as we plunged deep into what felt like the never-ending reaches of Sacramento's flat suburbia.

"So who's this Gareth person, anyway?" I said, recalling the encounter in the hallway at the station yesterday afternoon. "I don't

71

recall Travis saying anything about having an older brother."

"His cousin. Ray and Bill Nyland are partners in the car dealership. Gareth is Bill's son."

Glory Lou steered the sedan off Fair Oaks Boulevard and made several turns on narrow, tree-lined streets, finally stopping in front of a locked gate. Somewhere in this same neighborhood, behind a similar pair of shackled iron gates, I knew I'd find the "new" governor's mansion — La Casa de Los Gobernadores — built in the 1970s by wealthy supporters of then-governor Reagan, but never actually lived in by Ron and Nancy nor by any future governor.

Glory Lou spoke into an intercom box, the gates separated, and News Unit Five crept down a concrete driveway, halting in front of a garage almost as large as the *Sunset* magazine dream house centered between two massive valley oaks. Gareth Nyland answered the door, his feet still in slippers and a tie draped loosely around his neck as if we'd caught him in the middle of dressing.

"I see you didn't have any trouble finding the place. She's waiting for us in the island room." He led the two of us through a formal living room that held a florist shop's worth of sympathy arrangements, past a vast kitchen–family room area, and an entertainment center stocked with all the latest gadgets.

The "island room" turned out to be a glassed-in porch filled with wicker furniture, Hawaiian print cushions, a potted palm, ceiling fan, and fuchsia and ferns too delicate for a Sacramento summer. A tea trolley held a tray with fruit and croissants, an urn of coffee, a pitcher of orange juice, mugs, and glasses.

A tiny woman dressed in a red silk caftan rose from one of the white rattan chairs. "Thank you for coming on such short notice." Sapphire Ikeda and Glory Lou immediately embraced while I hung back, feeling awkward and out of place, wishing I could disappear behind the lush greenery. When Sapphire turned to me, I extended my arm, thinking a handshake might be more appropriate. She responded by squeezing me in a hug and whispering a second thank-you for taking the time out of my busy schedule to visit with her.

Without makeup, Sapphire Ikeda looked even younger than she appeared on television, could easily have passed for a woman in her thirties. Yet I knew she had launched her career as one of the first female news anchors on Sacramento television after finishing college in the mid-seventies, so that would place her at right around fifty. After her marriage to Ray Nyland and subsequent motherhood, Sapphire Ikeda had cut back on her daily TV duties, devoting her energies to special reports on gubernatorial swearing-in ceremonies and opening day of the Sacramento Jazz Jubilee, and station charitable events like the annual holiday toy drive. Even with only selective exposure, she remained an A-list local celebrity.

"We're the ones who should be thanking you for inviting us," Glory Lou said. "I can't believe you're doing this after all you've been through."

"It's called keeping busy. I believe it's the only thing that keeps me going. Please, help yourselves, and make yourselves comfortable."

Well, I did work out the previous evening, so one croissant couldn't hurt, could it? I rounded out the plate with a cluster of grapes and a handful of strawberries, poured a glass of OJ, and placed myself onto a wicker settee next to Glory Lou. As I nibbled on a strawberry, careful to make sure the juice dribbled onto the plate and not my cream-colored fleece pullover, I gazed from the glass enclosure across a manicured lawn, a gazebo designed to resemble a Japanese teahouse, a swimming pool, a tennis court, and a built-in barbecue. The vista faded into the morning mist rising from the American River that surged at the foot of the cliff marking the edge of the Ikeda-Nyland property. I couldn't see across the river in the fog, but I knew on the far bank I'd find the working-class suburb of Rancho Cordova. On a clear day and with the help of binoculars, I might even be able to pick out the modest tract home of Iris Fontaine, the boyhood home of the youth suspected of killing the young man who grew up on the ritzy piece of real estate where I was consuming my morning's second breakfast.

"You know what the hardest part is?" Sapphire said.

Glory Lou and I shook our heads.

"Not being able to see him. The coroner's office won't let anyone visit him until they finish and release him to the mortuary. Is it so wrong for a mother to want to see her child one more time?" She crumpled into the chair and raised a fist to her quivering chin.

"Of course not, hon." Glory Lou leaned forward and patted Sapphire on the knee. "Have they given you any sort of time frame?"

"Sometime today, so I'm told." She straightened her back and turned in my direction. "I'm so glad you were able to join us. I wanted to tell you in person how much I appreciate your kindness to Travis when he did his internship at your station."

"I didn't do all that much, really," I said. "Travis was a sweet kid with a lot of potential. There's no reason why he couldn't have been a success with or without my help."

"But he never understood that until you treated him with sensitivity and respect. For the first time, he realized there was something to life beyond hanging out with his friends and drinking."

As I recalled, my "sensitivity" consisted of refusing to cut him any slack, and expecting him to meet the standards of the rest of the broadcast team.

"Did you know, in the middle of that summer he spent with you, he signed up for outpatient therapy at the Footprints Institute?" Sapphire said. "On his own, with no pushing from either me or his father. It was as if for the first time he was really focused on getting his life on track."

"Like I said, he really was a terrific kid who didn't need much guidance."

"That's why I wanted to make sure you heard it straight from me." Sapphire's voice

76

took on the authoritative tone familiar to anyone who'd watched her newscasts over the years. "Do whatever you have to do to get to the truth. If that means giving airtime to the family of that young man the police think caused this tragedy, then so be it. I want to know what really happened to my son."

"I was out of line yesterday and I'm sorry," Gareth said from his seat next to the potted palm. "That goes for Ray and everyone at Nyland Automotive."

"Don't worry about it," I said. "Totally understandable, everyone's emotions are on edge."

"So you'll continue to pursue the story then," Sapphire said.

"Of course. I do have to wonder, though, why isn't your own station's news department launching an investigation?"

"I told them as far as I was concerned, they had carte blanche. But I'm afraid with all the budget cuts we've had lately, there isn't any staff left with the resources to do much more than rewrite the press releases from the police department. And at any rate, so far you've been the only media person in town willing to do any sort of digging."

I leaned forward, careful not to upend the plate balanced on my knees. "Even if I discover something that might prove to be less than flattering to you or the family?"

"My son may have had his share of problems," Sapphire said. "But crystal meth was not one of them. I'm not afraid of what you might turn up. I just want to know the truth."

I settled back into the vivid floral print cushions. "What happened after Travis finished his internship? I assumed he'd gone back to UCLA. I had no idea he was living in Sacramento."

"He did return to college, found a sober-living house near campus, finished his junior year with honors, and spent last summer abroad."

"He even talked about trying for an MBA and getting involved with Nyland Automotive," Gareth said. "Of course, the entire family was thrilled at the turnaround."

I daintily licked the last of the croissant crumbs off my fingers and deposited the plate on the tea trolley. "For certain, it's every parent's dream to see their children take an interest in the family business."

"That's why it's just so hard to understand what happened this past fall." Sapphire's voice trailed into a whimper and she sank into a cloud of red silk in the wicker chair.

"He started drinking again," Gareth said

with a long sigh. "He's clean and sober for over twelve months and then one day for no reason — bam! He's back to hitting the bottle."

"I'm sorry, but I have to ask: Was he ever in trouble with the law over his drinking?"

Sapphire's hand paused midway to raising a coffee mug to her lips, and she made a tiny nod in Gareth's direction.

"He had two DUIs before he'd even finished high school," Gareth said. "The DMV suspended his license until he turned twenty-one."

"Didn't you ever think it was odd, a young man in California not having his own car?" Sapphire said. "Especially considering the family business?"

"If I ever noticed, I must have forgotten." Truth is, the only thing that registered during Travis's internship was whether he showed up on time, not if he arrived by bus, bike, or behind the wheel of a shiny floor model from daddy's showroom.

"The sad thing is, he'd just gotten his driving privilege back this past fall and then . . ."

"Not another DUI?"

Sapphire nodded and squinted back tears. "Early last October, coming home from a club on the Strip."

"Travis was asked to leave the sober-living group home," Gareth said. "He petitioned the university for an academic leave of absence and came back here. The situation was clearly out of control. We felt we had no choice but to send him to Footprints Lodge."

Sacramento's equivalent of the Betty Ford Center. I knew of a couple of local media personalities who had checked themselves into the Footprints Lodge. Not that I would ever name names.

"He successfully completed the residential program and was back to attending AA meetings almost every night," Sapphire said. "Dr. Yount told us how proud she was at his desire to stay sober."

"She's head honcho at Footprints," Gareth said. "Travis even talked about maybe being able to return to school in the spring and pick up where he'd left off."

"He was living here at home then?" I asked.

"For a while. He'd recently moved into an apartment with another young man who'd recently just completed the Footprints program. We all thought it would be a good environment for him to transition into independent living. He came by on Sunday to pick up some extra bath towels. It turned out to be the last time I saw him." Sapphire plucked a handful of tissues from a container on the table, crushed them into a ball, held the tissues to her face, and sobbed.

As if the moment weren't already awkward enough, a telephone tucked away in the shrubbery began to trill.

"I'll get that," I mouthed to Glory Lou. I scanned the cluttered room for the source of the noise, finally located a cordless set perched on a glass-topped table next to a wooden carved tiki god. "Ikeda-Nyland residence," I said into the receiver in a low voice. I listened to the terse message, asked the caller to repeat it to make sure I understood correctly. A minute or so later, I stood in front of the cluster of wicker furniture where Sapphire Ikeda and Glory Lou waited.

"That was the coroner's office," I said.

7

Get me out of here. Just get me the hell out of here!

I was sandwiched between Sapphire Ikeda and Glory Lou on a thinly padded bench in the reception area of the Sacramento County Coroner's Office. A set of framed quilts on the wall provided a cozy touch to the otherwise bleak surroundings.

There was still time to bail, invent an up-'til-this-moment forgotten dental appointment, call a cab, and order the driver to put as many miles between me and this creepy place as quickly as he could.

Sapphire had insisted that Glory Lou and I accompany her to the coroner's headquarters, and after she'd said, "Don't make me do this alone" in a quivery whisper, how could we refuse? She'd changed out of the caftan and into a pair of black slacks and a gray cashmere sweater in less than five minutes, even managed to apply mascara and a film of red lipstick. Always the professional. We had the advantage of the midday lull in traffic and made the trip into the city's central core in only around twenty minutes.

Glory Lou piloted the news car with the expertise of someone not making her first trip to the county building. It stood on the edge of the vast University of California teaching hospital known colloquially as Sac Med. This is the facility where the region's most dire trauma cases are sent for treatment, and where Markitus Wilson continued to struggle for life. The emergency room of that institution, I suspected, supplied a good portion of the clientele of the establishment in which we currently cooled our heels.

"You're going to have to wait to view the deceased at the funeral home," the clerk behind the glassed-in reception counter told me. "I'm sorry, that's standard policy."

I'd put Glory Lou in charge of providing moral support to the grieving mother and assigned to myself the heavy lifting with the low-level bureaucrats. "Sure, I understand," I said. "But see, this is Sapphire Ikeda. From TV, right? And she just received a phone call from Detective Alvarado asking her to meet him down here. So how about setting aside your policy for a minute and buzzing Alvarado?"

The receptionist gave her teased and lacquered hairdo a fluff with her fingers, picked up the phone, and punched in an extension. She'd barely replaced the receiver before a pair of swinging doors pushed outward and Detective Dan Alvarado entered the lobby, followed by a young woman wearing blue cotton slacks, athletic shoes, and a white lab coat, and carrying a metal clipboard. I half expected to see a stethoscope draped around her neck to complete the ensemble until I realized such an accessory would be wasted on her regular customers.

Alvarado's face turned sour when he recognized Glory Lou. "I wasn't expecting a media entourage."

"These are my friends," Sapphire said. "I specifically requested that they accompany me."

"Lord knows, you can't expect her to do this alone," Glory Lou said.

Alvarado shifted his weight from one chukka-booted foot to the other. "Just so I'm not going to be hearing this spewed out over the airwaves of your radio station this afternoon."

"We can keep this off the record for now if you think it's crucial to the investigation," I said.

That seemed to satisfy the detective. He

pulled open the swinging doors and motioned for us to follow. Sapphire and I, both on the vertically challenged side, had to all but jog to keep up with the detective's lanky lope through a maze of corridors. I had only quick glimpses of gleaming metal trash cans, racks of white scrubs, stacked boxes of latex gloves, and black and red biohazard warning signs seemingly on every blank section of wall. At least the smells weren't as gag-inducing as I'd dreaded. Mostly I was aware of an overwhelming odor of bleach, plus the occasional whiff of a citrusy cologne that I assumed emanated from Alvarado. Still, it was all I could do not to vocalize the scream in the back of my head: get me the hell out of here!

Alvarado ushered us into a room about the size of one of the radio station's production studios, complete with the window filling the upper half of one wall. But instead of housing microphones, consoles, and cords, this room featured only a cheapie laminated wood table and three chrome and vinyl stacking chairs. Rather than looking out over a busy newsroom, the window provided a view of what, at first glance, could have been mistaken for a typical hospital operating room. There were the kettledrum overhead lamps, the glass jars and drawers of polished silver instruments, various hoses for sucking and rinsing. But you wouldn't expect to find a hanging scale in an operating room, nor a white board with notations of the weight, in grams, of every internal organ removed from the patient.

You would also hope that the patient lying on the stainless steel gurney would not be covered from head to toe with a white sheet.

Oh. My. God.

"Are you sure you're up for this?" Alvarado asked Sapphire.

"Absolutely." She stood poised in front of the window, every muscle straining, a wild animal about to pounce.

Alvarado nodded through the glass to the white-coated lab tech. She slowly rolled back the white sheet.

Okay, I'd watched a few episodes of *Six Feet Under*, and I thought I knew what to expect: the Y-shaped incision on the chest to allow access to the innards, the stitches leading from the neck around the skull, the opening where they'd removed his brain. What I hadn't anticipated was the utter and complete stillness of a human body from which the life force has fled.

I'd always privately thought of Travis Ikeda-Nyland as a golden boy, and not just because of his privileged background. He was lucky enough to have inherited the best physical traits of his biracial gene pool, and on his good days, i.e. days when he hadn't been partying the night before, he exuded an almost visible glow of youth and vitality. Now he was the color of ash, as cold and silent as the fog blanketing the Sacramento Valley. Even his sun-streaked hair appeared gray.

I heard myself sucking in air through my teeth. Glory Lou gave me a queasy look that told me she wanted out of here as badly as I did. Sapphire, meanwhile, never wavered from her post in front of the window, peering through the glass with fierce pride.

"We were hoping you might be able to help us identify this," Alvarado said. The lab assistant pointed a gloved hand at a dark spot on Travis's left bicep.

Alvarado flipped open a spiral-bound notebook. "Recent wound, knife or other sharp instrument. Four centimeters long, two and a half centimeters wide, and approximately one centimeter deep. From the extent of the healing that had already taken place, estimated time of the incision was two to three days before death."

"I have no idea," Sapphire said. "The last time I saw him was Sunday, but he was wearing a sweatshirt so I suppose I might not have noticed."

"Do you recall him saying anything about having been in any sort of altercation?"

"Absolutely not. I would have remembered something like that."

"How about a visit to the doctor? A dermatologist maybe?"

"No. What makes you ask?"

"The incision has almost surgical precision, like it was done with a scalpel. Maybe he had a mole removed? Or a tattoo?"

"Not that I was aware of. Couldn't a wound like this have been caused, when, you know . . . McKinley Park . . ." Sapphire's voice faltered for a moment.

"No, ma'am. Like I said, the wound had already started to heal. For another thing, he wore a dressing, a gauze pad and adhesive tape."

"Oh."

"It doesn't match any of our known gang initiations or goth rituals. Witchcraft, black arts, that sort of thing."

Sapphire whirled from the window and faced Alvarado. "My son was not involved in gangs or your so-called black arts. He was a fine young man from a good family who just happened to have a problem with alcohol. End of story."

"Of course, ma'am." Alvarado stuffed the notebook into an inside pocket of his blazer. "From what you're saying, you never saw this particular wound and never heard your son mention it."

"If I say sure, he cut himself as part of some bizarre fraternity hazing, would that speed things along? Would it put an end to this nonsense so I can start making arrangements for my son's funeral?"

I stood and inserted myself between the detective and the mother, doing my best to keep my eyes averted from the inert form on the other side of the glass. "I know we promised all this would be off the record. But what if I went on the air and asked my listeners if they know of any reason why Travis might have had what looks like a recent knife wound on his arm? You never know what might turn up."

"Bunch of nut cases, that's all that will turn up," Alvarado said. "Big waste of time."

"You never know. For one reason or another, some folks are reluctant to get involved with the authorities, yet they'll contribute information to a radio talk show when they know they can remain anonymous."

"Let me think it over and I'll get back to you."

I handed over a business card to Alvarado as he began shuffling us out of the homicide suite and into the maze of antiseptic corridors. Sapphire Ikeda hung back until the lab tech had finished replacing the white sheet over the empty shell that had once been her son.

"Lydia Ontiveras just called in sick." Glory Lou loomed over Josh in the newsroom. "If you're available to screen calls for the garden show this weekend, the shift's all yours."

"No can do," Josh said between chomps on a hamburger. "I'll be at odd con all weekend."

"Say what?" I asked from behind the computer at my desk.

"You're heard of *Space Odyssey*, right?" Josh had pulled up a chair and spread out his fast-food burger and fries on a corner of my desk. Now that our beloved Tiny's drive-in had closed up and the land had been sold to developers, we were stuck with the big national chains whenever the hamburger hunger hit. After the experiences of this morning, the only lunch I craved was of the same liquid variety that had given poor Travis Ikeda-Nyland such problems.

"Of course I've heard of *Space Od-*

yssey." Was there a soul on the planet within the reach of a satellite dish who had not heard of the perennially popular sci-fi TV series and its numerous spin-offs?

"There's this big fan convention in Sacramento this weekend. Marshall Dean Sheridan's going to be there."

"OddCon. I get it." I was pretty sure Marshall Dean Sheridan was one of the stars from the original series but didn't want to appear hopelessly out of the loop by asking Josh to verify that fact.

"What have you got going this weekend, you and the gray-haired ponytail? Anything exciting?"

"Nothing much. We'll probably just hang around, maybe go see a movie." I ignored his gentle put-down of older men (in other words, men over twenty-five) who continue to sport the hairstyle of a seventies-era rock star. I plead guilty, after a youth spent drooling over those icons in the pages of *Tiger Beat,* that I still find the look sexy as hell, whether in style or not.

"Anyway, I hear it's supposed to rain," I added.

In reality, I knew exactly what I was going to be doing during the upcoming weekend. As my computer had just reminded me, I was scheduled to climb aboard a Southwest

Airlines flight from Sacramento International to Burbank at seven thirty-five the next morning for my meeting with Doyle Bollinger at RadioLand.

"I need to borrow Josh for a few minutes."

I looked up from the monitor to see the figure of Dorinda Delgado bearing down on me.

"I've got to pick up a couple of cartons of station magnets at the Stow It for an event out at Arco Arena next week," she said. "You wouldn't believe how heavy those little suckers are when you try to lift a whole carton."

Like most radio stations, we rented space in a store-it-yourself complex where we kept extra supplies and old program logs. I'd been out there once or twice and noticed a couple of other radio station vans in addition to Sacramento Talk Radio. The owner must have been trading out storage space for commercial airtime. The only other tenant I'd ever made note of was a heavy metal band that had rented out a storage locker to use as rehearsal space, giving a whole new meaning to the term *garage band*.

"Why not wait 'til next week then." I didn't really care one way or another, but years of experience had taught me never to acquiesce too quickly to the whims of the sales department. Not to mention, Josh was supposed to be my employee, not hers.

"There's supposed to be a big storm coming in. Better to take care of it now than in the rain."

"No big deal, really," Josh said. He wadded up the greasy fast-food wrappers and lobbed them into a trash can.

"Up to you," I told him. The kid would learn soon enough. Let those sales sharks sense weakness, give them a taste of blood, and they'll come circling back for more, always more. They can't help themselves. It's just how they're programmed. "Just be back by two-thirty."

Detective Alvarado called the studio hotline during the five-twenty commercial break. "Been thinking about your idea."

"Going public with the business about the strange wound," I said.

"Talked it over with the rest of the investigating team. If you think you might be able to generate some useful information, it's okay by us."

I pumped my fisted hand in victory in the direction of Josh's call screener booth. Talk about being handed the perfect topic to finish the show, a tidbit to leave my listeners craving for more when I signed off for the weekend. Then the control room door opened, and in walked T. R. O'Brien, escorting a chubby woman wearing a silver necklace dangling with crystals.

8

Crap. I'd managed to forget all about O'Brien's commitment to that damn psychic. Sure, the phone lines went wild the minute I introduced Clarissa St. Cyr and mentioned her alleged abilities to communicate with the dead — or as she insisted on terming it, those who had "crossed over."

I don't think she was an out-and-out fraud, a charlatan who plants shills in the audience or memorizes the obituaries. I was willing to concede there are people out there like Clarissa St. Cyr who are more sensitive than most, who have developed their skills at picking up and interpreting the most minute of clues from other people: tone of voice, facial expressions, odors, gestures. But actually communicate with the dead? Forget it.

But why hadn't O'Brien warned me about the gimmick Clarissa was going to play with her own voice, going all high-pitched and breathy whenever she'd supposedly made contact with her spirit guide on the Other

Side? I found myself scrambling for the slider on the control board the first time she pulled that little stunt, riding gain to stabilize the highs and lows of volume, making sure that the VU meter — that bouncing needle that TV and movie cameras love to focus on whenever they set a scene in a radio station — never rose past 100 or fell much below 80. Potting up and potting down, referring not to something you'd cook in or smoke, but shorthand for the potentiometer controlling the electric current that sparked the magic of radio. Clarissa St. Cyr, I was to discover, would require a lot of riding gain.

"How about doing a reading for me?" I said into the on-air mike after I'd transitioned out of Captain Mikey's last traffic report of the afternoon. "Are you up for it?"

"The spirit guides are willing," Clarissa said, rattling a cluster of beaded bracelets on her right arm. "You must also be willing to do the work. Clear your mind and concentrate on the person you wish to contact."

I banished thoughts of Clarissa's loopy earrings getting tangled in headphone cords and called up the image I wished to remember him by. Not the lifeless figure on the coroner's gurney, and not the "restoration" he was probably currently undergoing at the mortuary Sapphire had finally selected. Instead, I conjured Travis as he was that summer he did his internship with me. Throwing his head back in laughter at some private joke in the call screener both. Riding his skateboard through the newsroom, all windmill arms and whoops of sheer youthful delight.

"I see a woman." That ghostly voice kicked in again and I made a grab for the control slider. "She's wearing her hair long and loose. She has bangs almost covering one eye, and she's dressed in a long, satin evening gown like one of those movie stars from the 1940s. Does that sound like anyone you might know from your past?"

"Other than Veronica Lake, not really."

"The spirit guides are giving me a closer look. The woman has red hair. Does that help?"

Well, duh! It wouldn't take a psychic to give the once-over to a carrottop like yours truly and deduce that she'd likely have a redheaded ancestor. She'd undoubtedly sized me up as the right age to have a grandmother who would have been a glamorous young woman in the Veronica Lake era. Trouble is, she was off by at least ten years. My red-tressed granny had married and borne children late in life, and would be wearing a flapper gown and sporting a shingled bob in heaven.

"I did have a grandmother with red hair, but I don't think she ever wore it long. Not as an adult, at any rate."

"I see the letter *G*. Possibly also the letter *N*."

Another obvious guess. *G* as in Grandma? *N* as in Nana? Clarissa had deduced I appeared still young enough that I likely wouldn't be attempting to contact a departed husband or boyfriend, yet old enough that my grandparents had probably shed this earthly coil.

"Sorry, no."

"I see someone else joining the red-haired woman. A dog? Yes, definitely a dog. Did you perhaps have a dog when you were a child?"

If you can't summon granny, then how about a beloved childhood pet?

"Sorry, but goldfish were about as exciting as it got in the pet department when I was a kid."

"Spirit is showing me a small dog, white with brown spots. I still see the letters *N* and *G*. And — yes! — the letter *B*. Are you sure you never had a dog?"

"Bing, bang, bong. I'm afraid not."

Pete Kovacs piloted his van down N Street while I filled him in on the events of my day — the meeting with Sapphire Ikeda and the visit to the coroner's office. "Sapphire called me on my cell phone just as I was leaving the station. She's starting to clean out this apartment Travis had been sharing with a guy he met in recovery."

"So soon?"

"She says she needs to keep busy."

"I'll say."

"Anyway, she found something she says I might want to have. I told her I'd be right over."

The red Dodge Prospector van halted at a traffic signal at Eleventh Street, the white wedding cake dome of the state capitol shimmering in the early evening gloom of midwinter. No tule fog, just a high cloud cover, the advance troops of the big storm the weather forecasters kept promising.

"Sounds like we're in for the perfect Saturday to hit the multiplex," Pete said. "There's a new Altman picture opening at the Century, and that Kubrick marathon at the Tower. I've always wanted to see *Dr. Strangelove* on a big screen."

"Me too, but Saturday's not going to work." I hated to lie to the most attractive man I'd met in a long time, but I just wasn't ready to drop the news about the potential job in Los Angeles and watch it sit there between us all evening like an obnoxious uninvited guest. What if I decided not to accept the gig at RadioLand? I would have stirred up a lot of anguish for nothing. "I promised Glory Lou I'd go with her to San Jose to help out with her niece's bridal shower."

"A bridal shower? You really are a trooper."

"Tell me about it. She's picking me up at some ungodly hour of the morning and we won't be back until late in the evening."

"Sunday, then. I hear it's supposed to rain all weekend."

I directed Pete to a street numbered in the thirties near the intersection with J, just a few blocks from McKinley Park. The Thrifty Thirties, just west of the old money mansions in the Fabulous Forties, consisting of modest bungalows constructed in the early decades of the twentieth century to house cannery workers in Sacramento's then-thriving tomato processing industry. The old Libby factory over on P Street had long since been turned into a health club and offices, and the once-humble cottages were now highly sought after by the capital city's metrosexual urbanites.

The apartment complex that had supplied Travis with his last shelter was of more recent origin, a two-story stucco box shoehorned into a deep, narrow lot. An oil-spotted slab of asphalt with diagonal white stripes provided a parking slot in front of each unit. All that was needed to complete the look of a fifties-era motel was a flashing neon sign and an ice machine.

A beater of an economy import in the first parking space bore a bumper sticker advising me that the driver was "Cruisin' Not Usin'."

"I think we found the right place," I said to Pete.

Weak light from a fixture over the door of the corner unit on the second floor illuminated a figure lounging on the top of the stairs. He stood and waved a hand holding a lighted cigarette when he saw us pile out of the van. "You must be the lady from the radio," he said. "I told Travis's mom I'd keep my eye out for you."

I introduced myself and Pete Kovacs. "And you must be the roommate."

"Chad MacKenzie." He looked no older than twenty-five, all spiky hair that appeared to have been styled with an eggbeater, tattoos of an intertwined Celtic design circling each wrist. I'm at the tail end of the generation that still associates tattoos with bikers, sluts, and sailors, but I know I'm rapidly becoming the minority. I can appreciate the beauty of ethnic and tribal body art, like the designs Chad MacKenzie displayed. What I don't get are the guys who emblazon the logo of their favorite fortified beverage across their chest, or the young ladies who etch the name of their prom date on their lower back, where it will peep out from low-rider jeans. What are these kids thinking? In about ten years' time laser removal of body ink will be a growth industry, I predict.

"Unbelievable," Chad said with a slow shake of the head. "One minute you're here, next minute you're gone. Man."

"Tragic," I agreed.

"He'd just completed ninety days of sobriety. Man, I just don't know sometimes."

"I know just how you feel. But maybe there is something we can do to make sense out of this sad situation."

"Like what?" Chad took a step back and sucked on the cigarette.

"Like figuring out what really happened in McKinley Park Tuesday afternoon."

Chad exhaled a slow stream of smoke. "The police have already been nosing around asking questions."

"Humor me. You told them —"

102

"I told them no, I never heard of Markitus Wilson, and never heard Travis mention the name. No, I don't know why Travis would have been hanging out in back of the swimming pool at the park Tuesday afternoon. And no, Travis wasn't into crystal meth, or any other of your so-called controlled substances."

"How about a young woman named Brenda Driscoll?"

"Never heard Travis mention the name."

"Did you happen to notice a wound on his upper arm?"

Chad turned toward the balcony and flicked ash over the edge.

"Like a knife wound," I said. "A fresh injury that would have appeared just a day or two before he was killed. You probably would have seen it covered with a gauze pad and tape."

"I might have seen him messing around with something like that in the bathroom Sunday night." Chad kept his gaze fixed over the balcony, at the diagonal white stripes of the parking lot and the row of oleander bushes barely visible on the far side. "I didn't pay that much attention."

"None of your business, right?"

"Right." Chad ground out the cigarette with a foot shod in a designer athletic sneaker the size of a tugboat and led us into the apartment.

The place was surprisingly neat for a bachelor pad, through I wondered if Travis's mom had gone on a sanitizing blitz in anticipation of my arrival. The usual futon, folded and covered with a brightly hued crocheted afghan. Rickety dining table with three mismatched chairs, garage sale or Salvation Army thrift store treasures. A board and brick bookcase that held more DVDs and CDs than books.

My attention was drawn to the top shelf, where a wood and brass plaque rested between two thick candles. The plaque was roughly eight by ten and around two inches thick. It included an outline of a pair of human footprints, the slogan "Celebrate Sobriety!", Chad's name, and a date in early October of the previous year.

"My first day of sobriety," Chad came up beside me when he saw me inspecting the plaque.

"Congratulations. Promise me you won't let this setback tempt you to weaken your resolve."

"Man, no relapse for the Chadster. I'm letting go and letting god."

The petite figure of Sapphire Ikeda stood in the doorway of one of the apartment's two bedrooms. She hefted a cardboard box marked "good clothes" in bold felt pen. Pete relieved her of the burden and began lugging it down the stairs, while Sapphire ushered me into the bedroom and placed a manila file folder into my hands.

"I found this in with a bunch of his papers from the university." She gestured toward a plastic milk carton that Travis had turned into a portable filing cabinet. "I thought you might want it."

I dropped onto one corner of a mattress, already stripped of its linen and blankets, and opened the file. Twenty or so sheets of cheap office paper, one piece of creamy stationery, one greeting card, an envelope from the drugstore filled with snapshots.

Jeez. The kid had printed out and saved every e-mail that I'd sent to him during his internship and after. Plus the formal letter of recommendation I'd written when he completed his work-study summer, and the greeting card I'd mailed when he returned to UCLA, thanking him for his hard work and wishing him well. I placed the file folder on my knees and shook the photographs out of the envelope. I'd forgotten about the day Travis had brought his camera to the station and posed himself in front of the microphone in the on-air studio.

"Are you sure you don't want any of these?" I said to Sapphire.

She shifted her attention away from a flimsy pressboard bookcase, where she'd been pulling off textbooks, DVDs, and music disks and placing them in a banana box scrounged from the supermarket. "I wouldn't mind keeping that wonderful letter of recommendation that you wrote, if it's okay with you. And a few photographs."

"Okay? I'd be honored to have you keep it. And help yourself to as many of the pictures as you'd like. I can always make copies."

We divvied up the contents of the file folder, and Sapphire returned to the task of emptying the bookcase. "Here, let me help." I made a grab at a thick tome from the top shelf. I figured I'd help her fill one more box, get Pete to cart it down the stairs, and we'd take off for the half-hour drive to Davis in plenty of time to meet our reservation at that Czech restaurant we kept hearing about.

The object that I'd grabbed turned out not to be a textbook but a plaque identical to the one that had held a place of honor atop Chad's living room shelf. It bore the name of Travis Ikeda-Nyland and a date a couple of weeks more recent than the numerals on Chad's plaque.

"He was so proud of that," Sapphire said. "He talked about his first day of sobriety like it was his new birthday."

I could tell she was dangerously close to tears, so I eased myself a few feet away to give her privacy. I pretended to be engrossed in a wall calendar thumbtacked next to the bedroom door. January depicted a rugged man rappelling up a snow-covered peak, and a slogan urging the reader to cultivate "an attitude of gratitude." I came close to joining Sapphire in the weep-a-thon when I realized Travis had filled nearly every block on the calendar with the time and location of the AA meeting he planned to attend that day. He'd also noted a dental appointment, a reminder to pick up his bicycle from the repair shop, and "Mom's birthday," circled in red, on the last day of the month. I double-checked the date for this past Tuesday. No mention of an afternoon meeting in McKinley Park, just a 7:00 pm Alcoholics Anonymous meeting.

I reached my hand toward the thumbtack in preparation of removing the calendar and tossing it in the box, giving the handwritten notations one last scan before I pulled it from the wall. My hand jerked to a halt when I focused on a name scrawled in pencil

on a date one week previously, four days before Travis's fatal encounter in McKinley
Park.

My finger quivered as I pointed to the
date and I uttered a quavering gasp, not un-
like the sounds Clarissa St. Cyr made when
she contacted the spirit world.

No listing of a time or place for a meeting.
No phone number. Just a name.

Reginald Fessenden.

9

Doyle Bollinger wanted to make sure I had plenty of time to make my eleven o'clock appointment with RadioLand, and had booked me on the first flight of the day from the capital city to Burbank. Smart move during the winter months, ensuring that my plane arrived at Sacramento International the night before and wasn't stuck in a storm in some other city. I arrived at the terminal early enough to board in Group A and to capture my favorite seat, next to the over-the-wing emergency exit. It's the closest thing to first class you can find flying Southwest.

The long-promised storm was spitting drizzle during takeoff and a thick layer of clouds made sightseeing a futile quest. I flipped through the pages of the news magazine I'd brought with me and finally, unable to concentrate, tossed it back into my canvas tote bag. I really should have focused on my upcoming meeting with Doyle Bollinger, rehearsing my answers to the usual job interview queries: Personal strengths?

Weaknesses? Why are you interested in a career at RadioLand? Why, indeed!

At the very least, I should have been fretting over whether I'd selected the right wardrobe for this meeting. I couldn't ask Glory Lou for advice and risk tipping my hand that I was thinking of jumping ship. The career advice books would recommend a conservative business suit, stockings, and pumps. Instead, I took a fashion risk and decided to go for what I hoped was a hip, Hollywood look: narrow black jeans, silk T-shirt screened in tones of red, black, and silver with the likeness of James Dean, strappy sandals, and a vintage black leather jacket that I'd pounced upon at last year's Junior League rummage sale.

Reginald Fessenden. Him again! So who was this guy, calling my show and pretending to be some old pal from high school? The genuine article, the Canadian inventor known as the "Father of Radio Broadcasting," had been dead for around seventy years. And what was his name doing on the calendar of a college intern who'd worked for me a year and a half ago? What was the connection? More to the point, what, if anything, did he have to do with the death of Travis Ikeda-Nyland?

My flight landed right on time and I managed to negotiate in less than twenty minutes the line-standing and form-filling that goes with checking out a rental car. As I steered the sedan out of Burbank and over the Cahuenga Pass, I found myself wishing RadioLand had popped for a convertible. It was one of those kinds of days in the Los Angeles Basin, brilliant blue skies, temperatures in the seventies, snow glittering from the tops of the San Gabriels like one of those old postcards with the orange grove in the foreground. Like most Northern California residents, I have a love-hate relationship with the southern half of the state, on the one hand resenting their theft of "our" water, and the weighty influence of Orange County conservatism on our politics. And yet, I couldn't help but groove to the energy level, the limitless possibilities, and hold out hope that maybe a little bit of that stardust would sprinkle on me.

I followed Bollinger's directions to a modern high-rise near the intersection of Hollywood and Vine, drove into an underground parking garage, and gave my name to the guard. Before allowing me to proceed, he made me pop the trunk of the rental car and scanned the undercarriage with a mirror on a pole. Now there's a level of security you don't often see in Sacramento.

111

Once inside the building, I followed another sentry's instructions to pose for a Web cam while he tapped information from my ID into a keyboard. Satisfied that I posed no national security threat, he directed me to the fifteenth floor.

"Hope you didn't have any trouble finding us." Doyle Bollinger met me as the elevator door slid open after bonging to announce fifteen. He was even younger than I remembered from the Broadcast Legends meeting where we'd met this past fall. Thirty, tops. Like Chad from the night before, he had one of those tousled hair styles that were supposed to look like he'd just crawled out of bed but had probably taken more time to achieve than I spend in front of the mirror every morning. He wore an oversize Hawaiian print shirt, khaki shorts, and canvas deck shoes. Gee, and here I was concerned about dressing too casually.

"I've been waiting a long time for this meeting." Bollinger ushered me into a corner office furnished in retro-camp: kidney-shaped coffee table, grass cloth wall covering, director's chairs with Hawaiian print canvas covers, antique long board propped in one corner. A set of vertical blinds had been opened to reveal a view of scrub-covered hills and the Hollywood sign.

"Thanks for coming in to see me on a Saturday."

I settled into one of the director's chairs. "I could have taken a sick day and come during the week, but it just didn't feel right." I wasn't just snowing him with evidence of how dedicated an employee I could be. Calling in with a pretend case of the flu when all I needed was some personal time off really did violate my personal sense of ethics.

"I'm just glad we finally got you down here to see the place, and to let me introduce you to RadioLand. We give our client stations a variety of formats to choose from: Young Country, Classic Country, Urban, Lite Rock, Soft Hits, Classic Rock, Golden Oldies. With our state-of-the-art digital processors, we can customize the sound for the individual market. Your average listener will never know he's not listening to a jock in his hometown."

"Fascinating." I hadn't heard him mention anything that sounded like news or talk in that list of formats, and wondered what kind of gig Bollinger had in mind for me. Classic Rock, I would guess.

"Our newest programming service is something we're calling The Studio, pop hits from the seventies, nostalgia for the tail end of the baby boom generation. That's where we see you fitting in."

"You mean, like disco?"

"Some disco, sure. But mostly just pop hits from around 1972 to 1979. The Captain and Tennielle, Starland Vocal Band, the Carpenters, Manhattan Transfer, Barry Manilow. Our research shows there's a huge untapped market out there for those artists, now that the teenagers of the seventies are hitting the big four-oh."

"I can't wait."

"You'll be able to record an entire four-hour show in just thirty minutes, because you won't need to sit through the music and the commercials. Our engineers will take care of all that. You just contribute those smooth, sexy pipes."

"You mentioned creating a customized product for every market. I'd think it would take more than a half hour a day to do the research and writing."

"No worries. Brianna — you'll meet her when you come back during the week — takes care of all that. She gets on the Internet and looks up the weather forecast for our various markets, even local news. So you can congratulate the mayor of Shreveport on his re-election, or the high school basketball team in Dayton for winning the state cham-

114

pionship. Just like you were there. The listeners will never notice the difference."

Unless they try to phone in a request, or an earthquake strikes after I've finished recording my bits for the next day's show.

"You'll be living in one of the most exciting cities in the world and only working a couple of hours a day. So you'll have plenty of time to pursue other opportunities. Voice-overs, commercials, animation. You should think about getting an agent. Of course, we'll own the rights to the Shauna J. Bogart name."

Of course.

Bollinger led me from his office down the hall. "Here's the studio where you'll be working."

Everything was digital, high tech, no dials to twist or sliders to push. "I feel like I've been beamed aboard the bridge of the *Starship Enterprise*."

"No worries. Austin will be your engineer." A skinny kid who appeared barely old enough to vote glanced up from a computer monitor. An unseen voice from a wall-mounted speaker intoned, "You're tuned to Lite 'n' Easy Hits for Buffalo . . . you're tuned to Lite 'n' Easy Hits for Oklahoma City . . . you're tuned to Lite 'n' Easy Hits for Boise . . . Milwaukee . . . Flagstaff. . . ."

Millions of people coast-to-coast listening to radio programs originating from this tiny room in a bland Hollywood high-rise? Produced by a couple of kids named Brianna and Austin?

"I'm sure you have questions," Bollinger said when he wrapped up the tour.

"For starters, why me? And don't tell me it's because you used to listen to me when you were a kid." I added a smile.

"Strictly a business decision. San Francisco is the first major market we've been able to penetrate with The Studio format. Most of our potential audience listened to you when they were teenagers. We did the research, and you tested incredibly strong with them."

I'd already decided I wouldn't take this job for anything less than sixty grand, five thousand more than my present annual income. Now that I'd actually seen RadioLand and realized they didn't want me to launch a new nationwide talk show, I upped the ante. It would take at least seventy-five thousand a year, plus benefits, to get me to introduce Barry Manilow songs and recite the time and temperature for all those listeners in Shreveport, Louisiana, and Dayton, Ohio.

Bollinger took me to lunch at a rustic,

greenery-filled eatery just off Melrose Avenue. "We offer full medical benefits, dental, life insurance, the works," he said between bites of a veggie burger. "Profit-sharing, and a bonus for every market in which you hit Number One in adults twenty-five to forty-four. Of course, we're prepared to buy out your contract at your station up in Sacramento."

"Sounds great." I played with my Caesar salad. I could just picture my obituary: She sold her soul for a dental plan.

"We're prepared to offer you eighty-five thou a year. Base."

"Dear God."

"I know that's not what you're used to." Bollinger apparently mistook my amazement for reluctance. "But that's just for starters. Once we sign up a few more major markets we can sweeten the deal."

I didn't know what to say, so I stabbed my fork at a piece of free-range chicken.

"Okay. What if we pick up your moving expenses?"

"This is a lot to think about," I said finally.

"Of course." Bollinger pushed his plate away and sat back on the wooden bench, his hands clasped behind his head. "Take a few days and mull it over."

"My boss is on vacation," I ad-libbed to buy myself time. "He won't be back in town until the end of the day Wednesday. I can't make a final decision until I've talked to him."

Bollinger ran his fingers through his rumpled hairdo, accentuating the bed head effect. "We were hoping to have this firmed up by the end of the week."

"Fine, then. Give me until Friday. End of the day." I was already pretty sure what the answer would be. How could I say no to that kind of money? And give up what — a boss who thought it was okay to broker time on my show to a psychic, and who expected me to bow and scrape to the whims of major advertisers? I just needed time to break the news to him, and say a graceful good-bye to Sacramento.

And to figure out how to make it work with Pete Kovacs.

I had a couple of hours to kill before I needed to return to the Burbank airport, and that included time to check in the rental car, ride the shuttle back to the terminal, remove my sandals, and step through security. I could have backtracked over the pass and wheedled my way onto an earlier flight back to Sacramento, but who knows how many days would pass before I'd get to enjoy this much sunshine?

Bollinger was more than happy to accommodate me when I requested to log on to one of his office computers after lunch, probably assuming I was eager to e-mail friends and colleagues with the news about his job offer. A few minutes of Google searching on "sober living," "student housing," and "UCLA" offered the name and address of a likely place, and MapQuest supplied the directions.

I got lost only once, circled around the huge VA hospital at Wilshire and the 405, then located what had obviously once been a fraternity house, faux white columns and all, sandwiched between Westwood Village and the UCLA campus. "The Thirteenth Step" was painted in gold letters on a sign hanging above the front door where undoubtedly Greek letters had once stood.

A young man paced on the porch and appeared to be talking to himself. I ventured up the sidewalk and discovered he was chatting into one of those hands-free cell phone rigs. When I reached the top of the three stairs leading to the porch, a second student closed the constitutional law textbook he'd been reading and rose to a sitting position on an aluminum lounge chair.

I introduced myself and confirmed that I had found the sober-living house in which Travis had stayed during his last two years at the nearby university. The fellow with the cell phone gave a name of Jared something, while the guy on the lounge chair said to call him what sounded like Tofu. It took a few minutes before I realized it was the currently popular nickname for males named Christopher. Topher, or just Toph. Both young men wore sloppy cotton T-shirts and baggy cargo pants containing enough cloth to cover a picnic table and still have enough material left for napkins. Do these guys honestly think the female of the species finds that look the least bit attractive?

"We heard what happened to Travis," Jared said.

"Totally," Toph added, which I gathered was his all-purpose expression to indicate extreme emotion.

I repeated the pair of names — Markitus Wilson, Brenda Driscoll — that I'd run by Travis's roomie up in Sacramento the night before, and received the same response from his Southern California housemates. Never heard of them, never heard Travis mention them.

"How about some fellow named Reginald Fessenden?"

"Wasn't he, like, a character on *Rocky and Bullwinkle?*" Toph contributed.

"You're thinking of Inspector Fenwick," Jared said, adding in my direction, "I'm positive Travis never mentioned the man. That name I would have remembered for sure."

"I don't mean to pry, but what's the story with this house? Do you have to be a graduate of a recovery program to live here?"

"Not necessarily," Jared said. "Some of us are here just because we want an alternative to the heavy party scene at the frat houses and the dorms."

"Some of us actually came here to study." Toph hefted the thick textbook over his head with one hand.

"So tell me, what happened to Travis last fall?" I settled myself onto a section of the lounge chair that Toph had just offered. "His family tells me everything was perking along just fine, he's working hard, going to AA meetings, getting good grades, doing all the right things. Then one day out of the blue he's off the wagon."

"Relapsed, big time," Jared said.

"But why? Did he break up with a girlfriend maybe?"

The two students looked at each other and shook their heads. "Not that he didn't have plenty of friends who were girls," Jared said. "He always said he was still searching for the special one."

"How about his studies? Any particular problems there?"

"Not that I know of. How about you, Toph?"

"Seems to me he was even more motivated than usual. I remember he talked to me one night for hours about how he was thinking about going to work for his dad for a couple of years, then go back for an MBA so he could really make a contribution to the family business."

"Anything else unusual or out of the ordinary that might have happened during those first weeks of fall quarter?"

"There was that guy who showed up to visit." Toph turned in Jared's direction. "Remember him?"

"Totally. He showed up late September or early October." Jared lowered himself to the wooden floor of the porch, arranged himself cross-legged, and pushed the cell phone rig off his head so it hung around his neck like a religious symbol.

"Some friend of his from back home in Sacramento, wasn't he?" Toph said.

"I'm pretty sure, yeah. Some guy he grew up with. I think it was the night he arrived that Travis went out partying. Big mistake."

"According to the house rules, he should have been asked to leave right then and there. But we covered for him, me and Jared. Looking back, we probably should have busted him that first night he came home drunk."

"Why do you say that?" I asked.

"It was like, one slip and he had given himself permission to screw up every night," Jared said. "He knew he had good ol' Toph and Jared watching his back, so that made it easy for him to keep on going out to parties and clubs. Next thing you know . . ."

"The DUI," I prompted.

"Yeah. The DUI."

"This guy from Sacramento, did you ever meet him? Did Travis ever mention a name?"

Jared and Toph looked at each other. "Travis introduced him once," Jared said, "but it was right when I was in a hurry leaving for class. He was a little bit older than Travis, I think, and for sure not Asian."

"Just your average white guy," Toph said.

"He had a weird name. Not as strange as Reginald Fessen-whatever, though."

I leaned forward in the flimsy aluminum lounge chair. "What kind of weird name?"

Jared's young face screwed up in thought. "I can't remember. Just weird."

"I think Travis mentioned a name to me once or twice," Toph said.

I itched to probe further, take the two young men out for pizza in the hopes that spicy grease might loosen a memory cell or two. But a glance at my watch reminded me that I'd better hit the 405 and start making serious progress back to the Burbank airport. I pulled two business cards out of my tote bag and handed one to each student. "If either of you remember the name, or anything else about this visitor Travis had last fall, I'd really appreciate it if you'd get in touch."

"Is it important?" Jared said. "I mean, will it help you figure out what happened to Travis?"

"Possibly. You never know. So feel free to get in touch anytime."

"If we think of anything, we sure will, Miz Bogart."

"Totally," Toph added.

Pete Kovacs was at my door, pizza box and six-pack in hand, within minutes after I'd changed into my favorite pair of comfy sweats, fed the cat, and poured myself a glass of wine. "Room service for Sacramento's favorite talk radio host. Tipping of the delivery boy is encouraged."

The bantering words were casual and friendly, but his voice had a flat strain and I didn't like the tightening of the muscles that I detected around his eyes and mouth.

"Come on in and get yourself out of that wet slicker." I carefully lifted the fragrant box from his hands, placed it on the dining table, opened the lid, and inhaled. Zelda's deep-dish cheese and mushroom. Our favorite.

Pete stepped out to the balcony to shake the water off his raincoat and drape it over a patio chair, seated himself at the dining table, and snapped open a can of beer. "You didn't really spend the day at a bridal shower in San Jose with Glory Lou," he said. "What gives?"

"What, what gives? I went to San Jose with Glory Lou. Why do you think I had to pour myself a glass of wine the minute I got home? I barely survived that bit where they cover the bride-to-be with toilet paper to look like a wedding gown."

"I ran a few errands this morning, just happened to turn on the radio to your station, and who do I hear on the air but good ol' Glory Lou."

Well, damn. She must not have been able to line up a fill-in call screener for the garden show and took the shift herself.

"So what gives?" Pete said. "Is it that pilot you've been spending so much time with?"

"Captain Mikey?" I made more noise than I needed to as I slammed down plates and forks next to the pizza box. "You know me better than that."

"Yeah." Pete gave me a sad smile and took a gulp of beer. "I do know you better than that. But I also know you're hiding something. Again I ask: what gives?"

I'd hoped for a little more time to sort out my feelings about Los Angeles in general and RadioLand in specific. Maybe place a couple of phone calls to colleagues in the business and get the scoop on Doyle Bollinger, just to make certain this gig really was the right career move. I had deluded myself into believing the longer I waited, the easier it would be to break the news to Pete.

"You're right." I seated myself and began transferring slices of the still-steaming pie to the plates. "It's time to give what gives."

10

I stood in my bathrobe and touched a button on the mantle, sending jets of gas flame dancing in the fireplace. Convenient, yes, but I missed the crackle and scent of a real wood fire. The rain continued to lash against the apartment windows, and I craved any source of cheer, no matter how faux.

Pete had tumbled out of bed while I was still snoozing and dashed outdoors to retrieve the Sunday paper. What a guy! Still, the mood inside the apartment tilted toward the chilly side, perhaps not as turbulent as the storm raging outside our doors, but nonetheless with clouds lurking on the horizon. Even the kitty seemed to sense the taut atmosphere and had skittered under the bed as soon as he'd finished wolfing down his morning helping of kibble.

Pete placed a steaming cup in my hand and settled in on the couch next to me. "When we move to Los Angeles, maybe we can get a house with a real fireplace."

I was about to reply that in L.A. we wouldn't *need* a fireplace. Wait a minute! Had I really heard him say what I thought I'd heard?

"You mean it?" I rose to my knees on the lumpy couch so I could face him directly.

"I'm not necessarily saying I'm all for it. But if we combine our resources, and especially with the money you'll be making, we ought to be able to afford a fireplace."

"But what about Retro Alley?"

"C'mon, I barely break even on the store. Ninety percent of my business is on-line these days. I could do it anywhere."

"But you love having that store. You thrive on all that personal interaction with the customers. Especially in the summer, when it's busy."

"I've been doing some thinking." Pete stretched and placed slippered feet on the coffee table. "I could keep the store, maybe take on a partner, and come back to Sacramento a couple of weekends a month to keep my hand in. After all, Southwest has flights practically every hour."

"Then how about the band?" When he wasn't playing shopkeeper, Pete pounded stride piano with a Dixieland band. How could he duplicate that in Los Angeles?

"The band may have to do without me.

128

There are plenty of musicians in L.A. I'm sure it wouldn't be that difficult to put together a new band and find a pizza parlor where we could play."

"Jeez, you'd do that?"

"I just wonder, are you sure this is the right move for you? Giving up talk radio and going back to being a disc jockey? I thought you hated how bland and sterile the radio music scene had become."

"Yeah, but look at the money they're offering."

"Have you thought about going to T. R. O'Brien and asking him to match the offer?"

"Of course I've thought of that. But let's be realistic; there's no way he could come up with that kind of dough. I mean, he's even brokering his airtime to a psychic and outsourcing Captain Mikey."

"If the money weren't an issue, would you still be interested in the job?"

"That's a difficult question to answer." I placed the mug on the coffee table and drew a chenille throw to my neck. "But I've got to consider my long-term career. Make my move while I'm still at the top of my game and all that. I mean, how long is O'Brien going to be able to keep the station competitive when he's continually outgunned by the big corporate broadcasters?"

"That's true. It's tough to be an independent these days, no matter what business you're in."

"How about you? Setting aside the money for a minute, given your druthers, is it Sacramento or L.A.?"

"In an ideal world, I'd like everything to stay just the way it is." He spoke slowly and paused to sip coffee. "But like I said before, I can sell kitsch and collectibles anywhere, thanks to the Internet. I'm more concerned about making a decision that's right for you."

"You know what I want to know?" I snuggled into the folds of Pete's flannel bathrobe.

"What?"

"What did I ever do to deserve to be so damn lucky?"

I could have cheerfully stayed on that couch for the rest of Sunday, cuddling with a very special man, watching the fake flames swaying in the fireplace, listening to the raindrops doing their tap dance against the windows, and trying my best to make one of the most important decisions of my life. In some ways, I wished Pete hadn't been so considerate. If he'd dug in his heels and said no way are we moving to L.A. and that's final, the choice might have been easier.

On the other hand, if he were that kind of jerk, I wouldn't be having a relationship with him, now would I?

Assuming I did say yes to RadioLand, I was probably looking at my last week as a talk radio personality in Sacramento. If the upcoming week really did represent my last five days on the air in Sacramento, then I wanted to go out in style. By my definition, style meant breaking a major local news story, giving the listeners a reason to miss me for more than a few days after I was gone. And right now, there was no story making bigger local headlines than the death of Travis Ikeda-Nyland.

The most tantalizing clue was the reference to Reginald Fessenden on Travis's calendar. But I didn't have the means to follow up until Monday, when I could go on the air and throw out a plea for the mystery man to call in. That left the only lead worth pursuing on a Sunday, the name Markitus Wilson had scrawled onto a scrap of paper just before leaving his grandmother's house. "Brenda." According to the fellow at the aerobics studio, she was modeling at an auto show this weekend.

I tore myself away from the comfort of the couch and scrounged through the recycle bin next to the front door until I found the weekend entertainment section from Friday's *Bee*. "Funny, I don't see any auto show listed in here," I said when I finished riffling the pages.

"The auto show?" Pete looked up from the commentary and opinion section of the current day's paper. "Wouldn't you rather go see that new Altman film?"

"Someone I'm interested in talking to is supposed to be working at the auto show this weekend. Strange, you'd think they'd at least list it on the local events calendar."

"The only local car show I know about is the Auto-rama and that's not for another month. Did you try the automotive section?"

Another plunge into the recycle bin retrieved the automotive section from Friday's paper, tossed into the oblivion of the plastic tub without ever having been read. I noticed that the ads for the Nyland Automotive Group were more subdued than usual, no garish yellows and reds, the grinning, thumbs-up photo of Ray Nyland missing from the logo. "No auto show here either," I said. "That's odd."

Odd?

There may not have been an auto show in the capital city this weekend.

But there was most definitely a show called OddCon.

It's easy to mock events like the *Space Odyssey* fan convention, those gatherings of folks obsessed with comic books, action heroes, sword and sorcery movies, or in this case, a television series that's been off the air for a good thirty years now. But as I look at it, these people at least are getting out of the house and doing something more interesting with their spare time than just sprawling on the couch and clicking the remote. As the saying goes, they have a life, albeit a fantasy life. At any rate, I'm the last person who should be making light of the whole science fiction fan scene. I mean, you can't get much geekier than belonging to the high school Audio-Visual Club.

I managed to bull my way into the ballroom of the two-star chain hotel off Interstate 80 on the city's north edge by flashing my California Highway Patrol media pass. Not that I'm cheap, but they were charging twenty-five dollars for a one-day ticket into OddCon, and that, as the fellow at the door informed me, did not include any enhancements. I shoved the ticket into a pocket and pushed my way through the crowd of amateur rocket jockeys, space cadets, and alien life forms, plus a minority of civilians, most of the latter wearing T-shirts proclaiming their allegiances to a favorite character, space vehicle, brand of computer, or galaxy.

For some reason, Sacramento is one of the home planet's hot spots when it comes to science fiction, fantasy, and all things nerdy. I'm guessing the reason, as usual, traces back to the omnipresence of state government, and the need for a ready supply of tech types to keep all those huge mainframes humming at places like the DMV and the Franchise Tax Board. That, plus being far enough away from Hollywood, but not too far — those convenient hourly flights — makes it the ideal test market for studio trailers and sneak previews.

Pete had begged off on the expedition, claiming the need to spend some time updating the Retro Alley Web site, and offering the opinion that I was embarking on the longest of long shots. I was beginning to think he was right as I scanned the dealer tables with their light sabers, paperback movie novelizations, action figures, character makeup, and costume patterns, searching for a booth bunny who resembled the athletic young woman whose photo I'd seen on the wall of the dance studio the previous Thursday evening.

Two pairs of arms waved in recognition

from a line that snaked from one end of the ballroom to the other, wrapping around the back wall of booths.

"Slumming it?" Josh Friedman said when I drew close enough to hear over the din of the crowd. His housemate, Andrew Stoller, stood at his side. Each wore a tiny lapel pin that pulsated with a pinpoint of red light. From what I could tell, they were roughly three-quarters of the way to the front of the line, which had stalled in front of a dealer applying temporary henna tattoos of the *Space Odyssey* logo. At least, I hoped it was temporary.

"Call it a field study," I said. "What's up with the line?"

"Marshall Dean Sheridan, that's what's up."

Oh, yeah. The star of the original series, and the marquee celebrity of this weekend's event.

"You guys are waiting in a line this long just for Marshall Dean Sheridan's autograph?"

"And a photo opportunity," Andrew said.

I slithered my way to the front of the ballroom, careful to reassure the autograph seekers that I was not trying to jump the line and risk getting beaned with a light saber. I recognized Marshall Dean Sheridan from the television commercials he'd recently appeared in for a regional chain of discount tire stores. He was stuffed into his old galaxy explorer's costume and was seated in an easy chair, his legs spread wide to accommodate a belly hefty enough to strike fear in any space invader. Three young women bustled at his side, sliding the fans' tickets through what looked like a credit card machine, then hustling them through the autograph session and photo op like a trio of intergalactic Santa's elves. Each wore a minidress and thigh-high boots, and each had a high-tech weapon strapped around her waist, the Jane Fonda–as–Barbarella look that never seems to go out of favor with the geek male.

One of them, I was pretty sure, was the instructor from the aerobics studio. She had the same thousand-watt smile, the short, geometric haircut, and the saucer-size hoop earrings, as well as the ideal leggy figure to display her out-of-this-world getup. T. R. O'Brien would have described the type as a tall glass of spring water on a hot afternoon.

I rethreaded my way through the crowd. Josh and Andrew had inched forward maybe two booths' worth, standing now in front of a dealer who promised to render your name in interplanetary code on a handsome plaque.

"How long is this autograph thing supposed to last?" I asked.

"Supposedly until everyone has a chance to get through the line," Josh said.

"Really? That's awfully generous of a star like Marshall Dean Sheridan."

The two young men looked at each other and snickered.

"Didn't you notice how they're swiping everyone's ticket up there?" Josh said.

"Yeah? So?"

"So that's how they check to see whether you've paid for any enhancements to your general admission ticket, like autographs."

"Paying for an autograph?" My voice rose into a shocked squeal.

"Thirty bucks for just the autograph, fifty if you want the autograph and the photo op," Andrew said.

"Jeez, you've already paid to get into the convention. Shouldn't the autographs be free?"

"For real. But it's like everyone else does it," Josh said. "Major League baseball players and all."

"You can't blame them for wanting to make a buck," Andrew said. "Maybe Sheridan won't have to do those lame tire

137

commercials any longer if he makes enough money this weekend."

"But this is *Space Odyssey!*"

I followed Josh and Andrew as they shuffled forward in the line. "I didn't see any cash changing hands up there."

Josh reached into the front pocket of his jeans and removed a business card–size piece of cardboard with a magnetic strip on the back. "They run your ticket through a machine and it tells them what you've paid for. Yours would come up just general admission. So they let you into the dealer room and the panels, but that's it. We've got the deluxe weekend pass. That means we have unlimited access for autographs and photos."

"Plus the costume ball last night, and the first-season-tribute brunch this morning," Andrew said.

I didn't even want to think about how much those two had paid for their unlimited access passes. Probably more than what Josh took home every week from being my producer. I pulled the comp general admission ticket from the pocket of my slacks. How soon would events such as OddCon start tucking those tiny radio transmitters into the tickets, like the ones that saleslady had demonstrated at Pete's store the other day? How much data on, say, the ticket holder's favorite character, or the number and type of dealer booths he visited, could be beamed back to a big motherboard hiding behind the curtains?

I estimated I had at least an hour to kill before the final Marshall Dean Sheridan fan would reach the front of the line and I finally had a chance for a private word with the woman I believed was Brenda Driscoll. I spent some time at a trivia contest that seemed to consist of one team hurling lines from a script and the other team guessing which episode it came from, and sat in on a panel discussion on biblical metaphors in *Space Odyssey* stories.

The model who I believed was my quarry was snapping the last of the fan photo ops with Marshall Dean Sheridan when I returned to the front of the ballroom. I waited for the final flash to pop and for a teenager in full *Space Odyssey* regalia to release her grip from Sheridan's shoulder, then waved and beckoned to Brenda.

"Sorry, we're closed," she said. "Sheridan's got a plane to catch."

"Not a problem." I flipped open my wallet, so the young woman could see my CHP media ID card. I was banking on her thirst for stardom to overcome any reluctance she might have had about talking to the news media. "You're Brenda Driscoll, right? I was hoping we could talk."

"About what?" She sounded wary.

Shouts and screeches erupted and a mini-stampede whirlpooled around the two of us as Marshall Dean Sheridan attempted to flee from a side exit.

"Let's find someplace where we can talk," I said. "How soon can you wrap things up and get out of here?"

She pressed the top row of her pearly whites onto her bottom lip. I could almost see the thought process at work, the fear of getting involved duking it out with the craving for publicity. If I had been a gambler, I would have placed odds on the latter coming out the winner. After all, this is a young woman who hired herself out as a model at a science fiction fan convention. The rungs on the show business ladder don't get much lower.

"Meet me in the lobby in fifteen minutes," she said. "By that statue."

Turned out I had to hover in front of the cheesy plastic likeness of the hotel chain's founder for almost a half hour before Brenda burst through one of the service doors. She'd thrown a purple plastic rain-coat over what I assumed were her street clothes, and had traded in the thigh-high boots for white sneakers.

"Sorry," she said when she reached the statue. "It took forever to find the guy who runs this thing and to get him to sign my time card for the agency."

"Not a problem. I imagine you know what this is about."

"Markitus Wilson. I'll tell you the same thing I told the cops. I haven't seen him in years, not since high school, and I had no idea he still had feelings for me."

"So you and Markitus went to high school together?"

"Cordova." She followed up with a graduation year from three years ago. "I was pretty sure he was hot for me back then, but as far as I was concerned, we were just friends. I was going out with his best friend's older brother all through high school."

"A regular teenage soap opera."

"I moved away from Rancho Cordova as soon as I could after graduation and haven't seen Markitus since." She spoke without hesitation and made eye contact. "This whole thing is just a huge, horrible surprise. Have you heard anything new?"

"I've been told he's still in a coma over at the Med Center." My "insider information" came from this morning's *Bee*, but Brenda didn't need to know that.

"Poor kid. Poor sweet, mixed-up kid."

"How do you suppose Markitus managed to locate you after all that time had gone by?"

"Maybe he saw me performing in the Solstice Revels."

We gave each other looks that said, "Yeah, right." Sacramento's culture-with-a-capital-*C* events like the Music Circus, the ballet, and the Solstice Revels might employ an attractive and talented African-American like Brenda Driscoll as a chorus dancer, but she'd be performing in front of a mostly Caucasian audience. The closest a young man from the Rancho Cordova 'hood would come to an event like Solstice Revels would be as part of the theater's cleaning crew.

"He could have seen one of the ads in the newspaper." She folded her arms across the front of the raincoat. "Who knows?"

"Who indeed. How about a guy named Reginald Fessenden. Sound familiar?"

She crinkled her nose as if smelling something foul. "Reginald who?"

"Fessenden. No one by that name has tried to get in touch with you lately? Markitus never mentioned him?"

"I told you, I haven't seen Markitus

Wilson since high school. Listen, I'm supposed to be meeting a girlfriend for dinner tonight so I'm going to have to run." Her rangy legs began striding toward the automatic sliding glass doors that comprised the hotel's grand entrance.

The rain had slacked off to a drizzle, and a few shafts of weak late afternoon sunlight reflected off the puddles in the parking lot. I wasn't sure what else to ask Brenda, but I didn't want her to escape after I'd devoted a good part of a Sunday afternoon to tracking her down.

"I hear you're up for a part in an indie film that they're shooting here in Sacramento," I said when I'd caught up to her. "That must be exciting." Get her chatting about her career, slow her down long enough for me to get the questioning back on track.

She halted next to a shiny orange coupe, a recent model with an angular shape like an old-fashioned train caboose. "Who told you that?"

"I think I read about it in Bob Graswich's column in the *Bee*," I said, not wanting to create any trouble for Benji at the aerobics studio.

She did that crinkly thing with her nose. "The film project's dead. Anyway, I've got an audition next week to be one of the Royal

Court Dancers. That's a lot more exciting than some low-budget film, don't you agree?"

"Definitely." I wasn't blowing smoke. Sacramento is obsessed with its NBA team, and the chance to join the Kings' dance team would most certainly trump a role in an independent film for an ambitious young woman like Brenda Driscoll.

"Wish me luck, then." She unlocked the orange vehicle and tossed the raincoat onto the front passenger seat.

"Break a leg." I watched as the box on wheels crept forward in the rain-slicked parking lot toward the exit to Auburn Boulevard.

The rear license plate frame bore the logo of the Nyland Automotive Group and the slogan "I Saved With Ray!"

So did about half the vehicles on the road in Sacramento.

11

I drove into the parking lot of the aging shopping center that housed the Footprints Institute and found a spot for the Z-car next to the beat-up economy import with the "Cruisin' Not Usin' " bumper sticker. A bright yellow and red banner stretched across the entrance made the office of the recovery institute hard to miss. As soon as I spotted the word "Today" I just knew "is the first day of the rest of your life" would follow.

I'm not necessarily knocking programs like Alcoholics Anonymous, though I do have reservations about the cultlike aspects, and the fact that the court can mandate participation in meetings that require a spiritual commitment to a Higher Power. Hello? The First Amendment? On the other hand, I work in an industry that's a magnet for neurotic, loner types — something about those tiny rooms with just you, the microphone, and the invisible audience — who drift into risky behavior. Booze, prescription painkillers, cocaine, gambling, you name it. I've seen too many promising careers destroyed by vices that had ratcheted out of control. I've also observed colleagues whose lives have literally been saved by programs like Footprints. So I try to reserve judgment, and if I had to choose an aphorism for myself, it would be There But for the Grace.

I hadn't bothered to make an appointment to see anyone at Footprints, riding the hunch that after the blizzard of press releases and requests for public service time with which they routinely bombarded the station, they'd be thrilled to have a real, live media person drop in. The receptionist all but tripped over himself in his eagerness to thrust an inch-thick press kit into my hands, and hustled me down a hallway past several closed doors.

The receptionist deposited me in the executive director's office. "What are the odds Dr. Yount would be in town this morning?" he gushed. "This is a lucky day for all of us."

"What a pleasant surprise!" A woman rose from a battered wooden desk in the cluttered corner office. "I listen to your show whenever I have the chance. I just so admire what you're doing to bring balance to the airwaves."

"And I've heard wonderful things about you and your program, Dr. Yount."

"Janice. Please, call me Janice, make yourself comfortable, and promise me there'll be no more of that Dr. Yount nonsense."

She could have been anywhere from forty to sixty, one of those soft, cuddly, auntie types with short, graying brown hair, a sagging chin under an unlined face, and a perpetual smile. An ever-so-slightly plump body was covered with a crocheted tunic in a zigzag of primary colors and black wool stretch pants.

No one could accuse the Footprints Institute of squandering donors' money on opulent offices for either the clients or the staff. The institute took up most of the storefronts of the small shopping center near Florin Mall, a beauty school at one end and a crafts store at the other being the only other tenants. Dr. Yount's — Janice's — office wasn't much bigger than a walk-in closet and offered only metal folding chairs for guests, on one of which I squirmed to find a comfy spot. On the shabby linoleum floor, I could make out the stains and fade marks where retail display cases and racks had once anchored. Janice still had one of those ancient tractor-fed dot matrix printers hooked up to her PC.

A framed poster on the wall behind Janice's desk featured a photograph of an ocean shoreline and a close-up of a line of footprints in the sand. I was too far away to make out the text, but I recalled bits of the story. Something about two sets of footprints, yours and God's, and when you see an imprint of only one pair of feet, well, that's the part where God is carrying you. Treacle-laced homilies such as this one usually set my teeth on edge. But if the footprints story gave my onetime intern the strength to turn his back, if only temporarily, on that bottle of liquid courage, then be my guest.

I told Janice I wanted to gather background information for a possible public service campaign.

"Our high school peer counselor program might make an interesting topic for your show," she said. "For our adult clients, we offer a variety of group therapy options, depending on the needs of the individual, as well as one-on-one counseling. Then, of course, there's Footprints Lodge." Her face broke into an even broader smile. "Our crown jewel, if you will."

She handed a brochure across the desk. "Many of our clients are in circumstances that require them to detox under the supervision of a twenty-four-hour nursing staff. Others who are new to recovery benefit from a structured, live-in situation as they make the transition to sobriety."

I scanned the brochure's cover, a photograph of a group of earnest-looking men and women seated in a circle in front of a cluster of pines, and the text: "Celebrate recovery in a serene mountain setting!"

"A serene mountain setting?" I said.

"We were lucky enough to acquire a beautiful facility in the Sierra foothills. Nature plays such an important part in the healing process, don't you agree?"

"Absolutely." Like I'm an expert.

"I'm just so excited about the work we're doing up at the lodge. I find I'm spending most of my time up there these days. It was only by sheer accident that you happened to find me in my office here in Sacramento this morning. Wasn't that a lucky break for both of us?"

I was about to answer affirmatively when a young man wearing the ubiquitous baggy cargo pants, sneakers, and an untucked flannel shirt entered the office. Greasy hair that might have been blond, given the benefit of a shampoo, drooped to his shoulders.

"Gavin, say hello to Shauna J. Bogart from Sacramento Talk Radio," Janice prompted.

Gavin grunted a greeting and began flailing away at the computer keyboard.

"We finally have the funding to upgrade our computer system," Janice said. "Gavin's got his hands full getting it all configured and hooked up. We're lucky to have him."

"For real. You know, I went to high school with a fellow who was clever like Gavin. I understand he's got a connection to your program. Reginald Fessenden?" I studied Janice and Gavin for any flickers of recognition. Janice maintained her upbeat exterior, while Gavin, to my untrained ear, never missed a beat on the electronic keyboard.

"You realize we can't disclose any information about our clients," Janice said. "Not even to confirm whether they even are past or present clients. Except to appropriate government agencies, of course."

"Of course." As a privacy advocate, I agreed one hundred percent with the policy. If it were up to me, I would have cut the government out of the information loop. Yet that same policy would make it difficult to pry any information out of Janice or her lieutenants about one particular client named Travis Ikeda-Nyland.

"You don't hear that name much anymore," Janice said. "Reginald?"

"Fessenden. Reginald Fessenden. If you should just happen to run across him, you might ask him to give me a call."

"It would be my pleasure."

I began gathering up the press kit and my down jacket. "Thanks, you've given me a lot of great ideas for the show."

"No, thank you." She rose and reached across the desk to clasp my hand. "I hope we'll be seeing you at Tennies and Tuxes."

"I beg your pardon?"

"Our big fundraiser of the year. A gourmet dinner served on the floor of Arco Arena followed by the chance to shoot baskets with your favorite Kings player. A lot of local media celebrities participate. It's really tons of fun."

"Sure, count me in." By the time her event rolled around on the social calendar, I'd be having my own tons of fun in a windowless studio inside a corporate office tower in Hollywood.

"You're well on your way to developing a pretty smooth stick." Captain Mikey put his initials on the pilot's logbook and handed it to me. "What is it that you're going to remember?"

"Hold the wing down to compensate for the crosswind?"

"Correct. And straighten it just before touchdown."

We stood on the concrete apron at Executive Airport after completing another hour of noontime traffic reports and a little flight instruction on the side. The weekend storm had cleared, giving us a luminous vista of the Central Valley and the snow-capped Sierra to the east. We'd spent most of the sixty minutes circling the downtown core, where a jackknifed big rig carrying a load of canned fruit cocktail had turned the 99–80 connector into a syrupy slowdown. The sun sparkled from the capitol dome and the windows of the government skyscrapers and reflected off the muddy waters of the Sacramento River churning toward San Francisco and the Pacific. On days like this, floating two thousand feet above the stresses and frustrations of those highways and cubicles far below, a person could fall in love with a city like Sacramento.

Michael waved a signal to a figure striding toward us from a row of hangars. "Hugh Stanton, one of the news guys at City Scope," he told me.

"I knew you'd want the chance to meet Shauna J. Bogart," Michael said to Stanton.

"A pleasure." Stanton shook my hand. He wore a knitted ski cap pulled down over his ears, wraparound sunglasses, and a fur-collared nylon windbreaker snuggled up around his chin. "So much for sunny California," he added.

"Hugh just relocated here from Florida," Michael said.

"Just wait 'til summer, when a cooling trend means the temperatures are only in the nineties," I said. The mercury hovered around the fifty-degree mark today, but the brisk breeze that had swept out the storm delivered an icy slap. "But for real, congratulations on the job at City Scope."

"It's only weekends and fill-in work for now," Stanton said. "If City Scope signs on with a few more stations, I'm supposed to be first in line for a full-time gig. I'm thinking about calling myself Sky View Hugh. What do you think?"

Michael had told me the story once about how he'd transitioned from Colonel Giordano to Captain Mikey. When he first took to the airwaves two decades ago, early listener comments and focus groups perceived him as too gruff and militaristic. A consultant suggested softening up his image by the addition of a cute nickname. Now it seemed as if every airborne traffic reporter had to adopt a gimmick, a *nom du aéro*.

"Sounds like a winner," I said. "I'll look forward to hearing you on the air."

We ambled through the terminal toward the parking lot, Michael and Hugh trading scuttlebutt about their new corporate owner at City Scope. I still felt the tug of the endless blue horizon teasing me back to the skies.

"Watch out, they'll try to make you wear an ID badge," I heard Michael tell Stanton.

"Forget it."

"That's what I told them. The last time I wore an ID badge was my last day in the air force. They have a problem with that, they can get themselves another flyboy."

"Amen to that."

Michael removed his wallet from an inside pocket of his leather flight jacket and withdrew what looked like a credit card. "What you want to do is let them give you the card, because you'll need it to gain access to the building."

"I'm supposed to show a card to a security guard every time I try to pick up my paycheck?"

"What security guard? It's a magnetic strip deal."

"Just like all the hotels are using instead of keys these days," I contributed to the conversation. We might as well have one of those magnetic strips surgically attached to our foreheads at birth, the way things were going.

"So like I say," Michael said to Stanton. "Accept the card, but do not let them get you to agree to wear it or they'll think they own you."

I usually have an easy time locating my car in a parking lot. You don't see a lot of Datsun 240Zs from the 1970s these days. Even overshadowed by tank-size SUVs and testosterone-laden pickup trucks, the jaunty yellow paint job and low-slung shape made the tiny car hard to miss.

On this particular Monday afternoon, my beloved Z-car sported another feature that made it stand out from all the other sedans, trucks, and vans in the Executive Airport parking lot.

A spray of glass chips next to the rear hatchback, dazzling in the sunlight as if someone had carelessly spilled a bag of rhinestones.

I spat out several expletives as I sprinted to the damaged vehicle. "I don't believe this," I said between swear words. "Here I'm gone only a little over an hour, it's broad daylight, and we're right in front of a busy street." I swept my arm toward Freeport Boulevard, just west of the airport parking lot.

"Could happen to anyone," Michael said. "Nobody and nothing is safe these days." He pulled out his cell phone and began dialing one of his contacts at the police department — like that was going to do any good — while Hugh Stanton trotted back to the terminal to see if he could find a broom and dustpan.

My first impulse was to check the dashboard. Whew! The factory-installed AM radio was still in place. Whoever did this had likewise ignored the CD player and the speakers planted in both doors. Maybe they'd been scared off before they had the chance to finish the job.

"What's that thing?"

I followed the direction of Michael's voice and spotted a dark, rectangular object resting on a faded beach towel in the back compartment of the Z-car. I tiptoed around the broken glass and eased my head and shoulders through the jagged wound to take a closer look.

It was a plaque from the Footprints Institute, just like the awards Travis and Chad displayed with so much pride in their apartment. In place of the name and date of sobriety, someone had slapped on a sticker: "True Power Comes From Within."

I withdrew my head and turned to face

Michael, still clutching the cell phone to one ear, and Hugh Stanton, who had started to make an awkward attempt at sweeping up the glass chips.

"If they wanted to send me a present," I said, "wouldn't it have been a whole lot easier just to call FedEx?"

12

Of course, no one saw a thing. No one ever does. The grizzled fellow in the control tower and the Asian newcomer who sold coffee and snacks in the pilot's lounge tsk-tsked over my misfortune, but casual sympathy was all they had to offer. As I predicted, when Captain Mikey finally reached his pal at the cop shop, he discovered the police don't even bother filing reports on broken auto glass incidents these days. "Your insurance will cover it no matter what," Michael said with a shake of his head as he snapped shut the cell phone.

By that time, I was busy punching numbers into my own mobile communications device. The hell with insurance! Someone at the Footprints Institute was obviously behind this act of malicious mischief. Who else would have access to blank plaques? That someone was going to pay.

The bubbly receptionist who had escorted me to Janice's office that morning informed me that Dr. Yount had already departed for the Footprints Lodge. "Can I put you through to anyone else? Our public relations director, perhaps?"

"Never mind." Whoever did this was obviously trying to send me a message — or a warning — else why the broken glass? The prudent course of action might be to lie low and wait for the culprit to expose himself. "If Dr. Yount calls in for messages, ask her to give Shauna J. Bogart a ring."

"Fe, fi, lo, li."

"Yeah, and I'm smelling smoke in the good ol' auditorium, Charlie Brown," I said into the microphone. "What's your point, caller?"

"Fe, fi, lo, li."

"Listen, Reg on a cell phone, you're going to have to do more than spout lyrics from an old Coasters' song if you want to stay on the air with Shauna J. Bogart."

"Fe. Fi. Lo. Li." He paused between each word. "Born in the days of old, an empire made of gold, I'll be riding gain with you near a fountain oh, so blue."

"You've got one more chance to start making sense or you're history."

"As I recall, you're the one who asked, nay begged, me to call the show."

Though I might quibble about the begging part, he was right. I had hinted, teased, and cajoled all through the three and four o'clock hours for Reginald Fessenden to call in. The listener who I was pretty sure was the legitimate item finally got through on Line Three at around five-fifteen.

"Fine. Score one point for the caller. Now it's your turn to convince me that you really are this blast from my past."

"If you insist." Reg made a put-upon sighing sound. "The junior prom. Shangri-la was the theme. You wore cherry blossoms in your hair. That time we rescued the flag from Mr. Bender's geometry class during the fire drill. Starbird Park."

I'd forgotten about Starbird Park, a square of city-owned lawn catty-corner from the high school. The smokers used to hang out at Starbird Park during the lunch hour. I ventured over to the butt-littered grounds only occasionally, just enough to remind myself who did I think I was fooling? Like I ever had the remotest chance of fitting in with the cool kids. I had to admit, this Reggie, whoever he really was, had done his research. It gave me the creeps worrying about which database he had managed to hack into to unearth this depth of detailed personal information about my high school days. I mean, how many people on this planet would be able to identify the phylum of the fake flowers I wove into my hair for the junior prom?

"You're supposed to be in the federal penitentiary in Lompoc. Insider trading, securities fraud. Bad boy."

"Yeah, well, sorry about your car."

"What?" My hand had been cupped over the button to cut him off the air if he'd continued to recite nonsense and twaddle. I withdrew my hand with a jerk. "What about my car?"

"I thought the broken window would be a nice theatrical touch. Guess I got a little bit carried away. But your insurance will cover it, right?"

As a matter of fact, the insurance company had already sent over a mobile auto glass installer who was busy at work repairing the Z-car in the station parking lot while I filled my three hours of airtime. But this sickhead wasn't getting off the hook so easily. "A little bit carried away? You . . . jerk!" I had to stop myself before I uttered a stronger word that would have gotten me in big trouble. "What a juvenile thing to do. You must really think you're still in high school. No, make that elementary school."

"I just wanted to get your attention.

Looks like it worked." He finished with a short, unpleasant laugh that made me cringe.

"If you really want to get my attention, you'll tell me why your name — or at least Reginald Fessenden's name — showed up on a calendar belonging to Travis Ikeda-Nyland."

"If you're suggesting what I think you're suggesting, I didn't have anything to do with it." The caller's voice had lost its cocky edge, as if he realized the time for making jokes was over.

"No, you just go around stalking local radio talk show hosts."

"I was only trying to help him, I swear."

I glanced at the clock, where the second hand swept toward the five-thirty mark. "We've got to take a break for news head-lines, traffic, and weather, but you stay on the line, Reg. I'm not through with you yet. Not even close."

"Fe, fi, lo, li." He managed to have the last word just as I touched the computer screen to activate the news break jingle.

The door to the control room opened and I heard the tinkle of what sounded like tiny wind chimes. Jeez, I'd once again managed to forget all about Clarissa St. Cyr. "Fe, fi, fo, fum, I smell the blood of an Englishman," she chirped as she arranged herself in the guest chair.

"Jack and the Beanstalk," I said.

"You realize, of course, that he's in terrible danger."

"You bet he is. If I ever meet him in person, I will personally break his face for what he did to my car."

"I'm serious," she said. "That caller is facing a very dangerous situation. I can feel it."

The Clunie Community Center stood in all its Art Deco glory in McKinley Park, only a few yards away from the spot where Travis Ikeda-Nyland had had an encounter with a bullet almost a week ago. I paused in the lamplight over the double entry doors, that eerie fact almost causing me to rethink my scheme. But the three-story red brick structure hosted an Alcoholics Anonymous meeting almost every night of the week and was within walking distance of the apartment Travis had shared with Chad Mac-Kenzie. If the young man had been serious about attending all those AA meetings he'd scheduled for himself on the calendar, the Clunie Clubhouse gathering would have been an obvious choice.

I lingered for as long as I could in the

lobby, as if I couldn't decide whether to join the rhythmic breathers in the yoga class taking place inside the auditorium, or press my nose against the glass door of the public library branch. In reality, I tried to convince myself that what I was about to do wasn't as sleazy as it felt. Back when I regularly read the women's magazines like *Cosmopolitan*, *Mademoiselle*, and *Glamour*, one of them, *Cosmo* probably, recommended AA meetings as a good place to troll for potential boyfriends. I remember tossing the slick publication against the wall in disgust, vowing that I would never be so desperate for male companionship. Now I was about to behave just about as dishonorably, pretending to be a longtime follower of the program just for the chance to snoop.

A rectangle of light pouring from an open door led me up the stairs to a meeting room on the mezzanine level. I peered into the doorway and made a quick scan of the thirty or so people grouped in a circle of metal folding chairs. My plan, if I spotted someone I recognized — like Chad — was to look confused and request directions to the ladies' room. From what I could tell, tonight's meeting was mostly an older crowd, no young men sporting copious amounts of body ink.

A man at the podium waved a greeting. "We're just getting started." I slipped in and found an empty seat near the coffeepot.

The guy at the podium read something that he called the AA preamble, ending with the reminder "Our primary purpose is to stay sober and help other alcoholics to achieve sobriety." He paused to give his audience time to digest this information. "I'm Jerry," he said. "A grateful recovering alcoholic for twenty-nine years." Applause, whistles, and thumbs-up signals responded to this confession.

"Any newcomers who would care to introduce themselves?" Jerry leaned against the podium and looked at me. A scrawny little fellow with wisps of white hair across a freckled dome and a scraggly gray goatee, he appeared as if he would have been around the forty-year mark when he started on his first year of sobriety. "Strictly optional, of course."

I had it all planned out, gave the first name that appears on my birth certificate, then said, "Another grateful recovering alcoholic. I've just moved here from San Francisco and thought I'd check out a few groups before I settle on one that feels like a good match for my needs."

I must have said the right thing, because

several in the group rewarded me with welcoming smiles and nods. It was a diverse
bunch, roughly a sixty-forty split between
male and female (maybe *Cosmo* was on to
something after all), everything from a pathetic shopping cart lady to polished men
and women who looked as if they had just
gotten off work at one of the capital city's
stuffy downtown law firms. But I didn't see
anyone who looked the right age for a kid
like Travis to pal around with, other than a
young woman who leaned back in her chair,
kept her arms folded against her chest, and
glared at Jerry with a look that combined
defiance and boredom. She sported the
classic goth look: gobs of black makeup,
black leather jacket, plaid miniskirt, torn
fishnet stockings, heavy black boots. A
fellow wearing tight bicycle shorts and a
shirt covered with sponsor logos had the
coltish body of a twenty-year-old, and I
thought he might have possibilities until he
identified himself as Trent, "celebrating
eighteen years of sobriety." Too old, unless
he'd starting tippling as a toddler.

Jerry announced the evening's topic
would come from chapter six of something
he called *The Big Book.* "We will intuitively
know how to handle situations which used
to baffle us," he read. "We will suddenly re-

alize that God is doing for us what we could not do for ourselves." He shut the book. "Who wants to start?"

It was time to segue into the second part of my plan. "I used to feel as if I understood that book thing that Jerry's talking about," I said. "But now I'm not so sure. I've been under a lot of stress, what with moving and starting a new job and all, and, well . . ." I lowered my head, stared at my hands resting on my knees, and spoke in a shamed mumble, "I started drinking again."

I waited for the murmurs of sympathy to die down. "I think I'm going to have to check myself into one of those twenty-eight day programs. I've heard the Footprints Institute has a good in-patient facility. I just wondered if any of you guys knew much about it and could maybe make a recommendation."

"Corey is back at Footprints Lodge." It was Trent, the bicycle guy. He guzzled water from a plastic gallon container like it was a jug of moonshine. "He relapsed."

"Gosh, I'm sorry." Jerry placed one elbow on the podium, cupped his chin, and scratched the goatee. "Would you like to share what happened?"

"Some sort of fight with his father over money. I only heard bits and pieces of their conversation over the phone. Not five minutes after he hung up, Corey's heading out to the 7-Eleven to buy a six-pack."

"Families and money. That's always a tough combination," Jerry said.

"Tell me about it." Trent downed another slug of H_2O. "The only bright spot in all this was the staff at Footprints. They made one of their regular calls to check on Corey's progress and managed to catch him early. Within twenty-four hours of when he'd started drinking again, they had him back in the lodge."

"Thank God for small mercies. Anyone else care to share?"

"I'm Vic, and I'm powerless against alcohol."

I let my mind wander during Vic's lengthy story about meeting his future in-laws and tried to make eye contact with Goth Girl, sending an unspoken plea to talk when the meeting concluded. I must have sent the wrong message, because she bolted the instant Jerry spoke the final lines in the Serenity Prayer and dismissed us for the evening. I hovered by the urn of coffee, pretending to neaten up the piles of paper napkins and packets of sugar substitute, keeping my radar tuned for someone to chat up.

"I hope you have a good health plan."

It was Mavis, a bedraggled woman whom I'd tagged as a probable resident of one of the homeless camps along the riverbank. But up close, I realized her tatty wool sweater was cashmere, and the battered leather handbag she carried bore a Louis Vuitton label. Her glasses, though smeared with fingerprints, were prescription bifocals and featured designer frames. Mavis was either one of the more eccentric residents of a Fabulous Forties mansion or an expert thrift store shopper.

"I hope so too," I said.

"You're going to need it if you plan to check into the Footprints Lodge. That's all they're interested in, you realize. Your money. Or your insurance."

"Yeah, well, that's managed care for you."

"That's the only reason they took Trent's partner back so quickly. They know his dad is loaded and will just whip out his checkbook and fill in a bunch of zeros, anything to keep his precious Corey out of trouble."

"So money talks. What else is new?"

"If you plan to check in, just watch your back." Mavis shook the Louis Vuitton bag in my direction. "And make sure your insurance is paid up."

Jerry waited until Mavis clomped toward

the door, then placed a paper cup under the spigot of the coffee urn. "Don't mind Mavis," he said to me as the cup filled with brown liquid. "She means well, but she's a bit opinionated."

"Nothing wrong with that."

"It's easy to be a critic, but the fact is, Footprints does wonderful work. It's amazing, as big as they are, and they still haven't lost the personal touch."

"How so?"

"Take Corey as just one example. A commitment to sobriety brought back on track by a timely intervention. I can't begin to tell you the number of similar cases I've heard about."

"Thanks for the information. You guys have been really helpful." I watched as Jerry stirred the contents of three packets of Sweet'N Low into his cup of coffee.

Jerry brought the cardboard cup to his lips and gave me a close look, as if searching for bloodshot eyes or trembling hands. "If you're looking for a place to detox, you'd be hard pressed to locate a finer facility than Footprints Lodge."

13

For once in my life, I didn't mind the Sacramento tule fog, even welcomed the shroud of thick gray moisture that sealed off the capital city from anything remotely resembling blue sky and sunshine.

There was no more perfect weather for a burial. Especially the burial of someone who had been young and full of promise.

I lurked at the fringes of the mourners at East Lawn Memorial Park — Sapphire Ikeda and Ray Nyland, Gareth Nyland and his parents, plus an assortment of neighbors, classmates, media colleagues, and business associates from Nyland Automotive. I tried to keep my eyes averted from the polished bronze coffin, poised above freshly turned earth, that housed the guest of honor.

A young woman inched herself in my direction. Goth Girl, from last night's meeting. So my hunch had been right, and I had located the AA meeting that Travis had regularly attended.

Goth Girl positioned herself halfway behind the trunk of a palm tree, stared me down, and beckoned at me through the morning mist.

Oh, well. I hadn't felt right about infiltrating the recovery group meeting anyway. Better that my cover be blown now than after I'd wasted more hours on the project. I tiptoed across the damp grass.

Goth Girl's look from the previous evening would have fit right in with the somber surroundings, but for some reason — a perverse sense of irony, perhaps — she decided to go for the all-American-girl image: freshly scrubbed face, brown hair in matching braids touching either shoulder, perky pink sweater topping a floral print skirt, white tights, pink mary jane flats, and so help me, a Hello Kitty purse.

"You're not really in the program," she said when I reached the palm tree. "You're that lady on the radio."

"Busted." I knew any attempt to maintain my anonymity would be futile with this tough cookie. "What gave me away?"

"You've got the lingo all wrong, for one thing. No one starts drinking again, like you said last night. You relapse. And you never heard of *The Big Book*. Puh-leeze."

"Ouch." So much for my budding career as an undercover agent.

"But you really gave yourself away when you talked about checking yourself into Footprints Lodge. No one goes to one of those live-in detox places voluntarily, trust me. You get sent there by the court, or you're told by your boss to either complete a recovery program or you're outta there. Or you get dragged there by your parents."

I expected her to add "like me" to the latter, but she just fiddled with the clasp of her silly plastic purse. "The only reason I'm at those tedious AA meetings is that my probation officer says I've got to," she added.

"You're a very observant young lady," I said. "How did you figure out I'm on the radio?"

"The manager at this clinic where I work after school listens to talk radio all afternoon. You have a very distinctive voice. And I recognize you from that billboard over on Howe Avenue."

That damn billboard. I'd howled in protest when T. R. O'Brien had unveiled plans to feature a group photo of the station's on-air personalities in the latest billboard campaign. "Hey, if we were pretty, we'd be on TV," I'd told him. But T.R. won as always. I cringed in horror when I drove through the intersection of Howe and Arden and encountered my gigantic, full-color mug.

"Congratulations." I extended my hand. "Shauna J. Bogart. Pleased to make your acquaintance."

"You can call me Camille." She placed a hand with bitten-to-the-quick nails in my palm.

"You know any of these people?" I jerked my head in the direction of the mob scene around the casket.

"Not really. I met Travis last summer through AA. We kept in touch by e-mail when he went back to UCLA, and I visited him a few times when he ended up back at the lodge. But he wasn't like my boyfriend or anything."

"Did he give you any ideas as to what prompted him to start drinking again this past fall?"

She shook her head, causing the beribboned tips of the braids to slap her shoulders. "He seemed fine, all excited about finally getting close to the end of school, and then going to work for Nyland Automotive. He had all these ideas about how he was going to revolutionize the car-buying experience, make it relevant for the Internet age, stuff like that. For real, that's how he used to talk."

"Did he ever mention someone named Reginald Fessenden?"

Camille traced a line in the duff ringing

174

the palm tree with the rounded tip of one of her shoes.

"You can trust me, I swear," I said. "Whatever you have to say stays between us if that's the way you want it."

"I promised." She spoke as if each word were being teased from her by a pair of tweezers. "But I guess it doesn't matter now." She shifted her gaze to the freshly dug grave. The clergyman had stopped talking, and the mourners were placing calla lilies on top of the coffin.

"You and I both know Travis wasn't killed because of a drug deal that went bad. If you really want to honor your friend, you'll help me discover the truth. So what about Reginald Fessenden?"

"I didn't want to do it," she said in a choked whisper. "But he made me."

"Who, Reginald Fessenden?"

"No, Travis."

"Travis made you do what?"

Camille responded by pressing her lips together and slipping a tear from the corner of each eye.

"C'mon, it's freezing out here." I gently grasped Camille's thin upper arm and steered her away from the grim scene being acted out over an open grave a few yards away. "Let's go talk in my car."

"You promise I won't get in trouble?" Camille said after she'd settled herself into the passenger seat of the Z-car and dabbed at her eyes with a tissue.

"You have my word."

"The thing is, Travis knew I worked in a medical office. I kept telling him I was just a file clerk, but he wouldn't take no for an answer. He said it wouldn't be that difficult for me to lay my hands on antiseptic, and pain-killers, and gauze pads and all that."

"And a scalpel."

"I tried, but they keep those things locked up all the time. So I used an X-Acto knife."

"That wound on his upper arm — you did that with an X-Acto knife?"

"I didn't want to!"

"What was it, some sort of gang ritual or something?"

"He was trying to remove this weird implant thing."

"An implant?" I twisted my torso in the tiny sports car so I could study Camille more closely. "Are you serious?"

"That's what he told me. He made me dig around with the X-Acto until I found this, this — thing."

"What kind of thing?"

"I don't know. It was gray and red, tiny,

about the size of a grain of rice. Travis made me flush it down the toilet as soon as I found it."

"Where does Reginald Fessenden fit in? Was he there when you gouged that thing out of Travis's arm?"

Camille shook her head. "It was just a name Travis mentioned. Something about how it was Reginald Fessenden who stuck this thing in his arm in the first place, and now he had to get rid of it right away."

"You sure it was Reginald Fessenden."

"You don't think I'd make up a name like that, do you?"

"Travis didn't tell you anything else about what this implant was, and why it was so important that he get rid of it?"

"Nope. He just told me to shut up and cut the thing out of him as fast as I could, and not tell anyone."

"You realize this sounds like something out of a bad science fiction movie."

"For real."

I gazed out the window of the Z-car at the black-clad mourners clustered around the flower-strewn coffin. In another few minutes, the bronze box would be lowered into the earth, taking with it the only tangible evidence of the veracity of Camille's story.

★ ★ ★

Camille kept insisting on referring to the reception at the Ikeda-Nyland estate that followed the burial as the after-party, like we had been invited to drop by Spago's after walking the red carpet at a Hollywood awards ceremony. Turned out, she wasn't far off the mark. Sapphire had decided on a luau theme, declaring that Travis would not have wanted his family and friends to wallow in sorrow. She'd hired a caterer to prepare pupu platters and fruit punch, found an authentic Hawaiian slack-key guitar player, and even managed to fly in fresh carnation and orchid leis, one for every guest. If this was another one of her "keeping busy" projects, I would hate to be present when she finally crashed from physical and emotional exhaustion.

Sapphire hooked an arm through my elbow and steered me to a quiet nook in back of the wooden tiki god statue. "Just between us, we got the coroner's report this morning," she said when we were out of earshot from the crowd.

"And?" I prompted.

"No alcohol in his blood, and no evidence of use of street drugs like crystal meth."

I let out a sigh. "You must feel relieved. And vindicated. I mean, how can anyone say this had something to do with a drug deal after this?"

She gave me a brief, tight smile. "I suppose you're right."

"This is good news, right? Then why the hush-hush?"

"You've heard of Vicodin, I assume."

"Prescription painkiller, sure. I got some from my dentist during my last root canal."

"They found a trace of Vicodin in Travis's system. And no, he did not have a prescription nor any reason to be using something like that as far as I know."

I turned the information over in my mind. The obvious answer was Dr. Camille, medicine woman. Hadn't she just told me she had access to painkillers through the medical office where she worked as a file clerk? Wouldn't Vicodin have eased the pain of amateur surgery during and after?

"Vicodin is fairly benign as prescription painkillers go," I said. "I'm sure there's an innocent explanation. Maybe he had a toothache."

"Maybe." She raised her chin and rearranged her facial features into the bland, reassuring visage favored by local TV newscasters. "Well. Mustn't be caught cowering in the corner or people will start talking."

I made one more round until I had satisfied myself that I really had sampled every variety of sushi being offered on the pupu platters, then headed back to the lanai to pay my respects one last time. I found Sapphire on the wicker couch deep in conversation in a language I assumed to be Japanese with a tiny, wrinkled Asian woman. Gareth and Ray Nyland, meanwhile, were surrounded three deep by various chamber of commerce and ad agency types. I drifted aimlessly through the greenery-filled room, finally coming to rest next to a glass-topped table where a thick photo album held center stage. I turned over the front cover.

Someone — Sapphire, I was willing to bet — had put together a retrospective of Travis's too-short life. Not just photographs, but documents and ephemera: his birth certificate, report cards, poems penned in seventh grade, even that letter of recommendation I'd written after he'd finished his internship at the station. I flipped through pages of school yearbook photos and snapshots of family vacations in Hawaii, two decades worth of proms, Christmas mornings, Easter egg hunts, childhood pets — an iguana, assorted kittens, a Jack Russell terrier named Bingo — and Pop Warner football teams.

"I had a dog like that once. Jumpin' Jack Flash."

I followed the finger that pointed to the photograph of the tiny dog to the tattoo-encircled wrist. Chad MacKenzie.

"Hey, think I can bum a ride with you?" he added.

"No problem." I was about to leave anyway, and Chad's apartment in the McKinley Park neighborhood wasn't that far from the station. "Just let me try to say good-bye to Sapphire."

"What happened to your wheels?" I asked as Chad strapped himself into the passenger seat of the Z-car.

"What wheels? Driver's license suspended, forbidden to operate or possess a motor vehicle in the state of California for the next three years. The only wheels people like me are allowed to have come on a bike."

"I thought you drove an old beater, a Honda or Toyota at least ten years old." I turned the key in the ignition. "Bumper sticker that says 'Cruisin' not Usin'."

"Give me a break. Even if I didn't have all those court restrictions hanging over me, you think I'd allow myself to be seen in something so pathetic?"

I was positive I'd seen the same vehicle parked Friday night in the lot of the apartment complex that Travis and Chad had shared, and then Monday morning in front of the Footprints Institute. If it didn't belong to Chad, then who?

"Do you know of anyone who might own a vehicle like that?"

"Look, someone like me does not associate with people who would drive something so pathetic. Get it?"

I was about to pull over on Fair Oaks Boulevard and tell the little snot he could walk the rest of the way home. But who knows, I might never again have this opportunity to pry information out of the person who spent more time with Travis during the last days of his life than anyone else.

"Just curious, how's your implant working out?" I reached across the stick shift and punched Chad's upper arm. Just a playful little tap, really. I banked on the element of surprise crushing his defensive fortress.

"What the hell do you think you're doing?" He jerked away from my fist and scooted to the far corner of the bucket seat.

"C'mon, I know all about the implants. Only I guess Travis's didn't work out the way he'd hoped."

"We're not supposed to talk about it. Something about patents and trade secrets. All of us had to sign a release."

All of us. So my instinct was correct, and Chad had a similar device hidden under all those tribal tattoos.

"I understand. But like I said before, I already know all about the implants. I'm just curious, that's all, about whether yours is working out any better than Travis's did."

"That's an interesting question." Chad extended his legs, digging his booted feet into the floor mat, and reached a hand into the front pocket of his black jeans.

"Yes, I mind if you smoke in my car," I said before he could fully extract a cigarette pack and lighter.

"Oh, man."

"Yeah, well, when you get your driving privilege back, you can smoke like a chimney in your own vehicle. But as long as you're dependant on the kindness of semi-strangers, you'll play by my rules. Now, about your implant."

Chad folded his arms across his chest and pouted for a few moments before he spoke. "Some days it feels like it's really helping to stop the craving for alcohol like they told us it would, other days I'm not so sure."

I'd heard of time-release implants to wean addicts off heroin, and a birth control device that seeped hormones into the system over a five-year period. Was the Footprints

Institute testing a similar device to lessen the pain of withdrawing from alcohol?

"Travis must have decided his wasn't working at all."

"I don't know what his problem was. All of a sudden, he's insisting he had to get rid of his device right away, and that I should have mine removed too."

I braked to avoid plowing into a Mercedes making a sudden right turn into the Pavilions shopping complex. "Did he give you any reason he was so anxious to have his implant removed?"

"He was real cagey about that, just kept yammering at me about how I needed to get rid of mine right away. I told him to forget it. If I decided to have mine removed, I'll ask the medical staff at Footprints to take care of it. Not some witch doctor girlfriend."

"Good plan. Did Travis ever say anything to you about someone named Reginald Fessenden?"

"I thought you said you knew all about the implant program."

"I also know we're still about twenty blocks away from your crib. If you don't want to end up walking those twenty blocks, humor me and tell me what you know about Reginald Fessenden."

"What's to tell? He's the head honcho, the big cheese, the chief kahuna."

"Meaning?" I gripped the steering wheel as the tiny car bounced across the H Street Bridge over the American River.

"Oh, man." Chad exhaled an exasperated sigh. "If you insist, Dr. Fessenden is the guy who runs the medical implant program for the Footprints Institute. Is that what you wanted to hear?"

14

"Doyle Bollinger called for you twice within the past hour." Josh faced me in the newsroom, hands planted on hips. "And there's some guy named Jared holding for you on the hotline."

"Call Bollinger back. Tell him I'm about to go on the air and I'll have to get back to him later." With only fifteen minutes remaining until showtime after dropping Chad off at his East Sacramento apartment and barreling back to the station, it wasn't much of a fib. That, and the little issue of not having decided for certain whether to accept the job in Los Angeles. I figured by the time my program had concluded for the day and I actually returned Bollinger's call, I'd get voice mail. It's always easier to dance and dodge on a recording than live and in person.

I punched the studio hotline from the phone on my desk and ignored my intern. Josh had to be curious about the number of calls I'd been receiving in recent days from the head of programming for one of the nation's biggest suppliers of syndicated radio programming. I'd certainly be suspicious if our roles had been switched. But no way would I whisper a hint to anyone at the station that I was considering a career change without talking things over with T. R. O'Brien first.

"So, like, you asked me to call you if I remembered anything about that guy who visited Travis last fall," Jared said. I pictured the student pacing on the porch of the sober-living house, talking into his hands-free cell phone rig in the Southern California sunshine.

"Absolutely," I said.

"This morning, I'm heading over to the Farmers Market to meet my mother for lunch. She's all over those Belgian waffles at Du-Par's. Then I'm all stuck behind this fender bender at Sunset and Fairfax . . ."

"And your point is?" I tucked the receiver between my ear and shoulder and began assembling notes and news clippings for my rapidly approaching airtime.

"So I'm stuck there like ten minutes just staring at the car in front of me. It's got this personalized license plate that says L8 AGAIN. Late again, get it?"

"So?" Late again was what I was going to be if Jared didn't hurry things along.

"So I'm thinking late again, late again, like with my mother and is she going to have a fit or what? And then I'm all — again!"

"Yeah, yeah. Cute license plate and all that, but what does this have to do with Travis?"

"That's what I'm trying to tell you. Again. That was his name. At least, that was what Travis was calling him."

"Again? What kind of name is that?"

"I know, I know. But I swear, that's what Travis was calling him. And get this — this Again guy was referring to Travis as Tin. Tin and Again. Weird, huh?"

"I'll say. And this was the guy who showed up to visit the weekend Travis starting drinking. You're sure about that."

"Yep. Tin and Again, straight to the bottle."

I was all set to ring up Doyle Bollinger — had the receiver in my hand and his business card in front of me — when Josh sent a message from his computer in the call screener booth.

LADY NAMED LEOTA ON LINE THREE. DOESN'T WANT TO GO ON THE AIR. SAYS IT'S IMPORTANT.

I stuffed Bollinger's card back into my pocket and tapped Line Three.

"You've got to come down to the Med Center just as quickly as you can," Leota said as soon as I greeted her.

"What's going on?" I couldn't tell from her frantic voice whether she was grieving or jubilant.

"Markitus is coming out of it."

"He's regained consciousness?"

"That's what I just told you, didn't I? He's back with us, praise the Lord, and he's talking."

"That's wonderful news." I kept one ear tuned to the network monitor for the chimes that would cue the end of the five o'clock newscast. "Does anyone else in the media know about this?"

"Not yet."

"See if you can keep it that way for another hour. I'll be there as soon as I finish the show."

More like ninety minutes elapsed, what with the agonizingly sluggish late afternoon commute traffic, between the time I took the call from Markitus Wilson's great-aunt and when I finally sprinted through the glass doors of the main hospital building at the sprawling medical complex. I located the correct floor for the Trauma Unit from the directory, and rushed into the elevator.

Leota extricated herself from a plastic chair in the waiting area as soon as she saw me emerge from the elevator. "Where's your tape recorder?"

"Digital." I raised my right arm so she could see the tiny recording device that dangled from a cord around my wrist. "No tape. Welcome to the twenty-first century."

"I just hope you can do something," Leota said with a thrust of her lower lip. "They're saying you and me can't come in. Only one visitor, and only immediate family."

"Is this true?" I approached the nurses' station and held up my wallet so that my CHP media pass would show through the plastic window. I flashed it in the direction of a dark-skinned woman wearing green scrubs. "Markitus Wilson is allowed only one visitor?"

The woman looked up from a patient chart. I had drawn close enough to read her plastic name badge. "This is the Trauma Unit," Kimberly Gupta, R.N., said. "We're not running a social club here. One visitor per day, and I believe Mr. Wilson's grandmother has been with him most of the afternoon."

Leota leaned over the counter and thrust herself in Gupta's face. "Markitus has something to say and Miz Bogart needs to hear it. This is going to clear his name and prove to everyone that my Markitus isn't a heartless killer like they all think."

"There's been a police officer stationed in front of Mr. Wilson's room 'round the clock since he was admitted," Nurse Gupta said. "If Mr. Wilson wishes to make a statement, he can do it to the appropriate authorities."

"Now why would he do something bone-headed like that? The cops are the ones responsible for him being in here in the first place."

"I'm going to have to ask you to keep your voice down. We have very sick people in here."

I put a hand on Leota's shoulder. "If I could make a suggestion, perhaps we could ask Iris to come out and relay to us whatever it is that Markitus said to her." It wasn't an ideal situation from a news standpoint, but even I knew better than to endanger critically ill and injured patients just for a hot sound bite.

Kimberly Gupta's face softened and I could feel some of the tension flow out of Leota's stringy frame. Gupta picked up a telephone receiver, and in less than five minutes Iris Fontaine joined Leota and me in the waiting area.

"I don't know what to think, I just don't

know what to think." Iris sank into one of the black plastic chairs.

"Why don't you start at the beginning." I touched a button to activate the recorder.

"His eyelids started fluttering a little after four, and at four-twenty he opened his eyes and smiled at me, just as natural as can be. I know it was four-twenty because I looked at the clock on the wall, like this is the moment my baby is reborn into this world."

"The Lord answered our prayers," Leota said. "He is merciful."

I paused to honor this moment of piety, then I said, "I understand Markitus has been talking, trying to tell us something."

"That's what I mean. I just don't know what to think." Iris brought a ropy-veined hand to her throat.

"Try me."

"You hear people talking about these near-death experiences. I wonder if that could be what happened to my poor Markitus."

"What makes you say that?" I braced myself for a description of a tunnel of white light.

"He just kept talking about movies. 'Grandma, I'm making a movie,' 'I'm going to be in a movie,' talk like that."

"The movies?"

"That's what he said."

"I take it he has no connection to the film industry."

"Shoot," Leota put in, "the closest that boy ever come to the movies was working behind the popcorn counter at the Century complex."

"I'm going to be in the movies," Iris whispered in awe. "Grandma, they're putting me in a movie."

"That's it? He didn't say anything about what happened in McKinley Park?"

Iris shook her head. "The nurses won't let me ask him anything, not yet. Let him talk if he wants to, but don't do or say anything that's going to stress him."

"Let me know if anything changes, especially if he decides to talk about McKinley Park. You have my cell phone number, right? Call anytime, day or night."

I hurried back to the Z-car, flicked on the dome light, scribbled a few lines of copy into my notebook, and dialed the station news hotline on my mobile phone.

"We're about to go on the air with the coach," the producer of Steve Garland's sports talk show told me. "Can't it hold until the seven-thirty local news update?"

"The prime suspect in one of the biggest homicides in the city has just started talking." I pounded my fist against the steering wheel. "No one else has this story but us."

"Yeah, well, no one but us has the coach agreeing to take calls about tonight's Kings game."

Tonight's Kings game! I'd forgotten all about that damn basketball team — and my commitment to be part of the half-time entertainment.

I slumped against the cement wall of the home team's tunnel at Arco Arena and tried to look as if I were reviewing my sins and contemplating my penance. One, I had shown up late — again. Two, I ignored the instructions to wear white-soled tennis shoes and a station T-shirt, and arrived in the same black turtleneck sweater, black slacks, and black low-heeled pumps that I'd been wearing since I left my apartment that morning. Third, I dared to question the appropriateness of the upcoming mid-game high jinks within hearing distance of the general sales manager.

"It's not your decision whether this is in poor taste or not," Dorinda Delgado had said to me.

"A publicity stunt involving Nyland Automotive on the very day they bury the owner's son?" I'd responded. "How could that possibly *not* be in bad taste?"

"If they'd wanted to cancel, they would have called us."

"Gee, you don't suppose they might have had more important things on their mind, do you?"

Delgado managed to borrow a pair of regulation sneakers with white soles in more or less my size from one of the Royal Court dancers. She loaned me a T-shirt from her personal stash, size XL with sleeves dragging past my elbows. Just the kind of polished image I like to project when I'm out in public.

I heard my name echo throughout the arena's public address system and took that as my cue to scamper onto the polished hardwood floor and join the rest of the on-air team. Now, I know professional basketball arenas look impressive when you're watching from the stands, but you have no idea of the sheer immensity until you've stood at center court, the roar of the crowd thundering from all sides, seventeen thousand pairs of eyes staring at puny, insignificant you. Well, maybe not all seventeen thousand. A lot of them were using the break to cruise the snack bars and line up for the bathroom. That still left the bulk of the sell-out crowd in the stands, waiting to be entertained. By me.

Me and my coworkers from the radio station. I was never so grateful to be part of a team, from the morning duo to the shrink whose show preceded mine, to even Clarissa St. Cyr, who'd tied little silver zodiac symbols onto the laces of her tennis shoes. The announcement of our names drew some cheers and applause from the crowd, but I registered a number of bored looks as well. Can't say as I blamed them. I could almost hear the collective sighs of disappointment. "You don't look anything like I pictured you."

The stars of Sacramento Talk Radio formed a double line on either side of one Cookie Fensterwald from Citrus Heights, selected at random from all of tonight's ticket holders to attempt to shoot a half-court basket. If she somehow managed to sink the ball, she'd win a new car from Nyland Automotive. The odds were ridiculous, especially for a petite legal secretary in her fifties. Even so, both the station and Nyland Automotive carried an insurance policy on the infinitesimal chance some lucky soul might actually win a so-called impossible game of skill.

No one was going to have to collect on

that insurance policy tonight. Despite the cheers and hand claps from the Sacramento Talk Radio staff, the thundering stomp of thousands of feet from the stands, and Cookie's best underhand fling of the ball, she didn't even reach the backboard.

I managed to slip away while the arena announcer gave a rundown of Cookie's consolation prize — "A Sacramento Talk Radio fun pack, including dinner for two at Paragary's Bar and Oven, a pair of tickets to an upcoming production by the Sacramento Civic Light Opera Company, a year's worth of oil changes from Jiffy Lube, and an official Sacramento Talk Radio T-shirt" — leaving my borrowed shirt and sneakers in a pile just inside the tunnel.

I'd had nothing to eat all day except for a few (okay, a dozen) pieces of sushi at Sapphire Ikeda's luau, and I could hear a King Dog calling my name. A few false turns in the labyrinthine ground floor of Arco Arena and I located the elevator that took me to the main concourse. I was within smelling distance of spicy sausage and fried dough when a female figure caught my eye. It wasn't just that she was stunning. Or that she was seriously overdressed for the occasion — long, slinky gown with strategic cutouts at the cleavage and waist level, glittery in the Kings' colors of purple and silver, more appropriate for Vegas than Sacramento.

Brenda Driscoll.

Now there was a young lady I needed to talk to, somehow convince her to tell me everything she knew about this movie being shot in Sacramento, and how she and Markitus Wilson fit in. Never mind that she clung to the arm of a considerably older gentleman, nor that they were strolling away from me. I tore away from my place in line at the concession stand and plowed through the throng in an effort to catch up. I didn't have the chance to study her companion very closely, but I did have an impression of liver spots, wild eyebrows, and one of those wattle things working under the chin. We're talking Senior Citizens Special here, folks.

I had fought my way close enough that I could have hollered and Brenda should have been able to hear me, when she and her male companion disappeared through a door. I caught a quick glimpse of the festive interior of one of Arco Arena's luxury skyboxes, then watched the door slam shut in front of me. "Flamm & Associates, Inc.," according to the discreet sign affixed to the door.

Flamm & Associates. Legislative affiliates.

Political consultants. Public affairs specialists. Call them what you will, it still spells *lobbyist.* And in California, with its term-limited amateur legislature, that equaled big-time power.

Maury Flamm had dropped by the station a few times, but I didn't feel as if I knew him well enough to knock on the door of his private suite and demand an audience with one of his guests. I was about to worm my way back to the concession stand and contemplate my next move when I recognized the state assemblyman who represented Sacramento reaching for the door to let himself in.

"Good job out there tonight," George Kanalakis said to me.

"Thanks, it was fun." I slithered in behind him like I'd been an invited guest all along.

I found myself in a chamber about the size of a medium-grade hotel room with furnishings to match, minus the bed. Even a TV set bolted to the ceiling. A wet bar boasted bottles of expensive booze, and the coffee table held picked-over trays of shrimp cocktail, teriyaki chicken on skewers, and roasted vegetables drizzled with vinaigrette. In the back corner stood a partially opened door to the biggest argument in favor of owning a skybox: the private restroom. I scoped out the thirty or so guests, finally spying Brenda and her gentleman friend ensconced in a row of seats on the missing fourth wall, facing the courtside action. Rats. I'd have to climb over four people on either side to reach her, and then I'd have to perch on the geezer's lap in order to have a conversation with her.

What was Brenda thinking, dating a gent easily three times her age, besides the obvious? Of course, I was aware that such things as escort services existed in the capital city. The weekly alternative paper carried pages of advertisements for escorts, models, and "therapeutic" masseuses every week. But was it worth it, no matter how wealthy and connected the client might be?

On Sunday afternoon, when I'd found Brenda Driscoll working as a booth bunny at a science fiction convention, I'd thought she'd sunk as low as you could go on the show business strata. I was going to have to reassess that observation.

Our host disentangled himself from a knot of a half dozen or so men and began striding in my direction. Even under the best of circumstances, Maury Flamm did not present a cheerful appearance. His tall, boxy frame, long face, and dark-circled eyes always reminded me of a separated-at-birth scenario involving Elmer Gantry and Fred Munster. Tonight, if he were being drawn by a comic strip artist, a black thundercloud would have hovered just above his rectangular head.

I thought about inventing a story of becoming lost while searching for someone else's suite. Arnold's maybe. But it had been an exhausting day, starting with a funeral and climaxing with a hurried trip to the Trauma Unit, and I still hadn't had anything to eat. Before Flamm could reach me and give me the old heave-ho, I made a dash for the door.

Ten minutes later, I balanced an already half-consumed King Dog in one hand and pushed open the plate glass doors of Arco Arena with the other, strode down the cement stairs, and began the hike across the parking lot. The game wasn't over yet and the vast expanse of asphalt was deserted. I trudged under the fuzzy glow of sodium vapor lights in the nighttime fog, past silent acres of sedans, trucks, SUVs, and sports cars, each in its white-striped niche. I wished I'd thought of commandeering a news car so I could have parked near the building, in the media zone. As it was, arriving a good half hour after tip-off, I'd had to abandon the Z-car in the outermost reaches of the huge asphalt field. I swallowed the last of the King Dog, wadded up the wrapper and napkin, stuffed them in the pocket of my parka until I could find a trash can, and hoped I'd remembered the correct lot letter and aisle number.

The clip-tap of my pumps against the pavement was the only sound I could hear, other than my own breathing. I finally spotted a shiny yellow hatchback between a white pickup truck and a deep purple Lexus sedan. I quickened my pace.

A human form emerged from the shadows between the 240Z and the Lexus.

"Ms. Bogart, I've been waiting for you."

15

I jammed my right hand into the pocket of my down jacket and pawed through the greasy food wrapper until my fingers found my keys. They might work as a weapon, especially if I managed to reach one of his eyes.

"That's quite a special vehicle you've got."

The voice sounded friendly, but I wasn't taking any chances. I took a slow step back and tensed myself to turn and run. A light pole stood a few yards behind me, and I mentally crossed my fingers that it contained a security camera.

"Can't a fellow admire a fine specimen of a vehicle? Vic Cortese from the River City Vintage Sports Car Owners Association." He raised a hand in an affable wave.

I held my ground and felt my fingers relax from their death grip around the set of keys. This happens every so often, usually a note or a business card left under my windshield from a collector wanting to know if I'm interested in selling. The answer is always no. My father bought the Z-car for me when I got my learner's permit under the delusion that a cool car would somehow improve my high school social status. Turns out, the yellow sports car has lasted longer than any and all of my romantic relationships, and after all these years it still manages to give me a tiny thrill every time I climb behind the wheel.

"I'm just not used to having people jump out of the shadows like that, late at night in a big parking lot," I said.

"Understood. Next time I'll try not to be so clumsy." He emerged completely from behind the Lexus, and I had the impression of a fellow who must have been quite a hottie in his youth, which I placed in the Eisenhower administration. A thick thatch of russet-colored hair, gray at the temples, mustache, a compact build in the beginning stages of sagging and softening. He wore a tan suede bomber jacket, black wool slacks, and tasseled loafers.

"You can't blame a woman for being cautious these days." I started to edge past Cortese and closer to my car. He seemed harmless, but I'd still feel better when I was safely inside with the doors locked.

"You just don't see many of these 240Zs

from the 1970s out on the road anymore. Especially one in vintage condition like yours."

"Thanks, but I'm not interested in selling if that's what you're after."

"Sell a beautiful piece of machinery like that? Of course not. But a woman like you, media celebrity and all, deserves to be seen in something new and luxurious."

"That may well be, but the Z-car is fine by me." Truth is, Pete Kovacs had been making similar hints of late about investing in a new vehicle, though his arguments focused on safety and reliability, little things like air bags and antilock brakes.

"The point is, I know people who could set you up in a brand-new set of wheels. How about a PT Cruiser? Or maybe a Mini-Cooper? No wait — I figure you for one of those hybrids. Save money on gas and help the environment. Everybody wins."

"What do you mean, set me up?"

"My associates might be willing to negotiate. Make a deal."

"This is starting to sound like one of those offers I can't refuse. Sorry, but I'm not interested." I had finally finished inching my way around Cortese and leaned against the driver's side door of the Z-car.

"Hey, it's not like that." Cortese raised

both hands, palms in my direction. "My associates admire your work and want to show their appreciation. What's wrong with that?"

"That's super, but I'm really not interested." Jeez, this guy was as persistent as a Mormon missionary.

"It's a shame, that's all, a talented, high-profile lady like you not having a new car to drive around town." Cortese reached into the inside pocket of the leather jacket, removed a business card, and handed it to me. "If you change your mind, here's how to reach me."

In the dim light, I couldn't make out the small type, only the logo of the River City Vintage Sports Car Association.

"I hope you understand exactly what it is that you're turning down," Cortese said. "My associates don't make this kind of offer very often."

"Tell your associates my car's not for sale, and neither am I."

Doyle Bollinger managed to ambush me by telephone at home the following morning. I felt naked and exposed without Josh to screen my calls, and without the excuse of a live radio show to attend to.

"I'm beginning to think you're having second thoughts about RadioLand," Bollinger said. "You've been playing so hard to get these past few days."

"Just busy, that's all." I sat at the table in the dining nook, a partially consumed toasted bagel on a plate in front of me and the cat rubbing my ankles. A blanket of white greeted me from the window, fog so thick I could barely discern the vehicles on N Street below me.

"You've given notice to your general manager?"

"First thing Monday morning," I lied. "He asked me to give him a day or two to talk things over with his business partners before I made it public."

"So we should have something firm from you sometime today."

"I thought you didn't need a final decision until Friday."

"That's before I knew some of the affiliates were going to be in town next week. What better way to introduce the new format than to have the host on hand for a meet-and-greet? We need to arrange to have you in Hollywood first thing Monday morning."

I slid the plate with the remains of my breakfast to the other end of the table. "I'll get back to you by the end of the day today for sure."

I placed my hands on my hips and examined the directory in the foyer of an aging office building in the eleven-hundred block of K Street, just a couple of blocks from the state capitol. At my sheepskin-booted feet, worn tile work announced the onetime location of Rosenstock's Shoe-tique. The windows of the ground-floor retail space had been covered with butcher paper, and a "for lease" sign appeared to be a permanent fixture.

I located Flamm & Associates, Inc., on the fifth floor. Beside Flamm's name, and next to each name on the directory, was a button and an intercom speaker. It looked like the foyer was as far as I would be able to penetrate, unless I could convince someone to buzz me through the thick glass security door and into the elevator.

The directory listed the Sacramento Civic Light Opera Company as one of six tenants on the third floor. I was willing to bet that, like most charities and arts organizations, the Light Opera Company would fall all over itself to welcome a drop-in visit by a media person. I placed my thumb on the button next to their name.

Twenty minutes later, I managed to extricate myself from the cluttered office of the

Sacramento Civic Light Opera Company. I lugged a media kit, a CD of highlights of last season's performances, an official stage crew T-shirt, and a pair of tickets to the upcoming revival of *Fiddler on the Roof*, and left a trail of promises to donate a schedule of public service announcements to help fill theater seats. I entered the elevator and punched Five. The iron bars of the door slid shut and the creaky grille-work cage began a sluggish ascent. My hunch had paid off that security would end at the ground floor. Once past the door and its electronic lock, a person could have the run of the entire building.

A simple wooden door with a plastic sign announced the home of Flamm & Associates. Odd for a major wheeler-dealer like Maury Flamm to have such unprepossessing digs. I supposed he preferred to throw his money around where it mattered, in the restaurants and watering holes around the capitol, not to mention that skybox out at Arco Arena. The door was closed, but a narrow, vertical window stood to one side of the entrance, presumably so the receptionist could keep her eye out for incoming traffic, and so someone like me could play spy.

I edged my way as close to the window as I dared and peered in at an oblique angle.

The view was partially obscured by a stack of four cardboard boxes stamped with the logo of one of Sacramento's major high-end commercial printers. Beyond the boxes, I caught a glimpse of a woman in a fuzzy purple sweater, and hair a shade of pink that could not possibly have been her natural color, tapping on a computer keyboard. A hulking male figure towered at her side and appeared to be reading aloud from a spiral notebook.

Rats. The pink-coiffed typist I could have dealt with. But not her plus Maury Flamm, who would undoubtedly recognize the unannounced media snoop from the basketball game last night. I was just about to retreat when Flamm snapped shut the notebook and disappeared into an inner office. Pink Hair's fingers halted their dance over the keyboard. She rose, turned her back to the door, and jerked open a file cabinet.

Now or never. Sure, Flamm could amble right back to the reception area. But I might have to lurk until lunchtime before this opportunity presented itself again. I opened the door and stepped inside as quietly as I could.

Pink Hair did a pirouette and faced me. "Got an appointment?"

What, no "Welcome to Flamm & Associates. How may we serve you?" What are they teaching young people in secretarial school these days?

"Gosh, I think I must have gotten lost. I'm supposed to be returning this stuff to the Sacramento Civic Light Opera Association." I hoisted the collection of promotional detritus in her direction.

"Try the third floor."

"Sure. Thanks." I took a couple of backward steps toward the door.

Pink Hair, apparently satisfied that the intruder was leaving, turned and buried her head in the open file drawer.

And leave I did. But not before I snatched a brochure from one of those boxes fresh from the printer.

The annual report of Flamm & Associates, Inc.

"Since when have federal prisoners been allowed to make phone calls to radio talk shows?" I leaned forward in the client's chair in Lisa Chandler's law office, a converted Victorian mansion within walking distance of the county courthouse and jail. Chandler was one of Sacramento's top criminal attorneys, and my guest expert whenever a major trial vaulted into the headlines.

"The quick answer is, they've been allowed to make phone calls, within certain limits, since the 1970s." Chandler sat behind a heavy, intricately carved wooden desk. She wore a green cashmere sweater set, and her light brown hair was caught in one of those scrunchie things at the top of her head, where it erupted into a fountain of crinkly curls. A small boy, maybe four years old, painstakingly constructed a Lego fort at her feet, the nanny having called in sick, according to what Chandler told me when I arrived. A space heater hummed in one corner.

"You're kidding. I thought you got that one phone call to your attorney and that's it."

"That's a popular misconception."

"I'm beginning to see why so many of my callers complain about pampered prisoners. What, are they sitting on the phone all day calling their bookies and their stock brokers?"

"The concept is, it's better in the long run if inmates are able to maintain ties with their families and community. They have to pay for the calls out of what they earn in the prison industries, or call collect, and no, they can't call just anyone. The numbers have to be on a list preapproved by prison authorities."

"And that list wouldn't include the call-in number for a radio talk show, I would hope."

"I sincerely doubt it."

"How about sending e-mails, setting up a Hotmail account?"

"No way." The fountain of hair swayed as she shook her head. "They may get computer access for vocational training and the like, but going on-line? No way."

"A real tech head might be able to figure out a way." I said it to myself, thinking out loud.

"Is this about that computer exec who got sent to Lompoc a few months ago?"

"Richard Snelling. Securities fraud, insider trading. He's supposed to be serving an eighteen-month sentence."

"Lompoc is hundreds of miles from here." Her voice registered skepticism.

"Over on the coast, just north of Santa Barbara," I agreed.

"How's he able to listen to a local radio show in Sacramento? Your signal doesn't reach that far, does it?"

"Not in the daytime. But these days, anyone in the world can listen to me, thanks to streaming audio on the station's Web site."

"But he wouldn't have Internet access in

prison, remember?" Chandler rested her head against the back of her chair, the curls fanning themselves into a crown.

"Maybe he escaped."

"Without the news media finding out?"

"Or he got an early release."

"Without the news media finding out?" This time, Chandler and I spoke in unison.

"There's an easy way to settle this." She turned to her computer and began tapping on the keyboard. I crept around the desk, careful not to stomp on any stray Lego blocks.

"Snelling, Richard P.," she recited from the monitor. "Incarcerated in the federal prison in Lompoc. Release date still almost a year away."

"You can look up names of prisoners on the Internet? You must be kidding!" I peered over her shoulder and at the familiar name, black type on a tan background, on the computer screen.

"You can find anything on the Internet if you know where to search. This one's easy, right on the official Federal Bureau of Prisons Web site." She rattled off an address ending with dot-gov. "Piece-a cake."

"Officially, he's still in the federal slammer. If he's calling a radio talk show and sending e-mails, he must have put together one helluva sweetheart deal with the warden," I said.

"Aren't you overlooking the most obvious explanation?"

"You mean, someone else is pulling these pranks."

"You have to admit, it makes the most sense."

"I suppose you're right."

Part of me wished Lisa Chandler hadn't been able to verify so easily that Richie's current address was a cell in a federal prison hundreds of miles from Sacramento. I would have preferred to believe he'd figured out a way to quietly escape.

The alternative — an anonymous, unknown stalker who had access to way too much personal information — was far more disturbing.

I tossed the results of my infiltration of the building housing Flamm & Associates onto the stacks of newspapers and press releases on my desk. Flamm's annual report, plus the press kit, T-shirt, and all the rest from the Sacramento Civic Light Opera Company. I lobbed the folder from the musical theater nonprofit into the recycle bin.

A leaflet slid from one of the folder's

pockets and landed face-up. A program from the Solstice Revels.

I flipped through the slim playbill until I found the head shots and résumés of the chorus members. Brenda Driscoll had used the same photo that graced the wall of the Jazz'n Motion dance studio, all pearly smile and gigantic hoop earrings. According to the one-paragraph biographical sketch next to the thumbnail-size halftone, she got her start in community theater "while still a student at Oakland's Castlemont High School."

Brenda had told me Sunday at OddCon that she'd attended Cordova High School with Markitus Wilson. A small fib, a matter of ninety miles separating the Sacramento suburb and the East Bay municipality, but a deception nonetheless.

I had to hand it to Maury Flamm; he put together one beaut of an annual report. My fingers caressed the embossed front cover, with the full-color photograph of the state capitol dome at sunrise, and the creamy inside pages with lush text in trendy fonts and artfully lit photography. But I didn't pounce upon any nuggets of information among all that gloss that seemed to have anything to do with filmmaking, ambitious young models/dancers, or my onetime intern. I scanned the list of the firm's clients: the Rice Growers Cooperative Exchange, United Citrus Producers of California, the Association of Northern California Mosquito Abatement Districts, the Federated Paving Contractors, and something called Citizens for Responsible Environmental Protection, which sounded to me like a cover for developers of flimsy tract homes and garish big box malls.

I skimmed the list one more time.

The Greater Sacramento Valley Automobile Dealers Association.

Lisa Chandler was right. You can find anything on the Internet if you know how and where to search. After a couple of false tries, I found the Greater Sacramento Valley Automobile Dealers Association in the electronic archives of the local newspapers. The most recent ink occurred this past October, coverage in the *Business Journal* of the group's annual meeting and election of officers. I scrolled through the article. Gareth I. Nyland, vice president for marketing for the Nyland Automotive Group, had been elected as one of five new board members, the new president being the CEO of Solon Imports.

Vic Cortese.

I easily located the Solon Imports Web

page and found the head shot of Vic Cortese among those of the Solon Imports sales staff, office crew, and mechanics. Definitely the same guy who startled me in the Arco Arena parking lot last night, almost causing me to lose my King Dog. I took another look at his mug and realized something else about Vic Cortese.

He was the "powerless over alcohol" fellow at the AA meeting Monday night.

I clicked the link that promised a biographical sketch.

"His many community activities include president of the River City Vintage Sports Car Association, member of the board of the Footprints Institute. . . ."

It wasn't as if everything became clear in a flash of light. But for the first time since Glory Lou had told me the name of the anonymous young man who'd been gunned down in McKinley Park ten days ago, I felt I was on to something.

So Vic Cortese and his "associates" wanted to offer me an incredibly good deal on a new car. Somehow I suspected it wasn't because they loved my show and wanted to express their admiration.

16

"What do you mean, he's gone for the day?" I planted myself in front of Mrs. Yanamoto's desk after demanding an audience with T. R. O'Brien.

"I'm sorry, dear." She looked up from her beloved IBM Selectric as she snapped in a new ribbon. Where did she find supplies for such an antique? "He and Dorinda Delgado had a meeting in Stockton this afternoon with the RV dealers' association to negotiate their annual advertising buy. I don't expect to see either of them for the rest of the day."

"Shoot." Now I wouldn't be able to call Doyle Bollinger with a firm answer this afternoon like I'd promised. At least I wouldn't have to confront T.R. with news of my upcoming defection for another twenty-four hours.

"Is everything all right, dear?" Mrs. Yanamoto fixed me with a canny eye. She'd been T.R.'s secretary and personal assistant for around forty years now, and had a finely tuned sensitivity when it came to dealing with neurotic radio types.

"Of course. Everything's fine." I pasted a smile on my face.

"Shall I pass along any message to T.R. if he happens to call in?"

"That's okay. I'll catch up with him tomorrow."

Kelly Ripa has one. So does *Good Morning America*, *The Today Show*, the *Bee*, and of course Oprah. So why should the Shauna J. Bogart Show miss out on the fun?

My book club was a bit different. Instead of featuring one title each month, I simply opened the phone lines and invited my listeners to call in with their picks 'n' pans from among the recent releases. I called it Whatcha Readin', and it seemed to be a big enough hit that I scheduled it as a regular feature every couple of weeks.

This afternoon, I invited a couple of guest experts into the studio: Kip Shore, one of the buyers at Tower Books, and Marisa Young, head of acquisitions for the Sacramento Public Library.

"You guys are doing great," I told my two guests just as a message from Josh scrolled across my computer screen.

LIZ MEYER FROM THE SACRA-
MENTO FILM COMMISSION HOLD-
ING ON THE STUDIO HOTLINE.
SHOULD I TELL HER YOU'LL CALL
BACK TOMORROW?

I excused myself, grabbed the receiver, and barked a greeting.

"Sorry, I don't know of anything," Meyer said. "We haven't had a major studio location shoot in Sacramento since 2000, when John Travolta and Lisa Kudrow did *Lucky Numbers*."

"I get the idea this is more of an indie project, probably low budget."

"Sorry, haven't heard of a thing. January just isn't the time of the year to be shooting exteriors and outdoor scenes."

"How about a project on the calendar for spring or summer? Maybe the film company was in town just to audition local talent and scout for locations."

"I've heard some talk about a made-for-TV movie possibly doing some filming in the Delta in late spring, but right now that's all it is — talk. Too bad." Meyer's voice took on a wistful tone. "We've got it all right here: Old West exteriors, government buildings, two major rivers, rice paddies, small towns that could stand in for New England and the Midwest. But all the location business is going up to Canada these days."

I could sense a pitch for publicity in the gearing-up stages. "It's a shame, for real." I thanked her for calling and sprinted back to the Tower Books buyer and the acquisitions librarian, and the listeners jamming the phone lines. For the next ten minutes, I functioned as little more than a ringmaster as my guests and the callers traded spirited volleys about their favorite books and authors. People actually reading books and sharing passionate opinions about them — this is great radio!

"Is that about the movie they're filming in McKinley Park?"

I had just introduced the four-thirty news break. I wrenched my attention away from the control board and toward Marisa Young. "I beg your pardon?"

"I just couldn't help but overhear that phone call you got from the Film Commission."

"What movie being filmed in McKinley Park?"

"This must have been, oh, about two weeks ago. I was just coming out of a meeting at the McKinley Park branch and I walked right past this film crew setting up by the duck pond."

"What did they look like?"

"I only watched for a few minutes. A young man with a camera, and another fellow with one of those boom microphones. It looked like one of those moronic action films, people running around with guns. I didn't recognize either of the actors, but I don't pay much attention to pop culture."

"Could you describe them?"

"I just remember they were young, three males and one female, one fellow and the girl were African-American, the other two guys white."

I leaned one elbow on the console and fixed my attention on Marisa Young, ignoring the gestures from Josh warning me that the newscast was about to end. He could always cover with a public service announcement, or the long version of my theme music. "I don't suppose you might have noticed the name of this film company, maybe a logo stenciled on the camera, anything else that might help identify them."

Marisa shook her head. "I thought it was strange at the time; the crew seemed so small, just the cameraman and the fellow with the microphone. You hear about these huge entourages in Hollywood, the stars' trailers and all that. This looked more like a student undertaking, or maybe a low-budget documentary."

If it had been a legitimate film project, the studio would have had to obtain a permit from the city, and that meant the Film Commission would have known about it. "You say this was around two weeks ago?"

Marisa dug into a canvas tote bag silk-screened with the declaration that "Librarians Do It in the Stacks!" She pulled out a thick day planner, flipped through the pages, and recited a date.

The Friday before Travis Ikeda-Nyland had his fatal meeting with Markitus Wilson.

"I just hope they're not making a movie out of one of my favorite books," Marisa said.

How did this movie business tie in to the Footprints Institute, if it did at all? I gazed through the glass into the call screener booth as if somehow I would find the answer in my reflected image.

"The movie is never as good as the book, you know?"

I could tell Marisa expected an answer, but I was too preoccupied with what I'd just heard. Two young people who match the descriptions of Brenda Driscoll and Markitus Wilson? Running around with guns? I opened the microphone, introduced Shauna J. Bogart and Sacramento Talk Radio as if on autopilot, mentioned the time and temperature, then let Marisa Young, Kip Shore, and the listeners have free reign while I tapped out a message to Josh.

CARE TO JOIN ME IN A LITTLE UNDERCOVER REPORTING PROJECT?

He responded with a string of exclamation points.

TOMORROW MORNING, THE FOOTPRINTS LODGE IN GRASS VALLEY. THINK YOU CAN SKIP CLASS?

LIKE, DUH!

I'LL PICK YOU UP AT 8.

WHAT'S UP? YOU GONNA CHECK YOURSELF INTO REHAB?

NOT EXACTLY.

Twenty women and two men stretched legs, arms, and torsos on the wooden floor and at the barre of the Jazz'n Motion dance studio. They wore either leotards and tights or stretchy workout shorts and bright tank tops, plus chunky white athletic shoes. A pumped-up disco-techno beat pulsated from a pair of speakers on either side of a waist-high wooden box that served as the instructor's platform.

My outfit consisted of a paisley leotard

and shimmery silver tights so new they still bore the creases from the packaging and exuded the aroma of fabric dye. Hey, at least I'd remembered to cut off the tags. My warm-up involved pacing before the front counter and staring at the clock.

Ten minutes after seven.

"It's not like her to be late," the receptionist told me. She exhibited a lean, mean workout machine in a form-fitting tank top that announced to the world that she "Gotta Dance," while her face had that creased, leathery look that made me vow not to skimp on the sunscreen. "Brenda's usually very reliable. Too bad, your first Funkercise class."

I strolled over to the front door and peered through the glass with the hopes of spotting a leggy young woman striding across the fog-shrouded parking lot. All I noticed was a white van parked along the curb in the passenger loading zone, "Ruehl Janitorial Services," lettered in black and red across the side of the van, atop a drawing of a ruler snapping in half. "We'll Break Every Rule to Satisfy the Customer."

"Does that van come around here every night?" I asked the woman at the reception counter.

"I don't know why they always have to

park right in front of our door. They usually take care of the bank and the chiropractor's office first, and then clean the studio when the last class of the day is over."

"Which would be this one, right? Brenda Driscoll's Funk-ercise class from seven to eight?"

"Except Tuesdays and Thursdays, when Benji does Cardio Kick-Start."

The minute hand had crept to thirteen past the hour. Several students were starting to don sweatshirts and gather up their gym bags, and I overheard some grumbling about expecting a refund for tonight's class.

"Have you tried calling Brenda?" I asked the reception lady.

"At seven on the dot. All I got was voice mail."

Well, Brenda Driscoll was a busy young lady. Auditioning for the Royal Court dance team, renting herself out as arm candy for an older gent in Maury Flamm's skybox, modeling at OddCon, appearing in a low-budget indie film, and leading an aerobics dance class three nights a week. Poor thing had probably gotten confused about the date, or had collapsed from sheer exhaustion.

"Maybe someone should check on her," I said. "Make sure she's okay."

"I'll try calling again." Gotta Dance picked up a phone and punched in numbers from a list pinned to the wall. She shook her head and replaced the receiver. "Just voice mail."

"What's her address?" I stepped behind the counter before Gotta Dance could object and began sifting through the sticky notes, steno pad, business cards, exercise equipment catalogs, and calendars that littered the desktop.

"Look, I'm not on the staff here or anything," Gotta Dance said. "I just help Brenda get everyone checked in for class. I don't know where they keep files on the instructors, and I'm sure I'm not supposed to give out their addresses."

"I understand. But I have a feeling Brenda might be in trouble of some sort." That's all I had at this point, a feeling, a sense of unease that grew more acute with the passage of each minute. Unease, plus frustration over a situation that threatened to delay my chance to confront Brenda and demand she tell me everything she knew about that movie allegedly being filmed in McKinley Park. And while you're at it honey, why'd you lie to me about going to high school with Markitus Wilson?

One of the male students, a Latino who

wore a white mesh tank top and solid white shorts, placed both hands on top of the counter. "What's going on here? We've never seen you before, and now you're insisting that Brenda's in trouble and that we're supposed to tell you where she lives."

"And your point is?"

"You could be the reason Brenda didn't show up tonight. Why should we help you?"

The young Funk-erciser had a point. If the tables had been turned, I would hope Mrs. Yanamoto wouldn't blithely permit a stranger to go through the personnel files at Sacramento Talk Radio and unearth my home address and god knows how much other intimate information. Little things like my Social Security number.

I couldn't think of any way to explain myself to the Jazz'n Motion gang and gain their instant trust.

So I did the next best thing.

I yanked open the top file drawer and began riffling through the manila folders over their yelps of protest. Aha! — Driscoll, Brenda, typed on a white label. I pulled the file and clawed through the scant contents until I found a W-2 form containing an address.

"You'd better stop right now or I'm

calling the cops." Gotta Dance emphasized her point by picking up the telephone receiver and shaking it in my direction.

One last peek at the address, then I dropped the folder onto the desk and sprinted toward the door.

I recognized the shiny orange box of a car parked on L Street near the intersection with Sixteenth before I was able to make out the house number. I found a spot for the Z-car in the next block and hiked back to the U-shaped arrangement of squat bungalows that must have started life as an auto court. Only a couple of blocks from the capitol and the ever-grinding gears of the state government factory, yet a throwback to an entirely different era and social class. My quarry's unit was toward the back. I opened the warped screen and knocked on the door. No answer. Not even any yaps from lonely pets or queries from nosy neighbors. Just a pizza delivery flyer hanging on the knob of the screen door and a political circular stuffed under the worn rubber doormat.

I tested the doorknob.

It gave a turn.

I kept my hand on the knob and pressed. Ever so slightly, I swear.

The door eased open.

I slipped my upper body through the

opening and fumbled for a light switch. "Brenda? Anyone home?"

Silence.

I gave up on finding a light switch, plucked my wad of keys from my pocket, squeezed the tiny flashlight on the key-chain, and arced the light across what turned out to be a small, tidy living room. A TV set and DVD player perched atop a white plastic cart, and an expensive stereo system and CD collection took up most of one wall. A combination phone/answering machine/fax, red light blinking with messages, shared shelf space with a potted bamboo, a good luck symbol according to Asian tradition.

"Brenda? Hello?" I crept inside the play-house-size bungalow and let the flashlight explore the shadowy corners of the living room. Nothing unusual. No replies to my repeated calling of her name.

Maybe she panicked when she realized she was running late for the aerobics class she was supposed to lead, and dashed out of the house so fast she forgot to lock the door. Then why was her car parked outside? Maybe she cowered in silence in the bedroom, terrified by the intruder in her living room.

"Brenda? It's okay. It's Shauna J. Bogart.

We met Sunday at that science fiction convention, remember?"

No sound except the creak of my footsteps against the aging wooden floor and my own ragged breathing.

A peek into a compact kitchen revealed nothing more interesting than a coffee mug and cereal bowl stacked in a drainer, and an open carton of low-fat milk on the black-and-white-tiled counter.

I edged my way around a corner and stood in the doorway of what I assumed was the bedroom. My hand groped along the wall for a light switch.

This time I found one.

I snapped the switch into the upward position and gazed into the bedroom.

The instant the soft yellow light filled the tiny chamber, I wished I hadn't been so damn snoopy.

17

It was almost eleven before I finally finished with the cops. I staggered into my apartment, tossed my backpack onto the couch, and made my way to the kitchen to give Bialystock his long-delayed dinner of kitty kibble and to fix myself a much-needed drink.

My answering machine signaled three messages. I skipped past the request from the *Bee* reporter to call back to clarify one of the statements I'd made earlier, and the invitation from something called Bereavement Network Resources to attend an upcoming support group meeting.

I heard Iris Fontaine's voice on the third message and felt my insides tighten. Had Markitus started talking again, confessed to the police officer standing in front of the door of his room at the Med Center? Had he taken a turn for the worse, lapsed back into a coma? Iris didn't leave any details, just asked me to call her as soon as I had the chance. Her tone of voice didn't give me the impression I should drop everything and return the call anytime day or night. Just ring her up when I had the chance.

I had the chance, but eleven o'clock was just too late for a call not clearly labeled as urgent.

Still, I knew it was one more thing that I'd stew about as I struggled for sleep, trying without success to banish from my mind the final image I had of the lovely young model/dancer.

I'd found her on the floor of the minuscule bedroom, wedged in an awkward heap between the four-poster and the dresser. Her long legs had crumpled beneath her like a marionette whose strings had snapped, and her head lolled at an odd angle. I glimpsed what looked like bruises next to the silver hoop earring on the sepia skin of her neck.

"Brenda?" I fixed my vision on the satiny purple kimono that covered her upper body, silently begging her chest to rise and fall with breathing, no matter how faint. "For god's sake, wake up!"

The form lay still and soundless.

Somehow I managed to stumble back to the living room, locate the phone, and dial 911 with quivering fingers. Sirens wailed in the background, drawing closer, before I had finished babbling to the dispatcher. I didn't need to see the grim face of the first paramedic who burst through the bedroom door to confirm what I already instinctively knew.

As far as I could tell, the police and the coroner's investigator believed my story. I mean, they wouldn't have sent me home if they thought I had something to do with Brenda Driscoll's death, and they would have been advising me to seek legal counsel if they thought I was a suspect instead of arranging to have a bereavement counselor call me. My story rang true because it *was* the truth: I believed Brenda Driscoll had a connection with the cops' Number One suspect in the killing of Travis Ikeda-Nyland. I had questioned her Sunday afternoon, and saw her, but didn't speak to her, last night at Arco Arena. I had wanted to ask her some follow-up questions and dropped in this evening at the dance studio to do just that. When she didn't show up to lead the Funkercise session, I became concerned, made a trip over to her house to make sure she was okay, found the front door unlocked and a corpse in the bedroom.

"Ask Markitus Wilson about an acquaintance of his named Brenda Driscoll," I said to the half-dozen officers packed in the bungalow's living room. "Ask him about the movie he and Brenda were making in McKinley Park. And while you're at it, check the enrollment records at Cordova High and see if they ever had a student named Brenda Driscoll."

The only thing I didn't share with the detectives was the possible connection with the Footprints Institute. It hung by the slenderest of threads, just a vague hunch. One day Travis enlists the aid of a friend to perform crude surgery to remove a medical implant, a gizmo that he'd received at Footprints Lodge. Next day, he's dead. That, plus a Footprints plaque heaved through the window of the Z-car, and a member of the Footprints board hinting that his "associates" had the power to see to it that I got a new car.

Just like that cute, shiny putt-putt parked in front of Brenda Driscoll's bungalow court. Sure, she could have saved up enough for a down payment on a struggling dancer's salary, and somehow managed to make the monthly payments if she lived frugally.

Or, she could have had an associate who made her a very good deal.

In return for her silence?

Just as I was holding back from the cops, I knew they were keeping information from me. In fact, they wouldn't even confirm that Brenda's death was due to anything other than natural causes. But it was all too obvious they suspected foul play, judging from the dusting for fingerprints, taking of photographs, and plucking of hairs going on inside the little house. And I know what I saw — those bruises around the neck. Nope, Brenda did not depart this plane of existence due to a brain seizure, or a heart attack, or a self-administered drug overdose.

Someone helped her along.

I sank into the couch, a glass of Chablis in one hand and the cat by my side, and watched myself on the eleven o'clock news. I was grateful the TV cameras had captured me from the waist up, where my down jacket covered the form-fitting paisley leotard, and had edited out the full-length footage. Flabby thighs encased in glittery tights would have been a scary television image.

A pounding on the door.

At twenty minutes past eleven?

I rose, eyeballed the security peep-hole, and flung open the door.

"Why the hell didn't you call me?" Pete Kovacs took a step inside the apartment and planted himself in the front hall, hands on hips.

"How'd you find out so soon?"

He jerked one thumb in the direction of the TV set. "So I turn on the late news, figuring I'll catch up on the headlines before calling it a night and what do I see? My girlfriend at the scene of a possible homicide. And not because she's covering the story — she *is* the story!"

"Look, I just got home after a long day and I'm wiped. Can't we fight about this some other time?"

Pete relaxed his combative stance and lowered his head. "Didn't mean to come on so strong. I just worry about you, that's all. Do you always have to be so damn independent?"

"I thought that was what you liked about me."

"I do, I do. I just, you know . . ."

"I know. You worry about me sometimes." I took him by the hand, led him into the bedroom, and let him come on as strong as he damn well pleased.

I hunched over the steering wheel of the Z-car and centered my vision on the white line on the right side of Interstate 80. My first winter in Sacramento had taught me the finer points of fog-driving: maintain a normal speed so some idiot doesn't plow into you from the back; it's better to be a follower than the lead vehicle; resist the urge to turn on the high beams as they'll only reflect off the moisture and create blinding glare. When it's so impenetrable you can't see more than a few feet ahead, stay in the slow lane and align yourself with the white stripe on the right side. And pray.

"Get into my backpack and find my cell phone and notebook," I told Josh.

Scrabbling sounds and a brush of flannel shirt against my shoulder told me Josh was doing as I'd instructed. I didn't dare take my eyes off the gray landscape and white line to check on his progress.

"Got 'em. Now what."

"You should find a number for Iris Fontaine toward the back of the notebook. Dial it, and then pass the phone to me." I stuck out my right hand, heard a series of electronic squeaks, then felt the weight of the mobile telephone against my palm. I transferred the phone to my left hand and placed it to my ear, keeping the steering wheel steady with my right hand. Hey, it's still not illegal in California to drive and talk on the phone. I figure it's no more distracting than any of the other activities that folks engage in while piloting a motor vehicle, things like eating, applying makeup, and yelling at their kids. Or listening to talk radio.

Iris Fontaine sounded awake and alert when she picked up the call. Good. I figured eight-thirty on a weekday morning wasn't too early to return a phone call.

"Oh my lord, that poor girl is dead," she wailed as soon as I identified myself. "I just heard it on the radio."

"I know. Too many young lives ending too soon."

"She was our biggest hope for proving that my Markitus didn't do it. And now she's gone."

"Listen, Iris, I've got to be realistic with you. I talked to Brenda Driscoll, and she claimed she hadn't had any contact with Markitus since high school. I imagine she told the police the same thing."

"If those lazybones ever got around to questioning her."

"I'm just saying, I don't know how helpful Brenda could have been in clearing Markitus."

"Then why did someone go to all the trouble of killing her, unless she knew something important and they wanted to shut her up?"

Good question.

"You tried to call me last night, remember?" I said.

"I was trying to tell you about these two

policemen who came to see Markitus. Detectives, weren't wearing no uniforms. They're wanting to ask him all about this Brenda Driscoll, and I'm thinking praise be, someone's finally paying attention to poor old Iris Fontaine. That's before I knew that girl had gotten herself killed, of course."

"What did Markitus have to say?"

"He didn't have nothin' to say, that's what. Nothin' that he hadn't already told me, and that I told you."

"That he was going to be in a movie."

"The same. Then they asked him what happened that afternoon when Sapphire Ikeda's son got killed, and he's saying he doesn't remember anything from the time he left the house and when he woke up in the hospital nine days later."

"I wonder if they could hypnotize him and see what he remembered."

"That's what one of those detectives started talking about doing. That's when the nurse jumps in and says no way is no policeman hypnotizing her patient without permission from the neurologist."

"Good for the nurse." I spotted a rectangle of red dots through the murk and increased my speed to catch up with the big rig and play follow-the-leader.

"That's what I said." Iris's voice crackled

through the cell phone speaker. "And next thing, she's telling these two cops that visiting hours are over, her patient is tired and needs his rest, and they'll have to come back some other time."

So basically it was the old two steps forward and one step back. Markitus had come out of his coma but remembered nothing except that he was going to be in a movie. And the one person who might have been able to amplify his story wouldn't be talking ever again.

"You told me the other day Markitus was working nights for a janitorial service just before he got into trouble."

"That's correct. That one with the ruler."

The white van from Ruehl Janitorial Services, parked every night in front of Jazz'n Motion. And a young man named Markitus Wilson slipping in with his mop and bucket at the very time Brenda Driscoll was winding up her Funk-ercize class.

Sounded like someone might have broken a rule or two to satisfy a customer.

I wound up my conversation with Iris Fontaine, passed the phone back to Josh, and cranked up the volume on the in-dash radio, riding gain on Glory Lou's honey-dripping southern voice. "Sources at the Sacramento Police Department say they are definitely treating the discovery of a young woman's body in a Midtown bungalow last night as a homicide. The victim has been identified as twenty-two-year-old Brenda Driscoll, a native of Oakland who apparently moved to the capital city two years ago to accept a part in a musical put on by the Sacramento Civic Light Opera Company. She recently auditioned to be a midseason replacement for an injured dancer on the Kings' Royal Court dance team. In fact, our sources confirm the team captain was planning to call her this very morning to tell her she had been accepted. We go live to Arco Arena, and a statement from the Kings' chief of public relations, Shane Emmerlich. . . ."

The freeway started a gradual climb, and the fog became less murky. I could make out the misty images of billboards advertising the Reno casinos, the ski resorts at the Sierra summit, and the Roseville Auto Mall.

"I know what you're planning to do," Josh said from the passenger seat. "You don't have to be so secretive about it."

"What, this morning at Footprints Lodge? I thought we went over everything yesterday afternoon."

"You know what I'm talking about. Los Angeles. RadioLand."

My fingers tightened around the steering wheel. "I don't know what you're talking about."

"You think I just fell off the turnip truck? Why am I all of a sudden fielding all these phone calls for you from this Doyle Bollinger dude? I dialed his number once, just to see who answered. This receptionist says I've just reached RadioLand."

"My, you're certainly turning into the little detective, aren't you?"

"So I look up RadioLand on the Internet and guess what — they're this big supplier of syndicated radio programming. And they're expanding their service, going to be announcing the acquisition of several major personalities any day now."

"Bollinger's just an old radio pal, that's all."

"Nope, not buyin' it. Why is this old friend calling two, three times a day, and getting all hissy and insistent when I tell him you're not available? You're going to quit, aren't you? Quit and leave us and go off to la-la land to work for the enemy."

Now who was getting all hissy?

"This has got to stay just between us," I said. "You're on the right track. I've been talking to RadioLand about a career opportunity with them. But I haven't given them a firm decision."

"I knew it!" I still didn't dare take my vision off the road immediately ahead, but I could just picture Josh folding his arms and giving his head a self-satisfied nod.

"But why?" His voice held a tiny quiver. "Sacramento's not that bad, is it?"

"The money, for starters. And security. I mean, look at what's happening at our shop. Outsourcing Captain Mikey."

"You won't exactly make things better if you leave."

"Radio is a tough business, in case you haven't noticed. Sometimes you've got to weigh the options, make a difficult choice, and move on."

"Just looking out for number one."

"Look, you're not helping any with the sarcasm. Like I said before, I haven't made up my mind and I haven't even said anything to T. R. O'Brien yet, so for god's sake mum's the word. Let's just forget about RadioLand for now and have some fun up at Footprints Lodge, okay?"

Silence from the passenger seat. I reached my hand across the stick shift and ruffled his frizzy blond hair with my fingers. "Okay?"

He made me wait another thirty seconds or so, then finally returned a flat " 'kay."

The fog dissipated just before we reached Auburn. Like a porpoise gleefully breaking the surface of the ocean after a long dive, the Z-car shot past the fog line into blue sky and sun, glorious sun. I took the Highway 49 exit and pointed the car north.

At a little over a thousand feet in elevation, the Sierra foothills community of Auburn is high enough to escape the gloomy blanket of vapor, but low enough to miss all but the most brutal snowstorm. Auburn shared sisterhood with a couple dozen villages and hamlets dotting the two hundred seventy-mile stretch of Highway 49, all dating to the Gold Rush days. Any of the historic downtown districts could have stood in for the Old West in a Hollywood film or TV western. The town of Jamestown, toward the southern end of the Mother Lode, had done just that in the third *Back to the Future* movie.

I'd heard there were still veins of gold running deep beneath these hills, but the cost of extracting it far outweighed its value on the world market. These days, the real treasure came from tourism and gentrification, most of these towns having been cutesy-pooed to the point that if an honest-to-god forty-niner were to hit town with pick and shovel, mud-caked boots, scraggly beard, and chaw of tobaccy, the horrified townspeople would probably bundle him off to the *Queer Eye* boys for a makeover.

The Z-car plowed through Auburn's modern commercial district, a strip of supermarkets, fast-food restaurants, and auto repair shops on the northern edge of town. Apparently it takes more than bed-and-breakfast inns, antiques shops, hand-sewn quilts, and organic blueberry muffins to sustain a village.

"Nice job on the getup," I said to Josh. He'd gone all out to create the impression of the dissolute slacker: black T-shirt crisscrossed with random wrinkles and bearing a scrawled demand to "Question Authority" (a sentiment I heartily shared), rumpled plaid flannel shirt with torn sleeve, worn tails out, brown corduroy pants sporting numerous shiny spots, sweat-stained sneakers, one lace undone. He hadn't shaved and he exuded an aroma of unbrushed teeth and unwashed socks, making me wonder if I would have to have the passenger compartment fumigated at the end of the day.

Josh grunted a thanks, then said, "I'm not going to have to actually check into this place, am I?"

"Of course not."

"And no medical experiments," Josh said. "No needles. I hate needles."

"Everybody hates needles. Now why would I do something like that to you?"

"Yeah, right. And no leaving me behind, no matter what."

"Absolutely, positively, no way." Unless we stumble across something really, really good.

Josh reached under the front seat, pulled out a bottle, and unscrewed a cap. I caught a whiff of a familiar odor.

"Is that beer?"

"Yeah! Is this great or what?" Josh tipped the bottle to his lips.

"Jeez, get rid of that thing right now. Do you want me to get arrested?"

"I'm the one doing the drinking. You're the designated driver."

"Hello? The open-container law?"

Josh swallowed and recapped the bottle. "I wasn't planning to drink the whole thing."

"Well, that's a relief."

"I just thought it would make it more realistic if I showed up with alcohol on my breath." He reached around the seat and stowed the bottle in the back compartment.

"You're a good kid, Josh, but you know something?"

"What."

"You don't always have to overachieve."

An additional twenty minutes of driving over the serpentine highway brought a warning from Josh that we were drawing close. "Make a right at that sign," he said after consulting the directions he'd printed out from MapQuest.

"Are you sure?" I slowed, flicked on the right-turn signal, and drifted over the shoulder to allow a pickup truck with a gun rack to pass. The sign that Josh indicated was obvious enough, a massive sheet of plywood attached to two tall poles. The paint had faded and peeled, but I could still discern the lettering. "Wertheim's Pine Rest."

"Positive. Check the mailbox."

My gaze followed his outstretched arm to a curved metal box atop a fencepost.

We'd found it, all right.

I turned right onto a gravel driveway lined with pines and entered the grounds of Footprints Lodge.

18

The drive crested a low hill and skirted a meadow lush with grass. I noticed a path winding through the meadow, and barrel-size pine logs spaced evenly along the trail. At first I took them to be benches. Then I noticed the Roman numerals, one through twelve, hacked into the logs, one numeral per, like the recovery movement's version of the stations of the cross. A man sat cross-legged in meditation at the base of the pine monolith carved with a *V* and *I*. He wore running shorts and a tank top, and I wondered if his lack of warm clothing was some sort of penance.

"Remember what we agreed to," I said to Josh.

"Yeah, yeah, yeah. You do all the talking. I just sit there and look pathetic."

I parked the Z-car at the end of a semi-circle of ten or so vehicles in front of a one-story, ranch-style building. A carved wooden sign, probably left over from the era of Wertheim's Pine Rest, dangled from the porch eaves and announced the location of the office. I stepped outside the low-slung sports car, stretched, and immediately understood how that man in the meadow could be wearing running shorts and a tank top in the middle of January. It had to be at least sixty-five degrees, bright with sunshine, just enough breeze to send the pine needles into a whisper of rattles but not brisk enough to chill. I raised my arms over my head, wished I'd worn something lighter than a fisherman knit sweater, jeans, and shearling boots, and inhaled the sweet aroma of pine-scented air. I took several deep breaths of the pure, clean oxygen, clearing my lungs of the damp rot that permeated the Sacramento Valley.

I'd already decided not to even try disguising who I was. Sacramento Talk Radio's fifty-thousand-watt signal blasted through most of Northern California and could easily be heard in and around Grass Valley. Someone would recognize me for sure. At any rate, members of the news media and entertainment industries are always checking into rehab. One more would not draw undue attention.

The lobby area of the office contained perky recovery slogans, maxims, and aphorisms on banners, plaques, and posters, just like the ones decorating the Footprints Institute's Sacramento headquarters. I parked myself on a bench under a blue and gold banner informing me that "Grace Happens," while Josh fidgeted in a metal folding chair. A rack underneath a frosted glass window held brochures from what appeared to be local tourist attractions. Another relic from Wertheim's Pine Rest? I snatched up leaflets for Discover Cornwall in Historic Downtown Grass Valley, Empire Mine, Malakoff Diggings State Park, and the Nevada City Antique Traders Association, just to have something with which to amuse myself should the wait prove to be a long one.

The frosted glass window slid open. I shoved the brochures into my backpack and watched as a woman's head and upper body filled the opening.

"Sorry to keep you waiting. Are you here for an intake?"

Light brown hair sheared off to about two inches long, nose and cheeks with a sprinkling of brown freckles, and a space between her two front teeth when she grinned after giving her speech. Her right ear held at least a half-dozen tiny round hoops that marched from the lobe to the top.

"My young friend here could use some help, and we're just checking out different facilities." I hadn't made an appointment but was willing to bet the staff at a place like this was used to having anxious friends and families show up on their doorstep, an inebriated companion in tow.

"You've come to the right place." She vanished for an instant, then reappeared through a side door.

"Hi, I'm Rhonda Barth. Welcome to Footprints Lodge, where the past is history, the future is but a dream, and the present is all that matters." She wore a plaid western-style shirt with snap buttons, tight jeans encircled with a hand-tooled belt and massive silver buckle, and cowboy boots. Rhonda Barth positively vibrated with that sort of hearty, outdoorsy energy that always makes me fear I'm about to get roped into joining a nature hike, or worse, participating in a campfire sing-along.

She slipped a finger into the back pocket of her jeans, removed a plastic card, and held it a few inches away from a rectangle of plain white plastic next to the door. I heard an electronic *ka-chunk* sound. Rhonda Barth pushed the door open and led Josh and me down a hall and into her office, a cheery room filled with calico print chair cushions, silk flowers, a glass apothecary jar filled with wrapped hard candies, and framed western landscapes, towering peaks and waterfalls, on the walls. A picture window offered a glance at a portion of the Footprints Lodge grounds. An orange iMac stood on a credenza along the back wall, the monitor facing the guest chairs.

Rhonda tossed the key card into a ceramic dish decorated with American Indian symbols. It landed with a tiny *chink* atop a cushion of paperclips.

I introduced myself and Josh and let her do most of the talking: programs tailored to the needs of the individual, certified counselors, facility fully licensed by the California Department of Alcohol and Drug Programs, detox under medical supervision, registered dietician, follow-up care for one year after completion of the program. Blah, blah, blah.

"We would need to do a full assessment first," she said. "I imagine, though, from what you've shared with me, that Josh would benefit most from our twenty-eight day residential treatment program."

I just loved the way she talked about Josh as if he wasn't even there. I nodded for her to continue.

"The residential program offers a structured environment for someone like Josh to develop the life skills that he'll need to stay clean and sober, one day at a time. We find that a serene, country atmosphere, away from the stress of everyday life, and full immersion in the concepts and philosophies of recovery — well, miracles do happen. We see them every day."

"We're especially interested in your medical program. I understand it's cutting edge."

"He'll likely require at least a day, maybe several, in detox. You can rest assured he'll have the best of care, supervision by our nursing staff, and access to medications should he need them to ease the pain of withdrawal."

"I was thinking more long-term. I understand you offer a program of medical assistance after a patient has finished the twenty-eight day program." I paused to assess Rhonda's reaction.

"We have so much going on here, sometimes it's hard to keep track." The cheery grin never faltered.

"Implants? Tiny devices that release medication to decrease the craving for alcohol?"

"Goodness, yes! We've just started running tests for the FDA. It's terribly exciting. How did you hear about it?"

"I do my homework." I'd given Chad MacKenzie a guarantee of confidentiality that I was not about to break.

"Your young friend could prove to be a suitable candidate for that program. But of course, we won't know that until we complete our assessment."

Rhonda removed a printed form from a file folder atop her desk and grabbed a pen from a leather-covered cylinder. I waited for her to start asking about Josh's medical history, childhood diseases, allergies, family legacy of alcohol abuse.

"I assume Josh is covered by an insurance plan?" The pen was poised above the line just under where she'd entered Josh's name.

"He's a full-time student at Sac State, so he'd be covered by the student health plan."

For the first time since our interview began, Rhonda's lips took a downward turn. "That may be a problem."

"Just out of curiosity, what kind of money are we looking at here?"

"That depends on so many factors, how much medical attention he'll need, how many days he'll need to stay in detox, we won't really know —"

"I know, I know, until you do a full assessment. Just a ballpark figure."

She tapped her lower lip with the pen. "Assuming he needs, let's say two days in detox, and then completes the twenty-eight day program, roughly in the neighborhood of twenty thousand."

Twenty grand? I tried not to look stunned. I mean, I shouldn't have been surprised, given what medical care cost these days. Shoot, even a root canal and crown will run you at least a couple thousand. But still, twenty thousand dollars! That's more money than a lot of people in America see in an entire year.

Rhonda must have sensed my astonishment. "It's a small price to pay for a lifetime free from the enslavement of addiction. Especially for a young man like Josh."

"My dad's good for the money if the insurance won't cover it." Josh spoke for the first time since we'd pulled into the Footprints Lodge parking lot. "Maybe you've heard of him. Mort Friedman? Friedman's Fine Furniture?"

"Of course!" The genial humor was back. "But let's hope it doesn't come to that. Give me a moment, and let me see what I can find out about the student health plan on the Cal State campuses."

She did a one-eighty to face the computer and began clacking on the keyboard.

My right hand snaked forward toward the ceramic dish on Rhonda's desk. I gingerly scooped up the keycard, careful not to disturb the paperclips underneath and make that telltale *chink.* Josh emitted a tiny gasp. I turned to him, gave my head a quick shake with lips pressed in a straight line. For god's sake, chill! I stuffed the keycard up the sleeve of my sweater just as Rhonda swiveled back in our direction.

"Could I bother you for directions to the nearest ladies' room?" I said. "That drive from Sacramento was just long enough, know what I mean?"

"Down the hall, third door to your left."

I left the office and scampered down the hallway. In which room would I find a nurse, a syringe, and a row of nervous volunteers waiting for their implants? Behind which door would I find the patient records, and how quickly could I locate the folder bearing Travis Ikeda-Nyland's name? Which office housed the person responsible for hurling a Footprints plaque through the back window of the Z-car? I paused in front of each door, listening for sounds of voices or activity. I didn't have a lot of time, and, just like the contestants on the old *Let's Make a Deal* game show, I wanted to make sure I made Monty Hall proud and chose the right door.

Then I reached a door at the end of the corridor, read the name chiseled into the brass nameplate, and realized the decision had been made for me.

Dr. Fessenden.

I gave the door a quick shove. Locked, of course. I held Rhonda Barth's keycard in front of the blank plastic rectangle next to the door and heard the muffled *ka-chunk* of the lock releasing itself.

A second *ka-chunk,* distant. The door at the end of the corridor opened, and a stocky female figure began lumbering in my direction.

I took a fast glance at a smock in garish primary colors, white slacks in an unnatural fiber, and white nurse shoes. I jumped back and scooted into the women's restroom.

The door began to swing open. A heavy white shoe and a leg sheathed in white polyester made its way through the opening. I leaped into a stall and waited for what seemed like an hour but was probably more like ninety seconds, until I finally heard the rustle of a paper towel, the squeak of the door, and footsteps retreating down the hallway.

I crept out of the restroom and crossed the hall, pushed open the door, and entered the lair of Dr. Fessenden.

Empty. Half-closed miniblinds over the one window sent stripes of sunlight over blank walls, a few nails protruding where artwork must have once hung. I made out a modern blond wood desk, the top bare except for a computer and telephone, leather in-box atop a credenza containing only a thin coat of dust.

I took a step toward the iMac. I knew I didn't have time to boot up and start nosing around in any electronic files that might remain, but I couldn't say no to the temptation.

Movement on the other side of the window. I looked up and saw a blur of primary colors. That damn nurse again! I heard the distant electronic *ka-chunk* of the outside door and footsteps in the corridor.

Busted! I turned and made a step toward the door.

An open cardboard box stood next to the door. I peeked inside and saw what appeared to be a few personal knickknacks that must have belonged to the previous occupant: a coffee mug, a rolled, rubber-banded poster, one of those Footprints sobriety plaques, and a jumble of books.

"May I help you with something?" The nurse had placed one hand around the door and peered inside.

"Silly me! I was just trying to find my way

back to Rhonda Barth's office. I must have gotten turned around."

"Two doors down and to the right. Here, I'll show you." I had the chance to study her in more detail, made note of dirty blond hair in a limp ponytail, bangs, and square, wire-rimmed glasses. A plastic name badge ID'ed her as D. Cooley, L.V.N.

"No problem. I'm sure I can find it on my own."

"Nonsense. I know how easy it is to get confused around here." Nurse Cooley put her hand on my elbow. I couldn't tell if she was being sarcastic or if she was genuinely accustomed to dealing with patients in various degrees of befuddlement.

Before I allowed Nurse Cooley to lead me away, I took one last peek inside the box.

Book with a worn red cloth cover, black vinyl stripe down the left side. Gold lettering and a gold logo.

A Blackford High School annual. For the year Richard Snelling befriended the only girl in the A.V. Club and took her to the prom.

19

"Have your father overnight a cashier's check," I heard Rhonda Barth say to Josh as I re-entered her office. "Or better yet, have him wire the money directly into our account."

"We're not quite to that stage yet," I said while nodding a thanks to Nurse Cooley as she backed away. "Josh and I have a list of several other recovery facilities in the area that we'd like to visit before we make a final decision."

"Why waste your time? Footprints Lodge offers the most comprehensive and up-to-date recovery program in the greater Sacramento area." She leaned forward and placed her chin in her hand.

"Would it be possible for us to tour the rest of the facility, see where Josh might be spending the next twenty-eight days?" I gestured with my left hand toward the window, while I let my right arm flop over the arm of the chair. I gave my arm a tiny shake. The keycard slid from inside my sleeve onto the floor. Josh twisted his mouth to prevent another whispered yelp of excitement.

"Of course!" Rhonda's gaze traced the direction of my left hand. "I was just going to suggest a tour." She snatched up a cell phone and rose from behind the desk. Her fingers poked through the paperclips in the ceramic dish, and her hands patted her pockets.

I scraped back the chair, rose, and hefted my backpack. "Is this what you dropped?" I indicated the blue-and-gray plastic card with the toe of my boot.

"Thanks," Rhonda exhaled a relieved sigh. "I'm such a ditz sometimes."

She led the two of us to an expanse of grass containing a scattering of picnic tables, a flagpole, a volleyball court and horseshoe pit, and a cement campfire ring. A half-dozen men and women sat in a circle on the grass, while a young man hunched over one of the picnic tables and scribbled in a composition book. On the far side of the natural amphitheater, a long bunkhouse-style building contained what I assumed was a dining hall and meeting room. Steam rose from a junior Olympic-size swimming pool surrounded by a chain-link fence. Beyond that, tiny cabins were planted across a forested hillside. I felt as if I'd entered a time warp, landing in a summer camp from a half-century ago, back when the two-week vacation to the mountains was a highlight of family life.

We played follow-the-leader on a packed earth path that curved gently across the large lawn and through a gate in the chain-link fence leading to a swimming pool. A young man stopped mid-lap in his expert rendition of the Australian crawl and hoisted himself out of the shallow end with powerfully built arms. He grabbed a white towel from a neatly folded stack and squished his way over to the cluster of molded plastic patio chairs where Rhonda, Josh, and I rested.

He was a magnificent specimen, a little over six feet tall with a classic swimmer's body, broad shoulders, and those brawny arms, rock-solid abs, narrow hips covered (barely) by a skimpy red Speedo, legs that seemed to go on forever. He ignored my stare and flung himself into a lounge chair, stretched out those fabulous legs, and toweled his face.

"We're just so proud of the progress Corey is making," Rhonda said.

"I'll just bet." He shook the water out of his hair puppy-dog style. "I know you really think I'm a loser. You all do."

"Now, now. The Fourth Step says to make a fearless and searching moral inventory. It does not say to beat up on yourself."

I pushed up the sleeves of my sweater and let the warm breeze caress my pale arms. "Corey, is it? I'm Shauna J. Bogart and this is my friend Josh."

"Corey Draper." He lifted a hand in a lukewarm wave.

"Do you happen to know a guy named Trent, lives in East Sac?"

"Do I ever!" Corey's handsome bronzed face grew animated. "You've seen Trent? How's he doing?"

"I saw him Monday evening at the Clunie Clubhouse. He seems to be doing fine." I paused to let Corey translate: fine, as in not drinking. "He's terribly anxious about you, of course."

"If you see him, tell him I'm counting the hours until visiting hours on Sunday afternoon."

"Visitors and swimming. Sounds like a pretty good life up here."

"You try it and see how you like it. They treat us like children."

"How's your implant working out?" The question was a gamble, as I had no idea if Corey was wearing one of the devices, or if he even knew about the program.

"Better I guess." He flexed the bicep of his left arm. "I haven't much felt like drinking since I ended up back in here, if that's what you're getting at."

"How do you feel about having a device like that hidden inside your body?"

"As long as it keeps me off the bottle and gets me out of here and back with Trent, I don't care."

The pager clipped to Rhonda's waistband chirped a command. "Sorry, you don't mind hanging out here for a few minutes?" She began to head toward the pool house.

"Are you kidding?" I spread both arms and leaned back in the patio chair. "I can't remember the last time I got to enjoy so much sunshine. And in January!"

"Terrific. I'll be back as soon as I can. And you —" she wagged a finger at Corey. "Aren't you due in group in five minutes?"

He responded by cinching the towel more tightly around his waist and moving his long shanks in the direction of the locker room.

"Don't ever leave me alone like that again!" Josh exploded as soon as it was just the two of us on the pool deck. Gone was the air of bored lassitude, back was Josh's typical bristling energy, like he'd just stuck his finger in a light socket.

"I knew you'd do just fine."

"As if! As soon as you left, Rhonda Barth called my father just to make sure he really would be willing to pay for my treatment if the insurance won't cover it."

Yikes. Now there was a development I hadn't counted on. My impression of Mort Friedman was that he liked me and was bursting with pride over his son's success at the radio station. But any parent might draw the line at their child's job description that included pretending to have a drinking problem severe enough to require residential treatment. "What'd your dad say?"

"She just got his voice mail."

I let out a sigh of relief.

"Yeah, well, what happens when Dad gets to his office and checks his voice mail?"

"Here, call the old man and explain." I dug into my backpack and handed my cell phone to Josh. "Be sure to tell him it was my idea. He likes me."

I was too edgy with nervous energy to just sit back and admire the scenery while Josh fiddled with the mobile phone and made things right with his father. So I rooted around in the backpack and retrieved one of those brochures I'd snagged earlier from the rack in the lodge's front office. Empire Mine State Historic Park. The cover depicted a sepia-toned photograph of a half-dozen gold miners, all bristly moustaches and soft cloth caps, hunkered down in what looked like the car of a roller coaster. I unfolded the leaflet and skimmed the text.

The richest mine in the Mother Lode . . . $120,000,000 worth of gold extracted between 1850 and 1956 . . . flourished in the 1890s under the direction of owner William Bourn, Jr., and the skilled tin miners he imported from Cornwall . . . tour Bourn's Empire Cottage, reminiscent of his famous Filoli mansion on the San Francisco Peninsula . . .

I sat up and let out a two-word exclamation starting with "Holy" and ending with something not so sacred. Josh gave me a quizzical look.

"Remember that caller from Monday's show?"

"Sure, your old pal Reginald Fessenden. What about him?"

A metallic *clank* and scraping noise announced the opening of the gate into the pool area. A female figure strode briskly in our direction. The head honcho herself, Dr. Janice Yount. I shoved the brochure into my backpack, while Josh sagged into the chair and let his eyelids droop.

"Shauna J. What a pleasant surprise!" Janice lowered herself into the plastic patio chair vacated by Rhonda Barth. She raised one hand to shade her eyes from the brilliant sunshine. "I broke away from a staff meeting just as soon as I heard you were here."

"I guess you've heard I'm here on personal business, not for anything having to do with my show."

Janice nodded and arranged her face in an expression of professional concern. "Josh is a lucky young man to have an employer who cares, who takes such a personal interest."

"Yeah, well, good help is hard to find."

"Indeed." Janice looked confused, as if trying to decide if I was serious or simply wisecracking. "I'm confident Josh will thrive here at Footprints Lodge. He wouldn't be the first local media person to go through the program, I can assure you."

"Somehow that doesn't surprise me."

"Our program is well-suited for artistic and creative souls. We encourage our clients to express themselves through journal-writing, poetry, painting, collages, music. We find it helps them access their deepest feelings. So often buried emotions are at the root of addictive behavior."

"How about filmmaking? Any of your clients involved in movies?"

Two lines appeared between Janice's eyes as she composed her answer. "We had a screenwriter go through the program about a year ago, but that's the only connection to the film industry that I can recall."

"I was thinking more in terms of an amateur project. Maybe video as a therapeutic tool. What did you call it? Encouraging creative expression?"

"If Josh is interested in video and would like to use that medium as a means of self-exploration, we'll give him all the encouragement in the world."

Janice stood and sidestepped over to the back of the chair where Josh sprawled in what appeared to be a semi-stupor. "Rhonda tells me she's finishing up Josh's insurance paperwork. So, young man" — she fastened both hands on Josh's shoulders, causing him to jerk to attention and stare in bleary-eyed confusion — "what do you say we march you back to the office and get started on the intake process."

Josh shot me a look of sheer panic.

I rose and stood in front of the chair, so that I was eyeball-to-eyeball with Janice Yount, Josh seated between us. "We're not quite ready to make a commitment yet. As I told Rhonda, we're looking at several local facilities before we make a final decision."

"Nonsense. Footprints is obviously the perfect choice and we've already gotten authorization from your insurance company. Now, why don't you head back to Sacramento while we get started on intake. You can return with whatever he might need, warmer clothes for the evening and, of course, his swim trunks."

"Not quite yet." I placed my hands under Josh's elbows and began tugging him in my direction.

"The situation is only going to get worse the longer you delay treatment." Janice spoke in a singsong voice, but I caught the clenched tension underneath the chirpy exterior.

"I'm sure you're right. But still, we've got to hurry to make an appointment at the next treatment center on our list. I'll call you when we make our final decision." I gave another tug, and Josh all but leaped out of the chair and into my arms.

"Very well then." Janice took a step back and flashed a phony smile in my direction. "Let me show you the way back to your car."

The three of us retraced our steps on the path across the football field–size expanse of lawn, Janice leading and Josh keeping his arm linked securely through mine. Janice turned and walked backward so she could face us while she talked. "Have you heard of an organization called Sharing the Pride of Sacramento?"

"I think so." I replied with the same wariness I would use if she'd just asked me if I'd heard of a company called Amway. Some civic booster organization, as I recalled. I had fended off numerous requests for airtime on the show, finally caved, and ran a few public service announcements for their annual golf tournament.

"Super! We're having one of our quarterly power breakfasts tomorrow morning. Why don't you come as my guest."

"Gosh, that would be a great honor." I paused, trying to decide whether the ordeal would be worth whatever information I might be able to ferret out. "Sure, count me in." What the heck, it was free eats.

"That's just wonderful. Tomorrow morning, seven, at the Hilton. I'll leave a ticket for you at the door."

We reached a curve in the path, and I noticed a stocky woman in a multicolored smock lumbering in our direction. D. Cooley, L.V.N. She gave a curt nod to Janice Yount as she stepped around her on the lawn. Josh and I shuffled our feet to the edge of the trail to allow Cooley to navigate past us. The nurse stumbled and brushed against my shoulder. As she hesitated to find her footing, I felt something in the palm of my hand. Tiny and scratchy, like a crumpled bit of paper.

Cooley made eye contact for only an instant, but I got the message: keep quiet and play along.

20

"Thank God that's over," Josh said to me from the security of the passenger seat of the Z-car.

"Just be grateful you're not going through the intake process and being sent to the detox ward." I stretched out in the driver's seat and thrust my hand into the front pocket of my jeans, where I'd slipped the twist of paper as soon as Cooley had handed it over to me. We were still in the Footprints Lodge parking lot, but I felt safe from prying eyes inside my own vehicle.

I smoothed the scrap of lined notepaper and read the penciled scrawl.

"Mother Magruder's, 11:30."

"What's Mother Magruder's?" Josh said.

"Get into my backpack and find that brochure about historic downtown Grass Valley; see what you can find." If Cooley meant by her note that she wanted to meet with me this morning at eleven-thirty, then I assumed it must be during her lunch break. Which meant somewhere in the general vicinity of Footprints Lodge and Grass Valley.

I steered the Z-car along the driveway and made a northbound turn onto Highway 49 toward Grass Valley.

"Here we go," Josh held the brochure steady against the dashboard. " 'Mother Magruder's, an old family favorite in the heart of Grass Valley's historic Main Street, features genuine Cornish pasties just like the gold miners used to carry in their lunch pails . . .' What's a pasty?"

"I think it rhymes with *fast,* not like those things strippers wear."

I reached the southern edge of the town of Grass Valley and made a right onto Empire Street. "So like I was saying out there by the pool, remember the guy who called the show Monday afternoon?"

"Yeah, your old pal Reginald Fessenden."

"Remember that poem he recited?"

"Fe, fi, lo, li?"

"Born in the days of old / an empire made of gold / I'll be riding gain with you / near a fountain oh, so blue."

"Sure, that poem. What about it?"

"I think we're about to find out."

The narrow road rose through a forest thick with pines. Around two miles after leaving the highway, I spotted the wooden sign for Empire Mine State Historic Park. I turned right into the dirt lot and parked next to a yellow bus from the Woodland Unified School District.

"A fellow named William Bourn owned the Empire Mine back in the 1880s and 1890s. Born in the days of old, an empire made of gold. Get it?" I climbed out of the car, grabbed my backpack, locked the door, and began crossing the parking lot to a low building housing the park office and museum.

"I guess so," Josh said when he caught up with me.

"So this William Bourn also built this mansion south of San Francisco. A huge estate called Filoli."

"Never heard of it."

"You wouldn't, because you didn't grow up in the Bay Area. It's a pretty common landmark for those of us who did." One of my favorite memories of the year I spent hanging out with Richie was the day we skipped school, drove up to Crystal Springs Reservoir in my then brand-new Z-car, hiked to the Pulgas Water Temple, and watched, fascinated, as the water destined for the faucets of San Francisco gushed from under the faux Grecian edifice into the reservoir. Sounds boring, I know, but it's actually a thrilling show. And free! We could see the upper levels of the Filoli mansion from the water temple, and told each other stories about the fabulously wealthy rock star who we imagined must live there.

"What's a Filoli?" Josh asked as we reached the door to the museum.

"The Bourn family motto: fight, love, live. Fight for a just cause, love your fellow man, live a good life." Sounded like a good plan to me.

"What about that fountain so blue?"

"Just give me time. I'm still working on that one."

The museum might have been worth a look, but it was difficult to tell, the place was so packed with schoolchildren, at least fifty of them, obviously on a field trip from that bus in the parking lot. Fourth graders, I imagined, the year of California history. I'd loved ever minute of it when I was their age.

I noticed several docents wearing teal vests covered with patches and pins, like the senior citizen version of Scouts, and would have liked to quiz them about the fountain. But they had their hands full and then some with the kiddies. The one ranger was deep in an animated discussion with two of the adult chaperones. I left four one dollar bills on the counter to pay for admission for two and pushed open the back door from the museum into the grounds of the old mine yard.

"Is this cool or what?" Josh's attention focused on the remnants of a shaky wooden railcar trestle, heading into the earth at a steep pitch. The chute that sent the miners deep into the shafts and tunnels that riddled this valuable piece of earth.

"We're looking for a fountain, remember? A fountain oh, so blue." All I could see was rusted bits of chain, wheels, and gears scattered about, and a barnlike structure covered in corrugated tin.

I tore Josh away from all the guy stuff surrounding the abandoned mine and followed the path to the Reflecting Pools marked on the leaflet. " 'You have just entered the grounds reserved for William Bourn and his friends,' " I read aloud as we strolled along the foot trail. In contrast to the industrial grittiness of the mine yard, this portion of the park was shaded with stately trees and carpeted with lush grass.

"Whoa, some cottage!" Josh stopped in the middle of the path. I put down the brochure and followed his stare.

Some cottage, indeed. I suppose compared to Bourn's mansion on the San Francisco peninsula you could call this two-story stone structure a cottage. It reminded me of an English country manor, complete with manicured lawn and rose garden. Prince Charles would feel quite at home in this little outpost of Britannia in the California Mother Lode.

"The fountain?" I reminded him.

I spotted a glint of something shiny in the middle of the lawn, as if the gardener had planted a mirror in the grass. I tiptoed across the grass, Josh following, until we reached a shallow pool of carved rock, three or four yards wide, a wedding cake tier in the center where water must have once erupted. Though the fountain was no longer operating, the pool was still filled with water.

Blue water.

In the distance, I could hear the chatter of dozens of children finally freed from the museum and let loose into the mine yard. I sent a message to my own Higher Power: Don't let any of them tumble down into one of those shafts. And please keep them away from the pool until I find what I came for.

"How'd they do that?" Josh asked. "Did they paint the bottom of the pond?"

I knelt and stuck my hand into the chilly liquid. "I think they put some dye in it. Food coloring, maybe."

"This Bourn fellow dyed the water in his fountain just to make it look pretty? Now that's what I call living the high life."

I'll be riding gain with you
Near a fountain oh, so blue.

Where was he? Richie. Reginald Fessenden. Hey, I kept my end of the bargain. I figured out your poem and found the damn fountain. Where the hell are you?

I rose, wiped my hand on the side of my jeans, and made a slow 360-degree turn. All I saw were pines and the pinkish stone of Bourn's cottage, the cloudless sky above and the emerald lawn at my feet.

"Could this be what you're looking for?" Josh's voice carried from the far side of the pool. He held an object about the size of a book in one hand.

"Where'd you get that?" I demanded as soon as I reached his side and saw what he carried.

"It was just lying right here in the grass, plain as day." He pointed with a sneakered foot at a rectangle of crushed lawn.

It was another one of those recovery plaques from Footprints Lodge, just like the one that had sailed through the back window of the Z-car at the airport on

Monday. Identical, down to the sticker affixed to where the patient's name should have been engraved.

"True Power Comes From Within."

I stuck a fork into the flaky crust of the meat-filled turnover that I'd ordered at Mother Magruder's and paused to savor the warm, aromatic steam.

"The lodge used to be a wonderful place to work," Nurse Cooley said. She'd doffed the colorful smock, revealing a robin's egg blue cotton turtleneck pullover, loosened the band around her ponytail, and invited us to call her Darla. "Then the Footprints Institute took over."

"Used to be?" I said. "I assumed Footprints had always run the place."

Darla shook her head and more limp blond hair escaped from the ponytail. "For a long time, the lodge was operated by a not-for-profit health care collective out of the Bay Area. They ran into financial trouble a few years ago when the dot-com bubble burst and they lost most of their big corporate donors. For a while, it looked like the lodge might have to close."

"And then the Footprints Institute came to the rescue."

"At first I thought it would be a positive

thing. Here they were, another nonprofit and with a good reputation for the work they were doing down in Sacramento. But it turns out all they care about is the bottom line. Money, money, money."

"They sure were eager to know about Josh's insurance coverage."

"Or whether my dad had the money to cover me if the insurance didn't come through," Josh contributed.

Darla paused to finish chewing a mushroom from her vegetarian special. "That's pretty typical, all right."

"Aren't you afraid someone will see you here with me?" I looked around the small eatery, six other parties of two and three clustered on mismatched wooden tables and chairs. The windows were covered with chintz curtains, and a ruffle of matching material accented the counter separating the dining room from the kitchen. A few battered miner's headlamps and tin lunch pails hanging from the flower-papered walls kept Mother Magruder's just this side of being tea-cozy cute.

"It's none of their business what I do on my lunch hour. Anyway, whenever Dr. Yount's on the premises, she always makes a big deal about eating in the dining hall with the patients, like she's just one of the common folk. So the rest of the senior staff, like Ms. Barth, all feel as if they have to follow suit."

"I would just hate for you to get into any sort of trouble by being seen with a potential patient, that's all."

"Listen, we all know who you are. It was all over the place within minutes of when you two showed up. This media person, this talk show host from Sacramento, is checking us out and we'd all better be on our toes."

"You're kidding." I let my fork hover midway from table to mouth.

"Why do you think I tried to stop you from snooping around on your own?"

"Cripes! Do you think they're on to me?"

"All I know is, the lodge is loaded with hidden security cameras. Another one of Dr. Yount's little improvements."

I took a bite of the savory chicken, potato, and carrot filling. Thus far, Darla Cooley hadn't spilled much more than the usual complaints of a disgruntled employee. So the lodge had been wonderful back in the good old days. Like almost everything, it seems. So the new management had their eyes fixed firmly on the balance sheet. Maybe they were forced to make some tough choices to keep the place afloat. So they appeared overly concerned about security. Isn't everyone these days?

"What's up with those implants?"

Darla wiped her lips with a paper napkin and smiled. "I was hoping that was the reason you came poking your nose in Dr. Yount's little kingdom. It's about time someone blew the whistle."

"There's something else going on than just an experimental program to lessen the craving for alcohol." I found myself whispering despite Darla's confidence no one worth worrying about would be spying on us in Mother Magruder's.

"The technology's been around for years to administer medications subdermally on a time-release basis."

"Like those birth control things."

"Correct. There's even a new device on the market to help addicts withdraw from hard drugs like heroin. But think about it — in order to release medication over a lengthy period of time, you're looking at a fairly large implant."

Darla held her thumb and forefinger about an inch apart. "Something around the size of a multivitamin capsule."

I forked another mouthful of chicken and potatoes and nodded for her to continue.

"Ever see one of those devices they're implanting into the volunteers up at the lodge?"

"Not in person, no." I recalled Camille's description of a gizmo about the size of a grain of rice that she'd extracted from Travis's upper arm.

"Ever had a dog or cat chipped?"

"Chipped?"

"Implanted with a microchip identification device."

"Oh, right, I've heard of those. If your pet gets lost, they can run a scanner over him at the animal shelter and track down the owner." I'd been meaning to have one of those injected into Bialystock but hadn't gotten around to it. After all, he was a contented indoor kitty, and the odds that he might make a mad dash for freedom from a loose window screen and separate himself from his tinned tuna seemed too remote to contemplate.

"Okay, then. That's what those things look like that they're implanting up at the lodge. Like a tiny microchip ID tag."

"But why?"

Darla took a swallow of orange-flavored fizzy water. "You've got to understand, this is all speculation on my part. I'm certainly not privy to any of the details of the program. Only hand-picked senior staff in Dr. Yount's inner circle get that kind of access."

"But you've got your theories. Otherwise, we wouldn't be having this conversation."

"I just think it's curious, that's all, the large number of returning patients who've received the implant. You'd think if they were receiving medication to stop them from drinking, the opposite would be happening."

"I'd wondered about that very same thing with Corey."

"And isn't it an interesting coincidence that these patients all got a personal phone call — usually from Dr. Yount herself — within hours of their relapse. Next thing you know, they're back on our doorstep. And isn't it interesting that all of the patients accepted into the implant program either have an excellent health plan or are independently wealthy."

"What are you saying, that these implants are some sort of tracking device? Dr. Yount is keeping her eye on her former patients and knows if and when they're backsliding?"

"All I'm saying is, that's what it looks like."

Josh look up from the beef pasty that he'd

been devouring in silence. "Begging your pardon, but I don't think that's possible. Those chips only work when they come in contact with a secondary device."

"What do you mean?" I asked.

"Like at the SPCA when they run the scanner over Fido's back to see if they can find his owner. The chip by itself doesn't do anything. It's the scanner that activates the chip and collects the information."

That saleswoman in Pete's store last week had said something similar, one scanner being able to inventory an entire pallet-load of goods in an instant.

"So Dr. Yount would have to have installed scanners in all of the bars, liquor stores, and convenience markets in the greater Sacramento area just to keep tabs on her patients," I said.

"All I know is, that's what I saw and that's what I think," Darla said.

I pressed the back of my fork into the remaining crumbs on my plate and allowed myself a moment to relish every buttery morsel. "How about Dr. Fessenden. How does he fit in?"

"At first I thought he was just another one of Dr. Yount's flaky so-called experts in the recovery business. He spent almost all of his time holed up in his office, or in the lab where they were running the implant program. But now I'm not so sure."

"How do you mean?" I pushed aside my plate and leaned forward.

"Ever since he got fired, I figured he must have been doing something right, else why would Dr. Yount have gotten rid of him."

"Dr. Fessenden got fired?"

"Either fired or quit. All I know is, there's lots of arguing going on behind closed doors, and then he's gone. Just like that." Darla snapped her fingers. "Didn't even bother to clean out his office."

I sank back into the wooden chair and tried to sort out this latest information. "When did this happen, this firing? And how long had he been affiliated with Footprints?"

"Around two, two and a half weeks ago. As far as when he joined the Footprints staff, I couldn't tell you for sure. I think the first time I saw him up at the lodge was around six or eight months ago. Why, is it important?"

"I might have known this Dr. Fessenden, that's all. What did he look like?"

Darla studied my face for a moment. "About your age, I'd say. Fortyish."

Gee, thanks.

"On the short side, kinda skinny, brown

hair, what was left of it. Mostly a few strands in this pathetic comb-over. Like I said, I hardly saw him at all."

It could have fit the Richard Snelling I'd known in high school, though in those days he had thick brown hair swooping down over his forehead and curling over the back of his shirt collar.

Then again, that description could have fit a good percentage of the "fortyish" men in Northern California.

Anyway, Richard Snelling was behind federal prison bars.

True Power Comes From Within. I tapped my fingers onto the steering wheel to the silent refrain of the inane phrase as I piloted the Z-car over the rolling hills and curves of Highway 49 south toward Auburn, Interstate 80, and civilization.

True Power Comes From Within.

Richie — or someone — had sent me the message twice on identical plaques, inspirational gifts from the Footprints staff to its clients in celebration of their commitment to sobriety.

True Power Comes From Within.

Of course!

True power did, indeed, come from within.

21

I torqued the steering wheel to the right. The Z-car skittered to a halt in a spray of gravel on the Highway 49 shoulder. A rusted barbed-wire fence separated the turnout from a pasture where cows grazed on the newly greened grass.

"What's up?" Josh said from the passenger seat. A lumber truck bombed past seemingly within inches, sending shudders of wind through the tiny sports car.

"Quick, where's the plaque?"

I twisted at the waist and flung myself into the space between the two bucket seats.

"There!" I hoisted the plaque into the passenger compartment and held it in front of me. Tiny screws on each corner held a sheet of brass to the top surface of a solid slab of polished wood. A ray of sunlight glanced off the shiny metal plate with its childlike outline of a pair of footprints and the command to "Celebrate Sobriety!"

"So?" Josh said.

"So! True power comes from within." I ignored the screws and began to claw at the edge of the thin metal sheet with my fingernails. It must have been affixed with an industrial-strength glue in addition to the decorative screws, because all I got for my efforts was a bent fingernail. I let out a tiny whimper of pain and brought my clenched fist to my mouth.

"Do you think this might help?"

I look over at Josh's outstretched arm. And at the nail clippers that rested in his palm.

"Yes!" I squealed in excitement, pain forgotten, and snatched the nail clippers from his hand. I didn't even bother using the pointy part as a screwdriver, just jammed the blade between the brass plate and the wood and used brute strength to rock the tool back and forth.

The top two screws popped and the cement began to weaken with a whispered suction sound. I used the blade of the nail clipper to bend the metal plate — the heck with celebrating sobriety! — and peeled it slowly from the wooden base, like I was trying to save a stamp that the post office had neglected to cancel.

"Oh, yeah!" My fingers touched something spongy near the center of the supposedly solid wood.

"Come to mama!" I made one last tremendous tug, pulling with all my strength from shoulder to pinky. The glue screeched in protest and gave up. The bottom pair of screws ejected themselves from the wood. I was left holding the mangled metal sheet in my right hand while the thick piece of wood rested on my knee, held steady by my left hand.

"Yes! Yes! Yes!" If one of those cows was eavesdropping, she might logically conclude that I'd decided to have my producer for dessert instead of the Apple Figgy they were serving at Mother Magruder's.

"What, what?" Josh elbowed his way past the stick shift to see for himself.

The center portion of the wooden plaque — normally covered by the brass sheet — had been hollowed out and lined with foam packing material. A white rectangular plastic box, about the size of a pack of cigarettes, nestled inside. I put my thumb and forefinger on either side and eased the box out of its hiding place. An electronic eye, like the business end of a TV remote control unit, stared at me from one end.

"What is it?" Josh whispered.

"I'm not sure." I placed the box back into the hollowed-out plaque with a hand that trembled. "But I'm pretty sure I know where I can find out."

I made the trip from the Highway 49–Interstate 80 interchange into the central core of Sacramento in a little over twenty minutes, which must have been a land speed record. The fog had dissipated to a thin veil, making freeway driving less treacherous than it had been in the morning hours. Traffic was relatively light in the hours after the noontime mini-rush and before the going-home gridlock, and the CHP must have been occupied elsewhere. I leaped out of the Z-car in front of Retro Alley and left Josh in charge of finding a place to park in Old Sacramento and feeding the parking meters.

The sound of rinky-dink piano music wafted from the door of Retro Alley, one of those ragtime tunes that Pete Kovacs loved, always reminding me of the clatter of someone dropping a tray full of silverware on a marble floor. I lingered in the doorway and watched him tickle the ivories at the upright piano. He was surrounded by two of his buddies from the Hot Times Dixieland Band, Herman the tuba player and the young dentist who played trombone. "We've got 'Take the A-Train' and 'Chattanooga Choo Choo' for certain," Pete said to them. "What do you say we add 'Orange Blossom Special' to the list?"

The California State Railroad Museum had announced plans for a series of living history weekends this coming summer, and Pete's band was on the short list of entertainers under consideration. An actual paying gig, no less. He'd told me the other night he considered it a sure thing, assuming the band could learn enough train songs in the next few weeks.

How could I ask him to give all this up and follow me to Hollywood?

"Don't forget 'The Atchison, Topeka and the Santa Fe.'" I placed one arm around Pete's shoulder and gave it a squeeze. My other arm hefted my backpack, the plaque resting on top.

I waited to exchange greetings with Pete and his pals, then said I needed to talk to him about something.

"Hoo, boy," Herman said, backing away. "I think I hear my cue to exit."

"And how," the trombonist said.

Both gave Pete sympathetic looks.

"I'm glad you're here," Pete said after the horn section had retreated. "Wait 'til you see what I found on the Internet."

He placed three sheets of stapled paper in my hands, color computer printouts of photos of Mediterranean-style homes — white stucco, red tile roofs, arched windows and palm trees, and carrying million dollar price tags.

"I found an interesting neighborhood in the Hollywood Hills. Whitley Heights, wonderful houses from the twenties. And it's all protected by a historic preservation district, so the developers can't come in and ruin it."

I pretended to study the top sheet. "They're fabulous, all right."

"Carole Lombard lived in Whitley Heights. So did Chaplin and Valentino. And it would be close to your work."

Historic preservation and long-dead celebrities from tinseltown's golden past. All it needed was a next-door neighbor who just happened to be in the market for a piano pounder for a traditional jazz band and Pete would have found heaven in the Hollywood Hills.

"I love it, but how could we possibly afford one of these homes?" I would have to pull in top ratings in every major market in the country, and Pete would have to sell an unbelievable amount of kitsch on eBay for us to come up with the cash for even a fixer-upper in that neighborhood.

"We could if we did house-sitting. You know Herman's niece, makeup artist to the stars?"

"I think so."

"She's heading off on location in Spain for at least six months and she's looking for a house sitter. We're going to need a place to live in L.A. Everybody wins."

"Yeah. Everybody wins." I rested the backpack on the glass counter that separated the retail section of Retro Alley from Pete's office area. "Remember that saleslady who was in here about a week ago with her high-tech inventory control things?"

Pete frowned in thought. "Oh, sure. Wal-Mart is going to require all its suppliers to use these devices and I'd better climb on the bandwagon or I'm going to be left behind in the dust, as useless as a Betamax player."

"She gave you some sales material, didn't she? A brochure or a flyer?"

"Possibly. If she did, I'm sure I tossed it in the recycle bin as soon as she left."

Damn! I scurried to the office side of the counter, yanked the blue plastic recycle bin from underneath Pete's rolltop desk, and began pawing through the contents.

"Good luck," Pete said. "I've probably emptied it at least twice since last week."

"You don't always take out every last piece. Case in point." I waved a handful of discarded envelopes from last month's Christmas cards.

Close to the bottom, stuck between inserts

from his SMUD bill and a *Sacramento News and Review* from three weeks ago, I discovered a full-color catalog on slick white paper, "I.D. Technologies Unlimited," in inch-high letters in red ink across the top.

"Ta-dah!" I held the slender booklet by both hands in front of my chest, a proud child displaying her crayoned artwork to daddy.

I spread the leaflet on the counter, opened the drawstrings of my backpack, and removed the white plastic box from its hiding place in the plaque. "See?" I tapped the photograph of the reading device in the catalog. "Don't they look the same to you?"

Pete studied the photo and the object lying next to it. "Looks like it to me, but I'm no expert."

The electronic sensor at the front entrance to Retro Alley bing-bonged, announcing the arrival of a customer. I looked up. It was only Josh, returning from parking the Z-car. He snatched up the sales catalog from the counter. "I.D. Technologies Unlimited? Is that why we broke the speed limit to get here?"

"What about it?"

"My housemate did a research paper on them last semester. He knows all about them."

"Here's the plan." I steered the Z-car under Interstate 5, leaving the Gold Rush–era historic district behind, reentering the twenty-first century in downtown Sacramento. "I'm going to drop you off at CSUS. Find Andrew — yank him out of class if you have to — and bring him to the station to take a look-see at this gadget. He'll have a car somewhere on campus, right?"

"Got it. Check. Yes, ma'am." Josh sounded testy.

"Look, you did a great job today. Better than great. Outstanding."

Josh stared out the window as we crept along in downtown traffic past Cesar Chavez Plaza and the Convention Center.

"Look." I tried again. "I know I run you ragged sometimes, making you skip class this morning and pretend to be an alcoholic, and then getting your dad involved, and then rushing back to Pete's store. But c'mon, admit it. On balance, you're having fun, right?"

"If we're supposed to be having so much fun, then why are you planning to leave?"

Jeez, not that again.

We rode in silence east on J Street, the government office high-rises gradually giving way to the Victorian-era homes and storefronts of the Midtown district.

"Someone left that plaque by the fountain at the Empire Mine especially for you to find, right?" Josh said as we idled at the traffic signal at Twenty-ninth Street. The I-80 business loop thundered overhead.

"Of course. It didn't exactly drop out of the sky."

"We're assuming it was left by the guy who called your show and read the poem about meeting you by the blue fountain."

"That fellow calling himself Reginald Fessenden."

"Do they give these plaques to everyone who completes the residential treatment program at Footprints Lodge?"

"I believe so. Travis had one, and so did his roommate. What are you getting at?"

"It doesn't necessarily follow that all of the plaques have been hollowed out and devices hidden inside. This Reginald Fessenden could have doctored that plaque we found especially for your benefit."

The kid had a point. I checked my watch. A few minutes after two. If circumstances — and traffic — fell in my favor, I had barely enough time to locate and tear open another plaque, drop Josh off at Sac

State, and blast over to the station before the notes of my show's theme music faded out.

"There's only one way to find out, now isn't there." I crossed Alhambra Boulevard and hung a left on Thirty-third. After a couple of false turns on the tree-lined residential grid of East Sacramento, I located the small 1950s-era building containing the apartment that Travis Ikeda-Nyland had shared with Chad MacKenzie.

I found the young gentleman leaning against the wrought-iron balcony, cigarette dangling from between two fingers. Loud music, jangling electric guitars, poured from the open door of his crib.

I made brief introductions and shouted over the deafening din of the stereo to explain what I planned to do with his sobriety plaque. "I promise to be careful, but there are no guarantees. If I ruin it, I'll certainly pay to have it repaired or replaced."

Chad ground out the cigarette on the railing and flicked it over the side to the asphalt parking lot one story below. "Why should I let you come in and mess around with my plaque?"

"Just trust me. C'mon, we don't have a lot of time to waste." I stepped through the open doorway.

"Hey, I never invited you inside my apartment."

Josh inserted himself between Chad and the entry to the apartment. "She's right. We don't have much time, and it is important."

I was about to interrupt, then realized Chad was actually paying attention to what my producer had to say. I felt dissed, both as a female and as a person who'd left her twentysomething years long behind. But if Chad would rather heed the advice of a guy closer to his own age than the words of an older, wiser female, then my best course of action was to back off and shut up.

"How important?"

"This might help shed some light on what really happened to Travis," Josh said.

"I guess it's okay. But be careful."

I found the sobriety plaque on the same living room shelf where it had perched during my first visit Friday evening. I used Josh's nail clipper to remove the top two screws. Gently this time, I slid the blade between the metal sheet and the wooden base and eased the two pieces apart just enough to slip my finger in the gap and probe toward the center.

I felt something spongy and soft. Foam packing material.

I smoothed the metal sheet, reinserted the

screws, and replaced the plaque to its point of honor on the shelf.

"Okay, Chad, here's the deal." I faced the young man and looked him in the eyes. "If anyone asks you about what just happened, we were never here, get me?"

"What's going on?"

"I don't know for sure. But if anyone tries to call you or ask you anything about your implant, or about your plaque, or about anything connected to your experience at the Footprints Lodge, just tell them everything's normal, everything's fine." I thought about Brenda Driscoll lying dead in the bedroom of her tiny downtown apartment. "In fact, if I were you, I wouldn't let anyone past the door of your apartment the next few days. Not even if it's someone you think is a friend."

"You're not being up front with me, so why should I play along?" Chad folded his arms across his chest, revealing intricate tribal art tattoos from wrist to elbow.

"Look, man." Josh again, intervening when he sensed both Chad and I were running out of patience. "I know she can be demanding at times. But do what she says. When we know for certain what's going on, we'll make sure you're among the first to hear."

"Another thing," I said. "Do you happen to know if there are other graduates of the Footprints Lodge living around here? Someone who might have a plaque similar to yours? Someone who goes to the AA meetings at Clunie Clubhouse perhaps?"

"That's why they call it Alcoholics Anonymous. 'Cause we're supposed to be, like, anonymous?"

"Yeah, and your roommate is lying under six feet of dirt at East Lawn Memorial Park. So, like, drop the attitude."

Chad's eyes shifted in Josh's direction, who gave him a small nod.

"There's this guy Trent who I think lives over in a little house on the next block, around Thirty-fourth and D. I see him out on that fancy racing bike all the time."

What I really wanted to do was race over to Sapphire Ikeda's estate out in Carmichael, find Travis's sobriety plaque, and yank off the brass plate. But there was no time for that, not even to detour one block to Thirty-fourth Street and see if we could locate Trent's house. Not if I wanted to drop Josh off at CSUS and make it to the station in time for my show.

"Remember what I said, and don't let anyone in for the next few days," I said as

Josh and I left the apartment. "Not even if it's Dr. Yount."

Especially, I felt like adding, if it's Dr. Yount.

I paced in front of the console in the broadcast studio, my attention barely registering on my guests, the callers, or the program log. All of my mental, physical, and emotional energy focused on the double-paned window separating the on-air studio and the call screener booth where Josh and his housemate tinkered with the white plastic box we'd found hidden in the plaque.

Andrew Stoller — Android to his closest friends — was a couple of years younger than Josh, a child genius who had won a bundle on the *Jeopardy!* teen tournament and entered college when he was only sixteen. He was a sweet-faced kid with black hair styled in a Moe Howard bowl cut and a diamond stud in his right earlobe.

I watched Josh as he tapped something into his keyboard. The letters scrolled across my computer monitor almost instantaneously.

FOR CERTAIN, IT'S A DATA COLLECTION DEVICE FOR MICRO-TRANSPONDERS. PROBABLY A CLONE OF THE DEVICE MANUFAC-

TURED BY I.D. TECHNOLOGIES
UNLIMITED.

I'd had the foresight to devote today's
show to the debate over whether the Sacramento Kings should be permitted to build a
downtown arena, and if so, how much
money — if any — the city should contribute to the cause. It was one of those frac-
tious local controversies that never seemed
to go away, one on which almost everyone
had a strong opinion. All I had to do was
stand back and juggle the phone lines.

I sent a message back to the call screener
booth.

DON'T THOSE THINGS REQUIRE A
HUMAN OPERATOR?

Someone, I would think, would have to
punch a button and activate the reader to
collect the data being sent by the transponder. And then turn the device off again.
How could that take place if the device was
sealed up inside a plaque? I supposed it
could have been designed to be permanently in the "on" position. But then,
wouldn't the battery run down after a few
days?

I had to wait through two commercial
breaks before I received the answer.

IT SEEMS TO HAVE A BUILT-IN
TIMER. IT TURNS ITSELF ON

AUTOMATICALLY FOR SIXTY SECONDS AT SET TIMES. LOOKS LIKE TWICE, MAYBE THREE TIMES EVERY TWENTY-FOUR HOUR PERIOD. INGENIOUS!

I burst through the door into the call screener booth at the start of the top-of-the-hour network newscast. "Let's make sure I understand this correctly. The device hidden inside the plaque turns itself on by way of a built-in timer. It sends out a signal. That signal activates the microchip implanted in some schmoe's arm. The chip sends data back to the reader. The reader stores the data."

"Right so far," Andrew Stoller said.

"Then how do you get the data out of the reader? I mean, I don't see anyone going around busting open these plaques and pulling out a floppy disk."

"Usually you'd have a mainframe some-where in the vicinity. That's how they work it in big warehouses. The reader scans a pallet of goods and then sends the data via wireless hookup to a mainframe."

"So I should be looking for a big com-puter somewhere in the neighborhood."

"Not necessarily. For a small-scale opera-tion like this, you could do it with a laptop."

I leaned against the foam soundproofed

walls of the closet-size booth. "You're saying someone could be driving around with a laptop and downloading the data being collected by this thing." I waved my hand in the direction of the reader, which lay in two parts atop Josh's desk, exposing its minuscule circuit board.

"Wouldn't even have to be a car. You could probably do this on a bicycle."

22

All of my instincts itched to go on the air with what I'd discovered. At the very least, warn any and all graduates of Footprints Lodge who might be listening to get rid of their Celebrate Sobriety plaques as soon as possible.

But, dammit, I was still missing too many pieces of the puzzle. What sort of data was the Footprints staff collecting? And what were they doing with it? There was still the chance this might be a legitimate medical experiment with only the noblest of motives.

Then why hide the scanners?

And why did Travis apparently feel so desperate to remove the chip riding under the skin of his upper arm that he had an unlicensed, untrained friend slice it out?

Something wasn't right. But I needed to fill in the gaps in my knowledge before I could go public with my accusations against one of the most respected charitable institutions in the Sacramento area.

Anyway, I wouldn't want Janice Yount to regret inviting me to the Sharing the Pride of Sacramento breakfast, now would I?

"You're listening to the Shauna J. Bogart Show on Sacramento Talk Radio. The downtown Kings' arena — yes or no? We'll take your calls right after this from Council-woman Marvella Kent . . ."

The on-air studio door popped open. Dorinda Delgado from the sales department, full steam ahead. Now what did she want?

"We need to pull all the commercials for Raley's," Delgado said.

"What's up?" The local supermarket chain could be counted on for a steady stream of commercials year-round. It wasn't like them to cancel.

"They want to save up their time and double up their exposure for Super Bowl weekend."

"Really pushing those chips and guac."

"Whatever." Delgado shoved a sheet of instructions in my hands. "Peg's updating the log starting with the five o'clock hour, so just make sure the correct spot scheduled for the four-fifty stop-set doesn't get aired."

"I think I can handle it."

Advertisers are always revising their copy or their broadcast schedules. That's the beauty of radio, you can change your message almost instantly. It wasn't out of the ordinary for Delgado or one of her salespeople to barge into the studio and make last-minute changes on the program log. Back when we did it all on paper, they'd make the alterations with Wite-Out and neat black ballpoint pen. These days, computers made the revisions even easier.

Delgado had come into the studio to make a similar change, pulling someone's spots from the schedule the afternoon the story broke about the shooting in McKinley Park, hadn't she? No, wait — she'd been carrying a compact disc in a jewel case. She wasn't pulling a sponsor's spots, just making a substitution. But which sponsor? And why the change?

And more to the point, why did any of this matter now?

I tried to shake the questions from my mind, but once the topic had imbedded itself in my brain cells, it wouldn't let go. As soon as I'd signed off to my listeners and thanked my guests, I found my way to the deserted sales area and Peg Waller's cubicle.

Peg was the station's traffic coordinator, a job title that had nothing to do with Captain Mikey's airborne reports but instead denoted the person in charge of scheduling the commercials on the program log. It's a thankless assignment, balancing the usually at-odds demands of salespeople, advertisers, and the ad agencies, and the on-air talent. It was six o'clock and Peg had already shut down her computer and departed for the day. I penned a note on a yellow sticky and affixed it to her monitor. "Last minute spot substitution during my show a week ago Monday. The client? Thanks, SJB."

"I was wonderin' when you were gonna git around to tellin' me." T. R. O'Brien sat in his favorite booth at the Salt Shaker and slammed his drink tumbler onto the tabletop with a rattle of ice cubes.

This was not starting at all well.

"Tell you what?" I peeled off my down jacket and slid into the seat opposite the boss.

"RadioLand?"

"Oh. That."

Did the entire city know about my planned defection to RadioLand? Had someone erected a billboard, hired a loudspeaker truck to spread the news?

"How'd you find out?"

O'Brien waved his good arm at me. "You've been in this business long enough.

You know how the rumor mill works. Missy, if you thought you could keep a thing like that a secret, you're not as smart as you set out to be."

A young woman in classic Las Vegas cocktail waitress garb refreshed O'Brien's scotch on the rocks and took my order for a gin and tonic. The Salt Shaker is a throwback, a genuine bar and steakhouse from the ring-a-ding lounge era, an outpost of adult high life in a sea of family theme restaurants. The fact that it was within staggering distance of several local radio and TV stations, including my own, made it a natural media hangout. I'd invited O'Brien to meet me at the Salt Shaker after the show, figuring it might be easier to break the news to him in dim light, surrounded by crushed velvet and mirrors, being pampered by a cute waitress less than half his age. So much for plans.

"You didn't answer my question. How'd you find out?"

"If you must know, I got a phone call from a buddy of mine that runs a bunch of stations in Tulsa. He's thinkin' about puttin' this new syndicated music program on one of those stations, and he wants to know my impression of a little gal named Shauna J. Bogart hosting a show like that."

"I'm really sorry you had to find out that way." I played with a paper napkin, folding it into squares. "I was going to talk it over with you before I told anyone else, honest. But things just kept getting in the way."

"Shoot, I'm not mad at you. Well, not anymore. I knew I couldn't hold onto you forever. You're obviously destined for a major market."

"Thanks." I hadn't realized how much tension I'd been holding in until I noticed my lips were trembling.

"But hits from the seventies? Reading liner cards that someone else writes? You've outgrown that. I thought that's why you went into talk radio, so you could express yourself."

"It is. And you're right." The waitress re-appeared with our drinks. I had to stop my-self from snatching mine off her tray.

"So it's the money, then," O'Brien said after he took a swallow of scotch.

"I suppose."

"Tell you what. I know I can't come close to meetin' whatever they've offered you at RadioLand. What if I throw in an extra five grand a year, plus a twenty-five hundred dollar bonus for every quarter that you maintain the number one position in the book?"

O'Brien didn't need to define which book he was talking about. When you work in radio, there's only one book, the Arbitron ratings.

"I'll have to think about it."

"You do that. Think about what you're giving up just for the sake of the almighty dollar."

"I suppose this means I'm off the air unless I tell you right now I'm one hundred percent certain staying."

"Now why would you be thinkin' I'd do a crazy thing like that?"

"Isn't that how this industry works? An air talent makes noises about leaving and management yanks them off the air before they can do any damage."

"I know you better than that. You wouldn't risk damaging my reputation or your own by pullin' some puddin'-head stunt."

I raised my glass and took a swallow to cover my emotion. All of a sudden, I really didn't want to leave. What, and give up the most fun I'd had in radio since I first broke into the business during the glory days of free-form FM in the seventies? Walk away from the best boss in the world at one of the last of the family-owned stations left in the country? But I felt as if I'd painted myself into a corner, all but promising Bollinger I'd take the gig. And getting Pete Kovacs all excited about house-sitting a historically preserved mansion in the neighborhood where Carole Lombard once shacked up with Clark Gable.

"Just think about my offer, Missy, that's all I ask." T.R. helped me into my jacket after we'd finished our drinks. "No matter what you decide, the door's always open at my station."

"I promise," I whispered as I bit back tears.

I sucked on a mint to mask the reek of gin and drove east on El Camino Avenue. This was the first chance I'd had the entire day to be alone, answering to no one, only to my own thoughts.

A fellow calling himself Reginald Fessenden starts calling my show, dropping tidbits of personal information that only my old high school pal Richard Snelling would know. Travis had noted an appointment with Fessenden on his calendar, and a Dr. Fessenden had an office at the Footprints Lodge.

The Z-car purred across Fair Oaks Boulevard, making its way toward the suburban community of Carmichael and the Ikeda-

Nyland mansion atop the American River bluffs.

I shook my head as if to clear the brain cells. The events of the day had left me drained and exhausted, and I half hoped to find the Ikeda-Nyland house dark, so I could just turn around, head straight for home, and fall into bed. But it was not even eight o'clock, and lights blazed from the multipaned glass of the living room window. Ray Nyland's voice on the intercom box invited me to drive on in.

"You're always welcome in our home," Sapphire Ikeda told me after I'd apologized for dropping in without notice.

"I was afraid I might be interrupting your dinner."

"We were just finishing up. Here, let me fix you a plate."

"Are you sure you have enough?" The fragrant aromas emanating from the kitchen made me want to run in and fall face-first into the pot. I hadn't had anything solid in my stomach since that chicken pasty almost eight hours ago.

"We have plenty. I haven't been able to swallow more than a bite or two ever since I got the phone call."

"I can imagine."

"Straight up five, a week ago Monday. I

was here in the kitchen, just starting to fix dinner. The five o'clock news had just come on the TV. Then the phone rang, and it was the police."

A glance at Sapphire's tiny figure, encased in a black and gold designer tracksuit, confirmed the claim about not eating. She'd gone from pleasingly petite to dangerously anorexic. As a fellow female on the short side, I know how the addition or subtraction of a few calories can make a huge difference on the waistline and hips.

Sapphire's gustatory offering turned out to be not a plate but a bowl filled with rice, broccoli, tender strips of beef, and a spicy ginger sauce. I stood at the counter of the vast, airy kitchen/den and tried not to fork down the leftovers too quickly. In the kitchen portion of the huge chamber, Sapphire finished rinsing bowls and forks and placing them in the dishwasher, while in the den, three men hunkered down around a computer. Two of them I identified right off as Gareth and Ray, while the third I pinned down as Bill Nyland, Gareth's father and Ray's brother. I'd met Bill Nyland briefly at the funeral, but that was the extent of my acquaintance.

"We found this CD while we were going through Travis's things," Sapphire said as she wiped her hands on a dish towel and rounded the counter. "It's really quite amazing."

I clutched the bowl and fork and followed Sapphire to the cluster in front of the flat-screen monitor.

"He was apparently preparing a Power Point presentation for the company's annual senior management retreat." Sapphire spoke in a low voice, like we were in a movie theater.

"Show her from the beginning," Sapphire said in a normal voice. Gareth, who'd seated himself in front of the monitor, clicked the mouse on the back arrow key, sending us to the first slide in the series.

Marketing to the
Next Generation of Car Buyers
a presentation to
Raymond I. Nyland
William I. Nyland
Gareth I. Nyland
and the Senior Executives of
The Nyland Automotive Group
by
Travis Ikeda-Nyland

Gareth clicked through the next slides, where Travis had laid out his premise. The

Next Generation — the eighteen to twenty-four-year-old first-time car buyer — doesn't relate to traditional advertising. Above all, young people demand authenticity. His solution: a series of commercials shot in the style of low-budget films. Each would feature the same three characters — twentysomething friends named Loren, Lindsey, and Fred — as they dealt with a slice-of-life experience in Sacramento. The advertising pitch, such as it was, came in the final frame: a shot of the back end of the trio's automobile, and the license plate frame from the Nyland Automotive Group.

I liked it. Even though I am far outside the target audience for Travis's advertising concept, it sure beat the usual efforts by Sacramento auto dealers, consisting as it did of geezer spokesmen in oversize cowboy hats urging us to "come on down," or inane jingles informing us that we can "find it all at the auto mall."

"Good stuff," I said between bites of rice and beef.

"Keep going," Sapphire said to Gareth.

In the next segment, Travis had outlined the specific vignettes in storyboard fashion. Loren, Lindsey, and Fred Make the Club Scene. Loren, Lindsey, and Fred Register for Class at CSUS. Loren, Lindsey, and Fred Go to the State Fair.

"I love it," I said. "It's going to be a risk for Sacramento audiences, but I love it."

I received no response from Sapphire and the Nylands, other than a clipped order from Sapphire to Gareth to "keep going."

Loren, Lindsey, and Fred Have a Picnic in McKinley Park.

23

I let my fork drop into the bowl. The clatter of stainless against ceramic and the hum of the computer were the only sounds in the den.

"Are you thinking the same thing I am?" I said after a long silence.

"Do you mean, are the police aware of this?" Gareth rotated in the swivel chair so he could face me.

"For starters."

"I personally burned a copy and turned it over to the police this afternoon, the instant I realized what Travis had put on this CD."

"What did they say?"

"You know the police. They never say anything."

"When did Travis put this together, do you know?"

"Beats me. Could have been last fall while he was still in school, could have been something he was working on up at Footprints Lodge."

"You could check and see the last time

the file was modified." Me, actually giving advice about computers? It had to be a first.

Gareth made a few clicks with the mouse. "Looks like the last time he worked on the presentation was this past September, the twenty-fifth."

Just before he had the visit from the mysterious stranger at UCLA, went on a bender, and ended up drying out at Footprints Lodge.

After this bombshell, my request seemed tame by comparison. Sapphire readily offered up Travis's sobriety plaque and Ray supplied a Swiss army knife. The brass sheet peeled away neatly — I was getting to be an expert at this — revealing the niche carved in the center of the wood, the foam liner, and the electronic reader device.

"I don't understand," Sapphire said with a quiver in her voice. The five of us — Sapphire, Ray, Bill, Gareth, and I — were huddled around a circular, glass-topped table in the breakfast nook, the remnants of the plaque resting on a woven placemat like a modern art centerpiece.

"I'm not sure if I do either," I said.

"Take a guess," Gareth said.

"I know this sounds crazy, but I think the gang up at Footprints is using microchip implants so they can spy on their former patients without their knowledge."

"You say this thing works kind of like a bar-code scanner in the supermarket." Gareth pointed a finger at the jumble of screws, plastic, wood, and brass on the placemat.

"More or less. It's quite clever, when you think about it. Everyone who graduates from Footprints Lodge gets a plaque. The people at Footprints know damn well most of their patients will treat the plaque as something valuable, like a college diploma. They'll give it a place of honor somewhere in their home."

"Just like Travis," Ray said. "It was the first thing he put up on his bedroom wall when he moved in with that MacKenzie fellow."

"So the odds are good the client will be within a few yards of the reader when the timer goes off. Just like that" — I snapped my fingers — "the data zaps from the microchip in some guy's arm to the reader hidden inside the plaque."

"But why?" This from Sapphire.

"That's what they call the sixty-four thousand dollar question."

"And what kind of data," Gareth said.

"Exactly. What kind of data are they collecting, and what are they doing with it?"

"You've gone to the police with this, I assume," Gareth said.

"Not yet. I mean, this could be part of a legitimate medical research project. Something that could revolutionize the way addiction is treated. Until I know more, I'm not comfortable with going public."

Bill Nyland spoke up for the first time. "What I want to know is, what does this have to do with that Wilson boy shooting our Travis in McKinley Park?" I placed Bill at around five years older than Ray, right around sixty, with ice blue eyes and steel gray hair trimmed in a military crew cut.

"We don't know for certain that that's what happened." I spoke gingerly, careful not to poke what was obviously a raw wound. "The police haven't charged Markitus Wilson with anything beyond evading a law enforcement officer as of yet."

"The police are clearly incompetent."

"You have to admit, Dad has a point," Gareth said. "This is all very interesting, these implants and scanner things, but what does this have to do with why or how Travis ended up getting shot in McKinley Park?"

I didn't know how to respond to that, so I just shook my head and shrugged my shoulders.

"Seems to me, Travis's presentation is

going to make it look even worse for Wilson," Gareth continued. "Here Travis was proposing to shoot a TV commercial in McKinley Park and what's the first thing Wilson says when he comes out of his coma — hey, Ma, I'm going to be in a movie."

If you asked me, it was a pretty thin thread. That TV commercial was just in the storyboard stage, Travis not even having made his presentation at the Nyland Group's annual retreat. What was Gareth suggesting — that Travis had decided to go ahead and film one of his proposed vignettes and recruited Markitus to appear in it? This janitor who'd never acted before in his life? And somehow, instead of shooting a television commercial for a car dealer, one of the cast ends up shooting real bullets?

"You make a good point," I said to Gareth. He nodded a thank-you.

"Look, I'm going to have to call it a night," I said. "Before I leave, may I ask a favor of all of you?" Hearing murmurs of approval from the assembled Nylands, I plowed forward. "Mum's the word for now about the implants and the reader device and all that." I repeated the advice I'd given to Chad MacKenzie, though in not quite so strident a voice.

Sapphire Ikeda followed me to my car. "I

understand what you were trying to tell us in there," she said when we'd reached the driveway. "But I'm still calling Detective Alvarado first thing tomorrow morning and telling him about the implant."

I turned from the driver's side door of the Z-car, where I'd just inserted the key into the lock. "I really wish you wouldn't."

"I'm trying to understand where you're coming from." Sapphire hugged her arms and shivered in the damp evening air. A security lamp above the garage door provided a circle of illumination around us, while a scattering of lights twinkled through the trees from neighboring homes. The vista beyond the Ikeda-Nyland mansion was a black nothingness where the bluffs met the American River.

"I appreciate that," I said.

"You're a journalist. So am I. You want to make sure you have your facts all checked out before you go on the air with a story. I get that. But this is my son."

"Just give me twenty-four hours. Please?" If I didn't have the pieces all put together by this time tomorrow, it would be a moot point. I'd be climbing aboard a plane to L.A. and saying good-bye to Sacramento forever.

"If I wait twenty-four hours, that means we're into the weekend and I most likely won't be able to reach Alvarado until Monday morning. Every day we lose means it's less and less likely we'll ever find out the truth about what happened to Travis."

" 'Til three o'clock tomorrow, then. If I'm not ready to go on the air and tell my audience about how the Footprints Institute is spying on their patients and what they're doing with the information, then you can call Alvarado."

"I wish I could say yes, but this is my son we're talking about."

I tried appealing to her instincts as a journalist. "I understand. But don't forget, you were the one who asked me to pursue the story. Please just give me a few more hours."

Sapphire nodded, as if turning over my line of reasoning in her mind. "You were the first news person willing to do anything more than just run with the news releases from the police department, weren't you?"

I leaned against the frosty metal of the Z-car, unwilling to say anything that might derail what sounded like a change of heart.

"Okay, 'til three o'clock tomorrow."

"Not a second longer."

The yellow sports car breezed through the light traffic of El Camino Avenue on the reverse trip to the downtown core. Only a little after nine, and the surface streets were almost deserted. Sacramento's like that, a profoundly middle-class, family-oriented city. Through the glow of light behind curtained suburban windows that I passed by on the roadway, I pictured dozens of bedside recitations of *Goodnight, Moon*, hundreds of alarm clocks being set for the early shift at one of the state office government factories.

I took the E Street exit from Business 80, cruised on Twenty-ninth to H, made a left, and crossed under the freeway, McKinley Park a dark expanse on my left. It was too late to catch any stragglers around the coffeepot at tonight's AA meeting at the Clunie Clubhouse. But it might not be too late to track down Trent, check his plaque, and see if he knew whether Corey had been presented with a similar inspirational memento.

It was a long shot, I knew. I had no last name, and Chad had given me only the tenuous lead of a small house near the intersection of Thirty-fourth and D Streets. But it wasn't that far of a detour from home, and at this point I had progressed beyond exhaustion and was operating on pure nervous energy.

The car crept along Thirty-fourth Street, my headlights and the occasional city street lamp providing the only hedge against the darkness. I swiveled my head from side to side, searching for a name on a mailbox, a bicycle, anything that might identify Trent's abode.

A brief burst of dim light a half block ahead as someone opened the door of a car parked on the street. The light disappeared when the driver shut the door. A banged-up economy import, at least ten years old. My headlamps glommed onto the reflective sticker on the back bumper:

"Cruisin' Not Usin' "

The beater hung a right on McKinley Boulevard, me in pursuit as I simultaneously focused on the pair of red taillights. I'd last seen this vehicle Monday morning in front of the Sacramento office of the Footprints Institute. Before that, I'd spotted it parked in the lot of the small complex one block over where Travis Ikeda-Nyland had shared an apartment with Chad MacKenzie. I'd assumed the car belonged to Chad, a charge he'd denied when I gave him a lift home from the funeral.

If the vehicle didn't belong to Chad, then whose name did appear on the registration card? It seemed too great a coincidence I'd spot the same vehicle twice — make that three times — in such a short time frame, and all in locations associated with the Footprints Institute.

Could this unimpressive heap be the missing link? Could those balding tires and sagging shocks be transporting a laptop to the homes of Footprints graduates, snatching the data stored inside their Celebrate Sobriety plaques?

The compact import turned right on Twenty-ninth and veered onto the Business 80 on-ramp. I gunned the Z-car and stayed on its tail. I figured at this juncture there was no use trying to disguise the fact that I was attempting to follow. I'd not tried to hide myself up until now, and the Z-car was too much of a standout to make an effective tail. Like Vic Cortese told me the other night at the Arco Arena parking lot, you don't see many of them out on the road these days.

The beater zoomed into the far left lane. Not bad for an older car that had obviously seen some hard driving. I floored it to keep up and strained to make out the numbers and letters on the license plate.

The small car hugged the left lane, merging onto Highway 99 while Business 80 made a curve to the west, completing its loop around the downtown core. Highway 99, meanwhile, angles south, eventually petering out near Bakersfield, some four hours' driving time distant. I hoped Bakers-field was not the driver's final destination. My gas tank would run dry and my bladder overflow well before then.

Just as I had drawn close enough to make another attempt at reading the license plate, the driver shot across three lanes of traffic, almost clipping a big rig, and disappeared down the Fruitridge Road off-ramp. Jeez — turn indicators? Ever heard of them?

For a split second, I was tempted to follow — signaling my intentions to my fellow mo-torists, of course — but a quick glance to my right and into the mirrors showed an eigh-teen-wheeler separating me from the off-ramp. A matchup between my cute little sports car and that behemoth would un-doubtedly turn into a remake of *Bambi Meets Godzilla.* I gave up the chase, took the next exit onto Florin Road in a sane and legal manner, looped under the freeway, and reentered, heading north, back to the down-town core and home.

"You should have seen Josh," I said into the telephone. "That kid is passing up a bril-liant career on Broadway, I swear."

I sat cross-legged on the living room couch in my favorite ratty sweats, Bialystock curled up at my side, and held the receiver between my chin and shoulder. One of these days, I'll have to invest in one of those hands-free rigs, like the one permanently affixed to Jared's head at the UCLA sober-living house, and save myself from a permanent crick in the neck. While I talked, I pushed open the drawstrings of my backpack and dumped out the detritus I'd collected throughout the day: the brochures promoting Grass Valley attractions, the plaque and its innards, the catalog from I.D. Technologies Unlimited, plus a pile of mail that I'd snatched from my "in" basket and stuffed in with the rest on my way out of the station this evening.

"I thought he looked unusually disheveled when the two of you dropped by the store this afternoon," Pete said. "Even for a college student."

Times like this, I realize the best thing about being in a relationship isn't the big, obvious stuff, like getting a delivery from the FTD guy on Valentine's Day, or having someone to smooch at midnight on New Year's Eve. It's the everyday moments, having someone to ring up at the end of the day, knowing he'll be genuinely interested in the latest goings-on in your life, no matter how trivial. Someone besides the cat who's happy to see you come home.

Some days, I let Pete do most of the talking, like the time he happened across the first paperback in the Travis McGee series, a first edition in pristine condition, tucked in the bottom of a box of *Reader's Digest* condensed books that had been dropped off after-hours in back of the Salvation Army thrift store.

But this particular evening, I did most of the yakking, pausing just enough to let Pete contribute a question or grunt of approval. Josh's performance at Footprints Lodge, and then finding the fountain of blue at Empire Mine.

"Oh, sure," Pete said. "William Bourn, founder of the Crystal Springs Water Company. He piped in the water from the Hetch Hetchy dam, hundreds of miles distant in the high Sierra. Talk about a tremendous engineering feat! All made possible from the profits from the Empire Mine. Built the Filoli estate overlooking the reservoir. It's now part of the National Trust for Historic Preservation."

Should have known the California history buff would have all the answers.

I continued on, filling Pete in on lunching with Darla Cooley, taking the plaque apart and discovering its electronic secret, enlisting Andrew's help to verify its identity. Meeting with T. R. O'Brien for drinks after work.

"That's not bad, salary-wise, for Sacramento," Pete said when I'd finished updating him on O'Brien's counteroffer to RadioLand.

"And I've got to admit, he's a great guy when you get beyond that curmudgeonly surface."

"So what'd you tell him?"

"Nothing, yet."

"Really dragging this down to the wire, aren't you?"

My hands worked on cruise control to open and sort the mail while I chatted with Pete. The thing about mail is, if you don't keep up with it, the pile seems to metastasize, engulfing everything else on the desk. I set up three piles, the largest destined directly for the recycle bin. A second, smaller stack consisted of invitations to civic and charitable events that deserved an RSVP, plus fan mail that Josh could deal with via a form letter. The puniest of the piles was reserved for possibilities, items that might have actual potential as a show topic.

Treat Your Valentine to a Chiropractic Adjustment. Pass.

From Gold to Grain: California Rice is Red Hot! Pass.

Farewell to Fleas — New Veterinary Treatment Offers Hope. Pass.

Which Circle of Dante's Hell Best Fits Your Lifestyle? Take Our Quiz! That one earned itself a toss onto the "possibilities" pile, just quirky enough that it might appeal to my listeners.

"If we get the gig with the Railroad Museum, we'll be making a commitment for the first and third weekend of every month from the first of May through September," Pete said.

I made an affirmative sound and slit open one end of a nine-by-twelve brown craft paper envelope.

"Plus the Fourth of July," Pete continued.

I let the envelope's contents fall into my lap, gave the black type a quick scan, and uttered an oath indicating intense shock and surprise.

"Too much of a time commitment?" Pete said. "I was afraid of that. Maybe we can negotiate."

"Not you, not the band," I said when I caught my breath.

"That damn cat playing too rough again?"

I clutched the telephone receiver with my left hand while I sifted through fifteen sheets of printed paper.

"You would not believe what I just got in the mail. As far as I can tell, it's from Brenda Driscoll."

24

At first glance, it appeared to be a script fleshed out from one of Travis's storyboards. "Loren, Lindsey, and Fred Go on a Picnic in McKinley Park." Only in this version, the plot took an unexpected turn shortly after the picnic basket and blanket hit the grass, and the climax had nothing to do with feeding leftover baguettes to the ducks or sneaking into a wedding at the rose garden.

In the script before me, Fred comes to Lindsey's rescue when an ex-boyfriend/ stalker shows up in the park. Fred pulls out a gun and fires a shot at the stalker, killing him instantly.

Somehow, I didn't think this scenario was going to inspire very many first-time car buyers to hurry down to a Nyland dealership.

A card was paper-clipped to the top left corner, one of those coupons for a free class at the Jazz'n Motion studio. On the reverse, Brenda — or someone — had penned the words, "Sorry, I couldn't. . . ." The writing trailed off after that.

Sorry I couldn't tell you the truth on Sunday?

Sorry I couldn't do anything to stop Travis from being killed?

Sorry I couldn't tell they were real bullets?

Sorry I couldn't write more, but someone's following me?

The flat brown mailing envelope consisted of a handwritten address, a blank space in the upper left corner where the return address should have been penned, a jumble of stamps adding up to almost three dollars, roughly double what it would have cost to mail this, and a Sacramento postmark dated yesterday.

I tried to picture the scenario, Brenda printing my name and the station's address on the front of the envelope, sticking on as many stamps as she had in her purse, scrounging up the first piece of notepaper she could find, a coupon from the exercise studio, paper-clipping it to the front of the script, and then scrawling the beginning of a message.

Then what? Distracted by a doorbell? Realized she was being watched? Pen ran out of ink? Something caused her to abandon the message, stuff the script into the envelope, seal it, and shove it into the nearest mail collection box. Maybe simply left it atop her own mailbox for the postman to pick up on his rounds.

How many hours — or minutes — elapsed before she completed that task, then opened the door of her apartment to let in her killer?

I couldn't remember ever actually attending a "power breakfast," wasn't even sure if I knew what, exactly, a power breakfast might consist of. I did feel confident, however, that the early morning event that Janice Yount invited me to would require a costume somewhat spiffier than jeans, sweater, and sheepskin boots. I'd recently begun to acquire a collection of classic, grown-up clothes, now that my social and professional life consisted of more than hanging around rock music clubs and coffeehouse open mic nights. I decided to team up the black leather jacket with a green silk blouse that nicely complemented the copper highlights in my hair (or so Pete once told me), pearl gray slacks in a lightweight wool, and low-heeled black pumps. I had to admit, it felt pleasant to experience quality fabric caressing my skin.

Even I could tell that my beloved back-pack, handwoven in a kaleidoscope of colors in Guatemala, would definitely be a fashion "don't" with this ensemble. Glory Lou had been bugging me to get rid of the backpack of late, and I was beginning to think she was right. The accessory fairly screamed early nineties postcollege bohemian. Glory Lou had recently passed along to me a black messenger bag she'd received as a premium at the last Radio-TV News Directors Association annual convention, a not-so-gentle hint to ditch the backpack, hon.

I dug the bag out of my closet, dropped it on the bed, and considered. Plain black canvas reinforced at the corners with black leather, and a thick shoulder strap, the bag was rigidly constructed and padded, presumably for hauling around a laptop. It definitely had possibilities as a briefcase-slash-purse. I transferred my essential girl stuff from the backpack to the messenger bag, plus wallet, pens, notepad, cell phone, and the digital recorder, hardly bigger than an eyeglasses case. I also tucked in the brown envelope holding the script, figuring I'd stop at the police station as soon as I could make my escape from the power breakfast.

This event must have been an oasis of excitement on an otherwise bleak social landscape because the Hilton's parking lot was already packed. The Z-car prowled up and down the asphalt rows, searching for an empty resting spot in a sea of expensive imports and high-end domestic vehicles, a densely packed parade of shiny chrome and high-gloss paint. Not a dented fender or cracked windshield or a spot of rust among them.

I thought I spotted an empty space in the next row. I accelerated and zipped around the end of the row. Damn! Not fast enough. An old economy import with a bashed-in driver's side door managed to sneak in ahead of me.

Not that beater again!

I backed up just enough to verify the "Cruisin' Not Usin'" sticker on the rear bumper and to study the driver without being noticed. A young man emerged from behind the beat-up door. I know I'd seem him somewhere before, dirty blond hair drooping over his collar, and that stoop-shouldered, caved-in-chest look that signified too much time spent in front of the computer and not enough time at the gym. He wore khakis, a blue blazer, and Hush Puppies, and carried what I assumed was a laptop in a black shoulder bag.

The computer guy who had dropped in to

tinker with Janice Yount's rig when I visited the Footprints Institute on Monday. Gavin, wasn't it?

He loped through the rows of parked cars, wove around the taxis and airport shuttle vans in the porte cochere, and disappeared into the lobby of the hotel.

I finally managed to locate a parking place and jogged as best I could in the pumps to catch up to Gavin. No luck. He'd had too much of a head start, and more suitable shoes.

"Shauna J.! I'm so glad you could make it." Janice Yount squealed, grabbed both my hands, and did the air kiss bit, plucking me from the throng pressing its way into the atrium banquet room. Dr. Yount had done herself up proud this morning, wearing aquamarine silk pants and blouse, plus a vest in a matching paisley print that floated from shoulder to floor, that rich hippie–earth mother look much favored by Northern California women who've crossed the big five-oh. She'd applied more makeup than I remembered her wearing before, and a tiny smudge of mascara appeared under one eye.

"Have you made a decision about a treatment program for your young friend?" She asked in a whisper after she pulled me aside.

"I don't think that's going to be necessary."

"Oh?"

"It looks like just spending an hour or so in your facility was enough to straighten him out. Scared sober, you might say."

"I'm just glad we were able to help out, no matter how small the contribution."

"Too bad we weren't able to complete our tour of the lodge."

We were almost alone in the lobby, the crowd having managed to squeeze its way into the banquet room. Janice placed a hand on my upper back and steered me to a registration table. A young man in a white shirt and tie took my business card and handed me a canvas goody bag with the "Sharing the Pride of Sacramento" logo screened onto one side. Great, now I had two bags to deal with. I was beginning to feel as if I were schlepping my way through the airport.

"You'll have to come up and visit us again under happier circumstances," Janice said as she draped the goody bag over my shoulder.

"I was really hoping I'd have the chance to meet Dr. Fessenden. I've heard so many good things about his work."

I studied her jolly expression for any sign of reaction. She might have winced, the tiniest tightening around the lips. "Next time!" she chirped.

We followed the eddies and currents of the crowd into the acreage of circular tables in the banquet hall. "I'm afraid they've seated me at the head table," Janice said. "So unnecessary, really." She offered to locate "fun people, I know you'll have a lot in common" and parked me at a table that included an advertising salesman from the *Business Journal*, a periodontist, three real estate brokers, and the owner of a chain of discount hair salons. The latter eyed my tresses with such professional curiosity I was afraid I might have to slap an imaginary pair of scissors out of her hand.

All of my tablemates, I noticed, sported lapel pins that pulsated with a tiny red light.

"Cool pins," I said after we'd traded introductions. "Where'd you get them?"

"Check your goody bag," one of the brokers suggested.

I groped through magazines, coupons, and what looked like a free sample of hair conditioner in the canvas tote. My fingers finally closed around a small, sharp object wrapped in plastic that proved to be a flimsy aluminum lapel pin featuring a rendition of the "Sharing the Pride of Sacramento" logo.

A tiny electronic button sat at the apex of the state capitol dome.

I inserted the pin through a buttonhole, careful not to make any snags or pricks in the silk blouse.

"Just pinch it in the middle to make the light work," the real estate guy said. "Here, want me to show you?"

"I'll figure it out, thanks." As if I'm going to allow any male besides Pete Kovacs to fiddle with my blouse.

"Just don't forget to turn it off afterward or you'll run down the battery," he said.

"Sure, thanks." I seriously doubted I'd ever want to wear this cheap gimmick after this morning.

The power breakfast turned out to be everything I'd dreaded. A typical civic do-gooder event, which is to say lots of ceremony, lots of cheers and applause, and lots of speechifying. I've never liked this sort of thing, have always instinctively distrusted any event involving mobs of people acting in unison. Even as a teenager, I was enough of a cranky iconoclast to avoid participation in pep rallies and assemblies. I usually escaped with Richie to the A.V. room, where we read *Mad* magazine while hiding out among the slide projectors and film strips on hygiene and safe driving.

The food wasn't bad, though.

I nibbled on scrambled eggs and hash browns and studied the head table, concentrating on Gavin, seated next to Dr. Yount. At one point, the young man actually ducked his head, shoulders, and arms under the table and came back up holding a laptop. It was all I could do to restrain myself from running up to the head table and snatching the machine out of his hands. I watched, a slice of toast wavering in one hand, as Gavin tapped on the laptop's tiny keyboard, whispered to Dr. Yount, pointed to the screen, then closed the machine. The computer vanished back under the table.

Back, I assumed, into the bag I'd seen slung over his shoulder in the parking lot.

Could Gavin be the missing link? The final factor in the collection of data from patient to plaque to laptop? That Cruisin' Not Usin' vehicle certainly got around: the Footprints office in South Sac, Chad's apartment, Trent's house, and now here.

I realized, as I scooped up another forkful of eggs and potatoes, that I faced an even bigger missing link, a gap big enough to drive a freight train through. I still hadn't discovered any connection between the Footprints Institute and the movie allegedly being shot in McKinley Park.

Those implants may be flying slightly under the ethical radar, but I had no indication anyone connected to the Footprints recovery program might be capable of murder to keep the implant program a secret.

"Now for the moment you've been waiting for, as we Share the Pride of Sacramento!" I recognized the master of ceremonies, the weekend weather guy for one of the local TV stations. "Let's start the new year right as we Share the Pride with one of our finest local nonprofit agencies, the Footprints Institute."

With some two hundred pairs of eyes focused on the head table, I used the opportunity to keep my hands busy under the tablecloth, switching all of my personal belongings from the messenger bag, and placing them into the Sharing the Pride goody bag. Then I removed all of the magazines, coupons, and samples from the goody receptacle and slid them into the messenger bag.

"We've helped literally thousands of people of all ages recover from the heartbreak of addiction." Dr. Yount's voice boomed from speakers on poles at either side of the head table. "As just one example, I'd like to introduce a young man who exemplifies everything that the Footprints Institute stands for. Five years ago, he was living on the streets. Today, he's a proud graduate of Footprints Lodge, has completed college, and is serving as our director of information technologies. Gavin Pruitt!" She flung both arms theatrically in the direction of the driver of the Cruisin' Not Usin' vehicle. He rose halfway, his head ducked in embarrassment, and reacted to the applause with a diffident wave.

Dr. Yount took her seat, and the weather guy returned to explain the concept of Sharing the Pride. An assistant with a hand-held microphone would travel from table to table inviting us to share news about our business or profession. In return for what the emcee called "sharing rights," the speaker was expected to make a donation of goods, services, or cash to the Footprints Institute. "Strictly voluntary, of course," the fellow at the podium said.

Yeah, right. Just like trying to "pass" during the group sharing portion of an AA meeting. I cringed, wondering how I could possibly flee and avoid this forced tithing. Everyone else in the audience appeared well prepared, checkbooks in hand. The very first speaker was none other than Vic Cortese, who offered a six months' lease on a new vehicle from Solon Imports. Why hadn't Janice warned me?

The woman traveling with the microphone reached my table. I waited for the salesman from the *Business Journal* to donate advertising space in the next four issues, and for the hair salon lady to make a long speech about the new European spiral perms, and then hand over a check.

My turn. I grabbed the microphone and stood. "Sacramento Talk Radio, the last of the independent, family-owned stations in the capital city, is proud to offer to Dr. Yount an hour of airtime this afternoon. It'll be her show, one hour from three to four, to get the word out about the good work of the Footprints Institute on the top-rated afternoon radio program in the city."

Dr. Yount beamed at me from the head table while the audience broke into applause. Now that's what I call Sharing the Pride.

Depending on how the rest of my morning panned out — and how cooperative the police might prove to be — she might very well end up sharing more than just her pride on my show this afternoon.

How about, say, a confession?

The microphone lady at last completed her rounds, and the crowd was starting to shrug into jackets, gather up purses and briefcases, and shake hands with their tablemates. I hefted the messenger bag and canvas tote with one hand and sprinted up to the head table. I hopped up the two steps of the risers and picked my way through table legs and microphone cords. I reached the chair that Gavin had vacated to chat with the TV weathercaster.

The black canvas briefcase squatted under the table, next to the chair. The bag that, presumably, held Gavin's laptop.

I placed my messenger bag under the table, next to the black briefcase, and clutched the souvenir tote bag containing my wallet, cell phone and digital recorder. And the script.

Using the tote bag as a battering ram, I managed to snake my way through the crowd and interrupt a lively conversation Dr. Yount was having with Vic Cortese just long enough to slip a business card into her hand and instruct her to meet me at the station no later than two-thirty. I slithered back to the still-vacated chair.

Then I did a bad thing.

25

Okay, the two bags didn't look exactly alike.

The trim on Gavin's briefcase appeared to me to be made of real leather, while I was fairly certain mine was constructed entirely from man-made materials.

And the orange juice being served this morning would have to have been laced with something potent enough to earn the drinker a one-way ticket to the Footprints Lodge for anyone to mistake the heft of a briefcase holding a laptop with a container stuffed with magazines, catalogs, and flyers.

But in the excitement of the moment — all that pride being shared! — little slip-ups have been known to happen, haven't they?

I exited the banquet hall, concentrating on projecting the image of a confident professional woman striding purposefully to her next appointment, a souvenir bag draped in the crook of one arm, and her briefcase dangling from her shoulder to her hip. I didn't dare break into a jog until I reached the parking lot.

The multi-story hotel cast a long shadow over the rows of parked cars. I glanced up and was greeted with actual sunshine, a few thin clouds against the blue sky. If things went well — in other words, if Andrew was home and able to hack into the laptop with ease, and if I was able to get in to see Detective Alvarado at the police station — I might be able to fit in a noon hour ride with Captain Mikey.

I pulled out my cell phone and punched in a number in Hollywood.

"Doyle's not around right now?" The receptionist had the Valley Girl vernacular down pat, turning every statement into a question.

"Do you have any idea when he'll be back?"

"I'm all, he had to take a meeting at Westwood One? I think he said he'll be back around eleven?"

"Tell him Shauna J. Bogart called and that I'll try him again later." I happened to spot the red light on the silly lapel pin from the power breakfast, still broadcasting its flashing red light from my blouse, giving me the appearance of a high-tech streetwalker. I pushed the center of the pin with my index finger to douse the light and made a mental note to unfasten the cheesy souvenir from my blouse as soon as I had two free hands.

"I could, like, put you through to his voice mail?"

"That won't be necessary. That's Shauna J. Bogart, B-O-G-A-R-T, and tell him I'll catch up with him later."

I returned to the car, hauled out Gavin's bag, and carried it across the street to the shingled bungalow that Josh shared with several other Sac State students. Their numbers and identities varied with the school terms, the only two constants being my intern and his best friend, Andrew "Android" Stoller. I crossed my fingers that Josh's genius housemate might not have any Friday morning classes.

"Not here," a bleary-eyed young Hispanic told me after I'd knocked twice on the door. He had a pierced eyebrow and wore a wrinkled T-shirt, tube socks, and checkered flannel pajama bottoms.

"Any idea where I might find him?" There was always the hope, no matter how slight, that the housemates posted their class schedules on a communal bulletin board just for the convenience of local talk show hosts who might come snooping around.

The student turned toward a book-strewn stairway leading to the second floor and hollered. "Hey, where's Stoller?"

I made out a muffled reply.

My host returned his attention to me, one arm draped along the edge of the open door and the opposite hand stuffed into the pocket of the pajama bottom, causing it to ride dangerously low on the hips. He grinned, revealing a row of orthodontically perfect white teeth.

"You might try Paradise Beach."

The question wasn't so much what Andrew Stoller would be doing at Paradise Beach in the middle of winter. The question was, what was an alpha geek like Andrew Stoller doing at Paradise Beach, period.

Featuring real dunes and a sandy shoreline, Paradise Beach is the closest place in Sacramento to a genuine California seaside playland. Nestled in an oxbow bend in the American River, the cove is an easy downriver hike from the Sac State campus. That fact, plus a scandalous reputation for tolerating nude sunbathing, makes it a popular destination for MTV-style beach partying by the collegiate set during the warm weather months. But somehow I was having trouble picturing Android — or Josh — participating in the debauchery.

Only two vehicles occupied space in the asphalt lot of the city park that fronted Paradise Beach on this January morning: a pickup with a camper top and a white panel van, the logo of the telephone company barely covered with white spray paint. Both were parked next to the trailhead of the footpath leading over the levee to the river. I left the Z-car next to the camper truck, grabbed the briefcase, and locked the car door.

From atop the levee that separated the river from the city park, I shaded my eyes and scanned the expanse of rock and sand, the leafless cottonwoods, and the sluggish waters of the American River. A couple of miles downriver, Markitus Wilson had crashed into this same waterway and gasped for life on a rock that protruded from the surface just past the shoreline. This morning, I was greeted with a scene of serenity, a lone fisherman in hip waders on the far horizon, and closer in, two people sitting on a log that had washed up on the sandy shore. One of them, I felt pretty certain, was Andrew Stoller.

I picked my way carefully over the loose stone that separated the levee from the sand. Why hadn't I thought to toss a pair of sneakers into the back of the car? Those damn pumps, even with a one-inch heel, were enough to turn the short hike into an ankle-twisting nightmare. A century and a half ago, the gold miners dislodged and overturned every rock and stone, sluiced every bit of gravel of this river in a frantic scramble for precious flakes that may have escaped the mining operations in the Mother Lode. The legacy of their rampage remained in the twenty-first century in the debris fields that lined both banks of the river from the point where it spilled over the edge of Folsom Dam to its final meeting with the mighty Sacramento.

It was, indeed, Andrew Stoller seated on the massive log, legs stretched out and feet dug into the sand. His companion was a young woman who pointed what looked like an old rooftop TV antenna toward the river. Andrew was tapping information into a hand-held communications device when I approached.

"What's up?" I tilted my head in the direction of the contraption after we'd traded greetings and introductions. The young woman was called Vandala, followed by a multisyllabic last name that she would have had to repeat at least three times before I would have gotten it. East Indian, I guessed, judging from the dark eyes and masses of black hair constrained by a set of bulky headphones attached to the antenna thing.

"We're otter spotting," Andrew said.

"That's just swell." Like I have time to contemplate the wonders of nature? I jerked the Velcroed flap of Gavin's bag and pulled out the laptop. "Think you could take a break from the critters and hack into this?"

"Hack?" Andrew gave me a look of innocence defiled. "You mean, like break into someone else's computer and snoop around in their files?"

"C'mon, don't give me that goody-two-shoes act." I shoved the slim electronic device into his hands. "You're just itching to see if you can do it, I can tell. Guys like you love a challenge."

"Does this have anything to do with that scanner I took apart for you and Josh yesterday?"

"I certainly hope so." If it didn't, I'd just committed a felony for nothing.

"I suppose as a professional courtesy to Josh's boss . . ."

While Andrew tinkered with the laptop, I watched Vandala as she aimed the antenna toward the river, bit her lip in concentration, jotted something on a notepad, then slid the headphones to her neck.

"Are there really otters out there?" From my stance in front of the log, I could hear the distant thunder of traffic on the H Street Bridge and on U.S. 50, and the whine of a jet lining up for a landing at Sacramento International. Could a mammal so untamed really live in the midst of this dense urban landscape?

"A few," Vandala said. "Not enough. That's why I volunteered to help the Department of Fish and Game with their tracking program."

"How does that thing work?"

"The otters in our study have a flipper tag, kind of like those things they put in the ears of cows. The tag emits a unique radio signal for each otter in the program. We volunteers go up and down the river, trying to pick up the signals."

"Wouldn't it be easier to use those microchip implants?"

"Like they're doing with dogs and cats? Two problems with that. One, when you're dealing with a wild animal, it's a lot less traumatic to attach a flipper tag than inject something under the skin. Two, when you're out in the wild, how do you get close enough to the animal with a scanner? Those things have a range of a few yards at most."

I gazed into the slow-moving river, at the golden reflections of sunlight where the water eddied around an exposed rock. After what I had learned about microchip technology and radio frequency ID devices, the otter tagging program seemed comfortingly primitive.

"One thing about those chips, they'll theoretically last the life of the animal," Vandala said. "The flipper tags are useful for two years at most."

"How come?"

"The battery runs dead. Don't forget, these tags are sending out a radio signal 24/7. You can't exactly train an otter to turn the thing on and off."

"And sometimes the tags fall off, I would imagine."

"Oh, yeah. Whereas with a chip, it's there for good."

Unless you hire a medical professional to remove it. Or convince an amateur friend to do the job with an X-Acto knife.

Andrew crowed and slapped his thigh.

"What, what?" I sprinted around the log and peered around Andrew's shoulder at the laptop screen. A chart of some sort, a grid filled with a random collection of numbers and letters.

"The smoking gun, for sure," Andrew said. "The missing link, the holy grail, the one ring to rule them all."

"What! Is! It!" I was tempted to grab the kid by the shoulders and give him a good shake.

"You just found the computer the Footprints people are using to collect information from their clients, that's what. From the implant to the reader to the hard drive, right here." He gave the top of the screen a little pat.

"And — ?"

"They're keeping track of the blood alcohol levels."

"What? How?" I seated myself next to Andrew on the log, careful not to snag my best pair of slacks on the rough wood. "Lemme see."

He adjusted the laptop on his knees so I could peer directly into the screen. I had to form a canopy with my hands to shade it from the sun's glare.

"Those letters down the left side are the initials of the people with the implants, or so I would assume," Andrew said. "See those numbers across the top? Those are the dates and times they collected the data. And those numbers underneath? Those are blood alcohol levels."

"How do you know those numbers are blood alcohol levels and not something else?"

Andrew made a couple of quick keystrokes and taps on the built-in mouse. "Take a look at the header." A block of type that had previously been hidden burst onto the screen.

Test Subject Blood Alcohol
Levels — January

It couldn't be more obvious, now could it? Andrew brought the grid back to the screen.

"How is a chip planted under someone's skin detecting blood alcohol levels?" I said. "I thought those things could only send pre-programmed data, like the name and phone number of a pet's owner."

"Sure, the cheap ones that they're using for inventory control and pet identification. But the sophisticated, cutting-edge chips are perfectly capable of medical monitoring. Data like the subject's blood pressure or cholesterol levels could, in theory, be transmitted to the nearest medical center. One of these days, the paramedics will be on the scene before you even know you're having a heart attack."

Yeah. And that oh-so-helpful counselor from the recovery program will be on the phone to talk you back into treatment before you even realize you've got a hangover.

I examined the column of initials running down the left side of the screen. C.M. was probably Chad MacKenzie. I was glad to see he was keeping his sobriety pledge. There was a T.W., with 0.0 noted for the previous evening. That could be Trent. Two and a half weeks ago, C.D. had had a blood alcohol level of 1.4. Corey Draper? The notations for T.I.N. ended two days before the death of Travis Ikeda-Nyland.

Now, let's get one thing straight. I have zero sympathy for drunk drivers, inebriated child beaters, and every other brand of sociopath who inflicts alcohol-fueled torment and tragedy on innocent bystanders. But I also feel passionate about a little concept known as the right to privacy, and that includes the right of the individual to drink himself blotto behind closed doors if that's what he wants to do. Long as he doesn't hurt anyone but himself in the process, it ain't nobody's business but his own.

Everything leading up to this moment on the beach next to the American River — the implants, the reader devices hidden in the plaques, the surveillance via drive-by laptop, the possibility of medical monitoring by microchip, even the playful otter with its flipper tag — filled me with unease and a vague queasy feeling.

And a sense of dread as to what this technology might hold for the future.

26

"It's almost ten," I said to Andrew. "I'm going to have to get the laptop back to its owner pronto."

"Don't you want to save the file?"

"Now how are we supposed to make that happen here?" I didn't have a floppy disk on my person or in my car and somehow I suspected Andrew didn't either. The floppy disk technology was just *so* last century, don't you know? But here we were, sitting on a log on the bank of the American River. It wasn't like we could easily plug into a printer and spew out a hard copy of the chart, or tap into a phone jack, access the Internet, and send the file to my e-mail account.

"Not a problem." He added a word that sounded like *hi-fi*.

"High fidelity?"

"Wi-fi. Wireless Internet Access. Most new laptops like this one are wi-fi enabled. Lucky for us."

I'd heard of wireless computing, but that

was about the extent of my knowledge. I don't consider myself a Luddite — I've accepted the station's conversion from analog to digital; I adore Internet research, and I wouldn't like to see if I could survive without my cell phone — but this wireless business was one step beyond my position on the learning curve. I gave Andrew a clueless look, shrug of shoulders, elbows bent, palms held out.

"It's as simple as getting into your e-mail through the Web and sending a message to yourself with the file attached. A simple Excel spreadsheet like this will be a piece of cake."

I let Andrew find the home page for my Internet service provider and locate the section that allowed us subscribers to access our e-mail via the Web. I'd used the feature occasionally while on the road, usually by finding a public library that offered free Internet access. I tried not to make it a habit. Wasn't the whole point of a vacation to get away from e-mail?

Andrew politely averted his vision while I typed in my user name and password. As if a little thing like a password would stop a tech head like him from breaking into my mailbox if that's what he wanted to do. I entered my own e-mail address into the TO field and even figured out how to click on the little paper-clip icon and attach the Excel file to the message.

"Just hit the SEND button? That's it?" I asked.

"That's it."

"But how — ?"

"Used to be, you'd have to find a wireless hot spot. But now, the entire city's been enabled for wireless computing."

I looked around and saw only river, trees, sand, blue sky, and that one fisherman knee deep in water. Not a cell phone tower or Web cam in sight.

"Don't bother looking," Andrew said. "Ever see a transceiver in a Starbucks? Not." He answered his question before I could ask what a transceiver might be. "They're much too small. But trust me, those Starbucks are hot for wireless. Same with hotel lobbies, the airport, and the Sac State campus. Like I say, the entire city. At the most, you'll see a tiny antenna, about the size of your little finger, in someone's home. A Wireless Access Point Router, attached to a box the size of a VHS tape."

"Couldn't someone intercept all these messages flying through the air?"

"If you're concerned about security, wireless isn't the way to be sending your message. Not unless you have access to a Virtual Private Network and major encryption to boot."

Let's face it, the future belongs to young brainiacs like Andrew Stoller. I just prayed that, like the superheroes in the comics, he would choose to use his special power for good and not evil.

I squinted my eyes as if I was about to make something explode and clicked the SEND button.

Gavin Pruitt gave me the hairy eyeball treatment when I showed up in the lobby of the Footprints Institute headquarters and turned in his briefcase. I couldn't say as I blamed him. My story of grabbing the wrong bag as I left the Hilton was so feeble even I was embarrassed. I concentrated on a trick I'd learned years ago from my father, the onetime state senator: talk fast, keep smiling, and get the hell out as quickly as you can.

"I'm just such a ditz," I giggled as I placed Gavin's briefcase on the front counter and accepted my messenger bag.

"I was just getting ready to call the cops," Gavin said as he clutched the briefcase to his chest.

"Well, then, isn't it lucky I discovered my silly error and hurried right over?" I gave my head a cute tilt. "Think of all the trouble I saved for both of us."

The door leading to the inner offices swung open. Janice Yount strode into the lobby. She'd removed the swirly, floor-length vest, leaving a solid column of aquamarine silk, and fixed that smudge of mascara under her eye. "Thank goodness you came as quickly as you did. We've been leaving messages for you at the station."

"I can well imagine." Think fast, think fast. "I didn't even check my voice mail, just turned around and drove straight out here as soon as I realized I'd taken the wrong bag. Got caught in traffic, wouldn't you just know it."

"Of course. Could happen to anyone."

"So Gavin's got his laptop, and I've got my bag. Everyone's a winner." My vision shifted from Janice Yount's beaming face to Gavin, back behind the front counter. He'd already removed the laptop from the briefcase, snapped it open and booted it up. Just great. What if Gavin could tell the file had been opened and read since the laptop had gone missing?

Rather than stick around and find out, I began to edge toward the front door. Janice was faster and managed to plant herself in front of the exit.

"I'm looking forward to claiming that hour of airtime on your station this afternoon," she said.

"Glad to be able to contribute to such a worthwhile organization."

"Is there anything in particular I should do to prepare?"

"Just relax and be yourself. You could talk about your upcoming public service campaign. Those television commercials you've been taping about the dangers of substance abuse among our young people. Like that spot about the college students in McKinley Park, and their encounter with the drug dealer."

"I beg your pardon?" She was either an excellent actress or was genuinely puzzled.

"Or you could use the opportunity to recognize some of your major benefactors. Like Vic Cortese."

"What an excellent idea! I'll start making a list."

"Sure is terrific to see such generosity from our business community. It's amazing how Vic Cortese can arrange for all these car giveaways from the Greater Sacramento Automobile Dealers Association."

"I suppose." Her unfailing expression of doubt and confusion was worthy of an Academy Award.

I made an exaggerated look at my watch. "Just look at the time! Got to scoot to my next appointment." I reached around Dr. Yount and pushed open the front door. That business about another appointment wasn't a complete lie. I'd rung up Sapphire Ikeda on my cell phone on the drive between Paradise Beach and the Footprints Institute office and suggested she meet me at the Sacramento Police Department headquarters. Allowing time for her to get herself ready and make the trip from Carmichael to South Sac, she should be pulling into the police station parking lot right about now.

"See you this afternoon," I turned and gave a perky wave before I broke into a jog in the direction of my car.

"You'll find my fingerprints all over this, I'm afraid." I slid the brown envelope in the direction of Detective Dan Alvarado across the wooden table. I was crowded into an interview cubicle at police headquarters with Detective Alvarado, Sapphire Ikeda, and Ray and Gareth Nyland.

"You say you got this in the mail last night," Alvarado said. He used tweezers to place the envelope in a large Ziploc bag.

"That's correct." I repeated the story of grabbing the mail from my "in" box at the station and taking it home, finally getting around to opening it late in the evening, and discovering the anonymously sent envelope with the script. "I came over here as soon as I had the chance."

"You say the contents of this envelope might have some bearing on the Ikeda-Nyland case."

"I'm positive." I handed one set of paper-clipped sheets of slippery fax paper to Alvarado, one to Sapphire, and kept one for myself. "Sorry about the quality, but that's what happens when you use your little home fax machine as a copier. You'll find this is the pertinent scene, where this character named Fred shoots a drug dealer who interrupts his picnic in McKinley Park."

I gave them a minute or two to read, Ray and Gareth Nyland crowding in on either side of Sapphire. I hadn't invited them, but if Sapphire felt more comfortable having her husband and nephew for moral support, it was fine by me. Bill Nyland, I guessed, had stayed behind to mind the store.

"So what's your theory?" Alvarado returned the flimsy sheets to the table and removed his reading glasses.

"My theory? Aren't you the one doing the investigating?"

"You're a smart lady, and like you said, your fingerprints are all over this thing. So humor me." Alvarado leaned back in the chair and placed his hands behind his head.

"Isn't it obvious? Someone arranges for Brenda Driscoll and Markitus Wilson to come to McKinley Park, the day Travis is killed, with the idea that they're going to play-act in a movie, probably a short indie film. They recruit Brenda through the Sacramento Civic Light Opera Company. They ask her to find a young African-American male to play the part of her boyfriend. Maybe she tries several of her friends through the theater company and the dance studio and no one's available or interested, who knows?"

"Go on."

"Then she remembers the guy who shows up to clean the dance studio every night. He's obviously smitten, will do anything she asks. When she mentions the possibility of working on a film project with her, he leaps at the chance."

"What does this have to do with Travis?"

"I was just getting to that. They lure Travis to the park with the idea that they're going to tape a commercial for his dad's car dealership. But when he gets there, he discovers an entirely different film project is taking place, a plot involving drug dealers and a shooting. With Travis himself as the victim."

I heard a slapping noise as Gareth slammed a copy of the script onto the table. "You're trying to tell me Wilson thought he was following a movie script and shooting blanks? Give me a break!" A flush of crimson crept up his flabby neck and spread to his cheeks. "Like the creep couldn't tell the difference between blanks and real bullets?"

"Could happen, if he never handled a gun before, neither a real one nor a theatrical prop," I said.

"For a first-time user, he certainly managed to get off one hell of a lucky shot."

Now there was a point I'd not considered. "There's a card from the Jazz'n Motion dance studio attached to the script," I said to Alvarado. "When you check it for prints, be sure to compare them to the fingerprints your people took off the corpse of Brenda Driscoll. Oh, yeah, don't forget to check it against a sample of her handwriting."

"You keep talking about 'they,'" Gareth said. "Who do you suppose 'they' might be?"

Who, indeed? Janice Yount, desperate to silence a former patient who'd figured out that microchip in his arm was doing a lot more than reducing his craving for alcohol?

"I'm still working on that part."

The meeting over, the Nylands piled into a brand-new luxury sedan with dealer plates and cruised from the police station parking lot. I sat in the Z-car, the door slightly ajar to let in fresh air, and contemplated my next move. I wished I had a printed copy of that file Andrew and I had found on the Footprints computer, with its list of initials running down the left-hand side. I'd have to drive back to the station and see if Andrew's magic with wi-fi really worked if I wanted to hold a hard copy in my hands.

Tin and Again, straight to the bottle.

Travis Ikeda-Nyland — T.I.N. on the list of Footprints clients.

Tin, the odd nickname he'd been called by the visitor the weekend he'd fallen off the wagon big time, last autumn at UCLA. Tin and Again, according to what Travis's pal Jared remembered.

What if *Again* wasn't a word, but someone's initials? Just like T.I.N. A.G.I.N.? A.G.N.? I didn't recall seeing that combination of letters in the chart of Footprints patients, but I had taken only one short look at it out there on the log next to the American

River. I'd have to drive back to the station to find out for certain.

I used my cell phone to ring the station and check for messages.

Two calls from the Footprints Institute, one from Gavin and one from Janice, both wanting to know if by any chance I'd walked away with their laptop.

Captain Mikey, informing me the weather looked promising, inviting me to join him for a spin in the traffic plane if I could make it out to the airport by eleven-thirty.

Doyle Bollinger, insisting that I must call him with my decision no later than five o'clock today or he was going to rescind the job offer. "I sense a good deal of reluctance on your part, and I need a team player who's one hundred percent committed. There are plenty of other unemployed radio people out there who would kill for this gig if you don't want it."

I tapped in the number in the 310 area code.

"He just went to lunch?" The RadioLand receptionist informed me. "Can I take your name and number?"

"It's Shauna J. Bogart."

"For sure? Doyle wants you to call him on his cell? You've got the number?"

I broke the connection and hit the speed

dial to hook me up with the individual I most wanted to speak to, the one person in the world whose thoughts mattered to me the most.

"He's up in Oroville for most of the day," Pete Kovacs's assistant said. "I don't expect to see him until late this afternoon."

Of course. Hadn't Pete told me the night before about the out-of-town trip to appraise a collection of antique lunch boxes, including an original Hopalong Cassidy?

I gazed out the windshield of the Z-car, past the Sacramento Police Department's collection of law enforcement vehicles, across busy Freeport Boulevard to the flat field beyond a chain-link fence.

I could pick up the phone and dial up Doyle Bollinger on his cell, interrupt his lunch, and tell him the good news: Shauna J. Bogart is one hundred percent committed to RadioLand.

I could drive back to the station, print out the file I'd purloined from the Footprints laptop, and begin assembling my notes for this afternoon's interview with Janice Yount.

Two years ago, when the Sacramento police and fire departments announced plans to leave their longtime homes in the downtown core and move into an abandoned shopping mall in the southern suburbs, it didn't feel right to me. I could understand the lure of easy freeway access and acres of free parking, but the police headquarters of a city with big-time aspirations like Sacramento just *belongs* downtown.

Today, though, I was grateful the PeeDee had moved into that loser shopping center at the corner of Freeport and Fruitridge.

Directly across the street from Executive Airport.

Michael had the two-seater Bonanza warmed up and ready to taxi down the runway as I sprinted through the terminal and across the apron.

"Sorry I'm late," I swung the canvas tote bag into the right-hand seat.

"For you, it's worth the wait." The fellow in the left-hand seat wore a ski cap, wraparound sunglasses, and a nylon windbreaker with fur collar pulled up around his neck. That new guy from City Scope, Hugh Stanton. Sky View Hugh.

"Where's Michael?" I clambered into the tiny aircraft.

"Tied up in a meeting. The folks at City Scope asked me to fill in. Some new sponsor who needed to be schmoozed. You know that old story."

"Do I ever. That's radio for you." I strapped myself into the seat belt.

Stanton taxied to the edge of the runway and turned the nose into the wind. "Let's see how well you do on the run-up."

"Magnetos. Carb heat. Controls. Flaps." Already I could feel my tension lifting. "Vacuum. Mixture. Trim. Beacon. Seat belts." For the first time in what felt like weeks, I focused on something other than a crucial career decision and the death of Travis Ikeda-Nyland.

"Excellent. Check for traffic on final approach."

We waited for a Piper Cherokee to complete its landing — the plane attempting to land always has priority — and began rolling for takeoff.

"Care to take the stick?" Stanton asked.

"As long as you're there to step in if I start to lose it."

"You won't lose it. Michael tells me you've got all the right moves. All you lack is confidence and experience."

I tightened my grip on the throttle and pushed it in, sending the plane racing down the runway. The airspeed reached almost seventy miles per hour, and the ship felt lighter, as if it were straining to loosen its earthly ties.

"Pull back, slow and smooth," Stanton said in a calm voice.

The nose lifted skyward, the runway dropped away, and I was surrounded by nothing but blue sky and a few thin, high clouds. If I'd been flying with Captain Mikey, I would have whooped and clapped my hands in the sheer joy of the moment. In another hour, I'd have to return to the world of Doyle Bollinger, Sapphire Ikeda, and Janice Yount. But for this short time, I had managed to literally float above it all.

We followed Captain Mikey's usual practice of tracing a figure eight over the capital city, checking on conditions on the major freeways: Interstate 80, U.S. 50, Interstate 5, Highway 99, and that oddball business loop around the downtown core, the 29–30 and the W–X freeways. Stanton monitored the station with an AM radio mounted to the control panel and made his reports with a handheld two-way radio.

The icy peaks of the Sierra began to come into greater focus. Stanton, who'd taken the controls after I'd finished the takeoff, had veered off the figure-eight course. We were heading east into the foothills, following Interstate 80.

"It's a pretty day for sightseeing, but I've got to head back to the station when the noon hour newscast is over," I told Stanton.

He responded by removing the ski cap and wraparound sunglasses.

"Hugh? Shouldn't we be turning around right about now?"

"My dear, when I'm riding gain with you, we've got all the time in the world."

27

"Dr. Fessenden?" I felt as if my jaw were dropping all the way to the ground two thousand feet below.

"Oh, please. Reginald Fessenden died in 1932."

He fit the description Darla Cooley had given me up at Footprints Lodge yesterday — slender, short, with a few wisps of brown hair arranged across the top of his head. If he wasn't Dr. Fessenden, then who was he? High-tech multimillionaire turned federal convict Richard Snelling? My pal Richie from high school?

A dozen responses burbled to the surface of my intellect, most of them having to do with kidnapping, theft of an airplane, unethical medical experiments, and homicide. I finally voiced the most insistent: "Are you out of your freakin' mind?"

"I don't believe so." He spoke with about as much emotion as if I'd asked if he preferred paper or plastic to bag his groceries. "But thanks for asking."

He reached into the back compartment of the Bonanza, retrieved a wadded piece of purple cloth, and tossed it into my lap. "One for me and one for you." He zipped open his windbreaker, revealing a purple T-shirt with white iron-on letters.

The Reginald Fessenden
Royal Riding Gain Academy

There were only two of these that I knew of in the entire world. Richie owned one, and I had the other — that is, until the day I threw it back at him in a fit of teenage pique. I smoothed out the musty fabric on my lap to reveal the same homemade logo.

I was sitting next to Richard Snelling. My junior prom date.

"You escaped from federal prison!" I didn't need to shout to be heard over the thrum of the engine, but I did anyway.

"Who says I escaped?"

"Then why aren't you in a cell in Lompoc where you belong?"

"Look, I can't go into the details. Let's just say there are people who are very highly placed who are interested in microchip technology and its human applications."

"I can see where the prison system would find such research most interesting. So you finagled a secret deal, your very own work-release program. Officially, you're still locked up in the federal pen. Unofficially, you're serving your sentence at the Footprints Lodge. At least until you managed to get yourself fired."

" 'Fired' is such a negative word. Just say I had philosophical differences with Dr. Yount."

"I suppose Travis Ikeda-Nyland somehow stumbled across the true identity of Dr. Fessenden up at the Footprints Lodge, and that's why he had to die."

"I had nothing to do with the death of that young man."

"Then who did?"

"I wish I knew. All I know is, I tried to help him. As soon as I realized what was really going on up at Footprints Lodge, I told him to get rid of his chip as soon as he could and to spread the word among the other patients who received them."

"I think the Footprints Institute is responsible for Travis's death. They realized Travis was about to blow the whistle on the implants. Rather than risk all that negative publicity, they shut him up forever."

"That's an interesting scenario, but like I just told you, I have no idea."

"I don't know about you, but that microchip implant stuff gives me the creeps." A shudder of revulsion ran up and down my spine just thinking about an electronic Big Brother, no larger than a grain of rice, monitoring my bodily functions and tracking my movements.

"Did you know there's a resort in Spain where guests have the option of receiving a chip that recognizes their ID and their credit balance? No need to carry around money or a credit card or proof that you're old enough to buy a drink. Just wave your arm in front of the scanner and it's handled. The ultimate credit card and personal ID, all in one easy-to-carry package."

"Let me guess, folks at that resort are lining up to have those damn chips stuck under their skin. They can't pop that needle fast enough." Never underestimate the sheeplike behavior of the vast majority of human beings.

"No different than getting a piercing or a tattoo if you want to be cool."

"They'll have to tie me up and hold me down before I ever allow a chip to get planted inside me."

"That genie is already out of the bottle, my dear. My thought was, get in on the ground floor and harness the power for benign, humanitarian purposes, make the genie serve mankind rather than the other way around."

"And you thought the Footprints Lodge might be the perfect testing ground? What were you smoking!"

"When you're a federal prisoner you don't get to be choosy about your assignments."

"I assume the whole point was to track clients who either had generous insurance plans or who were independently wealthy, and to scoop them back into the program the minute they relapsed. Welfare cases need not apply. When you started raising ethical considerations, that's when Dr. Yount did the equivalent of firing you. She called Lompoc and told them to come and take their prisoner back. What happened then, you somehow managed to flee?"

"Don't forget, I'm not the only one with something to hide. Dr. Yount can't afford for her program to get a lot of scrutiny right now. The research program was scheduled to conclude at the end of this week and a federal marshal will arrive in Grass Valley tomorrow to escort me back to Lompoc. I plan to be there like a good boy."

"And in the meantime, you earned yourself a couple of weeks of freedom to mess with my mind. Why?"

Richie raised his hand for silence and

cocked his ear toward the AM radio. The host of the noon newscast had just introduced the final traffic report of the hour. Richie grabbed the two-way and ad-libbed a flawless description of a slowdown on Business 80 heading out of downtown over the American River Bridge. We were miles from visual contact with the city core — just east of Roseville, following Interstate 80, from my bird's-eye view — but he must have figured a tie-up on that notorious stretch of freeway was a safe bet.

"Sitting in for Captain Mikey, this is Sky View Hugh for Sacramento Talk Radio." Now is the point where he should have returned the handheld walkie-talkie to the clip on the control panel. Instead, he gave the coiled wire a strong yank. The cord snapped from the transmitter box mounted under the control panel.

"Hey, what do you think you're doing?"

He grinned demonically and tossed the useless communications device into the back storage compartment.

"You're going to have to pay for that, I hope you realize."

"I'm good for the money. I'm a multimillionaire, remember?"

The plane banked and I realized Richie was gradually changing direction, heading north, sending us farther away from our home base. I scanned the instrument panel and kept one eye on Richie, waiting for the moment I could grab the radio connected to approach control and send a Mayday to the tower back at Executive. Even the interplane radio would be better than nothing. I might be able to raise another pilot.

"If you're thinking of using one of those radios, I wouldn't bother if I were you," Richie said. "While I was waiting around for you to show up, I had plenty of time to disable them."

"What'd you do to Captain Mikey? Disable him as well?"

"Didn't I tell you he got tied up in a meeting?" he chortled. "Tied up, get it?"

"Yeah, real funny."

"He's fine, honest. Just managed to get himself locked up inside an empty hangar. After I get you all settled in your new abode, I promise I'll return his airplane and release him from the hangar. I'll even pay for the gas. So quit stressing."

Settled in my new abode? I wasn't liking the sound of this one bit. "There's still the little issue of kidnapping. You know — moi?"

"Kidnapping? Doesn't that involve holding a person captive against her will? After you find out what I've got planned for the two of us, you'll be begging me to let you stay. Trust me."

"What new abode?"

"Just one of my many properties. A ski lodge north of Lake Tahoe. Very remote, very secluded, very romantic. You'll love it."

I could have flung back any number of snotty replies, but it wouldn't help my situation to seriously annoy the person who actually knew how to land this plane. I dropped my voice into a seductive purr. "Sounds fascinating. Can't you give me a little hint? Just one?"

"Remember all those kids in high school, and how mean they were to us? The cheerleaders and the football players, the guys with the muscle cars and the girls with their own charge accounts at Macy's?"

"Of course. You don't forget a thing like that."

"What if I told you I've planned a little reunion. A chance for us to enact our own personal revenge of the nerds."

"Sounds super." Actually, it sounded anything but. What did he have in mind when he talked revenge, a Columbine re-enactment?

"They're all going to receive an engraved invitation to an ultraexclusive class reunion at the Filoli mansion. All paid for by one of my dummy corporations."

"So they won't have any idea who's really issuing the invitation. Clever."

"Red carpet, limos, caviar, French champagne. I'm working on hiring Elton John to entertain."

"I just can't wait!" I did my best to sound naïvely enthusiastic and to hide the sarcasm I really wanted to vent.

"Just picture it: Those so-called cool kids, with their pathetic suburban lives, their PTA meetings and their car pools and their dead-end jobs that won't even pay a pension if they manage to hang on long enough to retire. And here they are, being treated to the most fabulous party they've ever imagined in their miserable little lives. Then you and I show up — surprise, surprise — your mystery host and hostesses, the king and queen of the high school reunion: dashing tycoon Richard Snelling and that girl from the A.V. Club who grew up to be famous talk show host Shauna J. Bogart. Won't they be sorry!"

"You're going to all this trouble just because some jock gave you a wedgie in the locker room in ninth grade?" I didn't even try to mask my true feelings. "That was over twenty years ago. Get over it!"

"Where's your sense of fun? Just imagine the looks on their faces."

"You've still got a whole year to serve on your sentence. Do you plan to lock me up at this remote ski lodge until you're free to throw your coming-out party?"

"I'll be out in less than a month. An early release for good behavior, part of the deal we negotiated in return for my donating my genius to their little human microchip project."

"But why all the games? Why throw a plaque through the window of my car, why all the strange phone calls to my show, fe, fi, lo, li and all that?"

"Breaking the window was a little over the top, and I apologize. To answer your question, I knew I had to earn your respect. You wouldn't have been able to resist a puzzle to unravel. Something we have in common."

"And you've been following me around the past few days? Planting the plaque next to the fountain at the Empire Mine when you knew I was on my way?"

"Following was hardly necessary. I knew you'd come poking around Footprints Lodge eventually, and then find your way over to the Empire Mine. Those docents were more than willing to help a fellow leave a little gift for an old classmate once I made a generous donation to their museum restoration fund."

"But why me? I mean, if you want to make a real impression on those cool kids from high school, why not hire a supermodel to be your escort for the night?"

He took his attention off the horizon and gazed at me with empty brown eyes. I attempted to gauge his expression but came up blank.

"I've always had a crush on you. I thought you knew."

"You carried a torch for twenty-plus years?" A picture flashed in my mind of being held captive in his ski lodge, dressed and fussed over like a doll, a one-of-a-kind museum piece to be trotted out and displayed to the public on special occasions. "That's not love, that's obsession. Now turn this plane around and take me home!"

"Make me."

Fine. He wanted to play games? He picked the wrong person to mess with!

I knew better than to fight with him over control of the Bonanza. Sure, I had a throttle and wheel at my hands and a set of rudder pedals at my feet, a duplicate of the controls at Richie's position. But I knew in a struggle over which set of controls the plane would obey, the victor would be the person with the most sheer body strength. Richie wasn't the most physically prepossessing guy in the world, but he'd still have the advantage of male muscle mass. Not fair, but that's the way human anatomy works.

More to the point, any struggle over control of an airplane is going to have only one outcome — a fast, one-way trip to the ground.

But, shoot, I wasn't going to let this lovesick lunatic fly me to some prison of a ski lodge miles from civilization without putting up a fight.

I admit, I wasn't thinking with calm logic at this point. I let anger and adrenalin take over. I looked around for a weapon, anything to get myself out of this predicament. I slid my left hand down the edge of the seat. My fingers touched something flat and metallic, warm from the sun beating through the windshield. Captain Mikey's aluminum clipboard, the one he kept strapped to his thigh for taking notes on traffic conditions.

I held the clipboard with both hands, raised my arms, and shook it in Richie's direction. "Turn this plane around this instant!"

"Why should I?"

"Turn around, dammit!"

I didn't mean to hurt him. Honest. But I

misjudged the distance, forgot for a moment how cramped the cockpit truly was. Somehow in my furious flailing with the clipboard, I managed to make contact with the top of Richie's head. I must have hit just the right strategic spot, because he slumped forward onto the control wheel.

The plane responded the only way it could. By nosing downward.

Yikes!

I summoned all the upper-body strength I had to push Richie's inert body back from the wheel. He slumped to the far side, against the hull of the aircraft. I detected a trickle of blood on his forehead. I wanted to make sure he was okay, but the needs of the rapidly descending aircraft took priority.

Gripping the control wheel with both hands, I eased upward. The craft leveled off and I finally took a deep breath. We'd just missed what could have been a fatal stall.

"Richie? Richie!" My fingers probed for a neck artery and detected a pulse. "Wake up! For god's sake, wake up!" I slapped his cheeks gently like they do in the movies.

No reaction. Richard Snelling may have been still alive, but he was down for the count.

I clutched the handheld microphone. "Mayday! Mayday!" No answer either from approach control or the interplane radio. Wait — there's still the back-up transceiver attached to the outside antenna. "Mayday!"

Silence. No answer but the hum of the engine, the rush of the wind, and my own ragged breathing.

One small aircraft with a half tank of fuel, radios dead, an unconscious aviator, and a student pilot with only a few hours of flight instruction under her belt.

No question, I was up that infamous creek with the scatological name.

28

I shrieked the name of that well-known creek repeatedly and without pausing for breath until I got the panic out of my system.

First things first. Get this bird heading back to the home nest! I executed a slow bank, reversing the direction from northeast to southwest.

Think, think, think. What would Captain Mikey tell me if he, instead of a comatose felon, were buckled into the next seat? Don't lose it! Use that space between your ears for something besides holding your hat. Smooth and steady does it.

Smooth and steady. The terrified thoughts tumbling over each other in my mind began to recede, replaced by a transcendent calm.

Richie had thought he'd deprived me of all methods of communication when he disabled the two-way radios.

He forgot about a girl's second-best friend.

I grappled around in the back compartment, located the canvas tote bag from the Sharing the Pride breakfast, and fished out my cell phone. I suppose the textbook thing to do would have been to call 911, or ring up directory assistance and ask the operator to put me through to the control tower at Executive Airport.

Instead I called the station.

Glory Lou picked up on the second ring. I had to pause to let her utter a series of "lordy" and "as I live and breathe" as I told her of the pickle I currently found myself in.

"Are you finished?" I said. "Good. Now here's what I want you to do."

The Bonanza glided over the city of Sacramento, the trees, skyscrapers, parks, and rivers arrayed before me like my own personal kingdom. From my aerie high above the urban center, I picked out the Sacramento Talk Radio tower, the capitol dome, the sandy shore of the American River where I'd met with Andrew Stoller this morning, and the Business 80 bridge with — yes! — a traffic tie-up, just like Sky View Hugh had reported.

"Four-two Tango Delta, we've made visual contact," Captain Mikey said to me. Four-two Tango Delta, 42TD, the unique identification painted in huge letters on the traffic plane's fuselage.

"Check," I said, even though I knew there was no way he could hear me.

So far, so good. Glory Lou had followed my instructions to the letter, had called airport security and told them to start searching empty hangars for a pilot locked up inside. Captain Mikey reported directly to the control tower, where he ad-libbed a continuing set of directions to the station via telephone. Back at the station, Glory Lou patched the phone line through the control board, sending Michael's instructions booming over the airwaves, straight into thousands of radio sets in cars, homes, and offices throughout the capital city — and into the AM radio mounted atop the instrument panel in my winged capsule.

"Wouldn't it be easier for Captain Mikey to talk you down over the cell phone?" Glory Lou had asked.

"I'm going to need both hands for the controls," I said. I swear, if I get out of this thing in one piece, first thing I'll do is invest in one of those hands-free cell phone rigs. "Plus this is going to be the most exciting story to unfold on the radio since *War of the Worlds*. Think of the ratings!"

The glass square of the Executive Airport

tower rapidly approached. On the ground near the runway, I spotted the ambulance that I'd directed Glory Lou to order for Richie, and a fire truck that I'd not asked for and hoped I wouldn't require. I noticed several TV vans parked haphazardly nearby. One of the Sacramento Talk Radio news cars was just pulling up to join the welcoming committee.

Now it was all up to me.

I'd tried landing the traffic plane once before but had choked on the final approach. Landing just felt so *wrong* to me, the aircraft actively resisting my attempts to bring her to the ground. The ship had been built for staying aloft, after all, not being chained to a concrete tie-down area. Captain Mikey had sensed my discomfort, taken the wheel, and executed a neat three-point landing.

Today I didn't have that safety net.

I rotated my head from side to side, checking for other aircraft in the vicinity. Captain Mikey had just assured me that the tower had put a hold on all incoming and outgoing traffic until I'd safely touched down, but I wasn't taking any chances. Better a swivel neck than a broken neck. I took a glance at the sock. No wind to speak of.

Bare tree branches and the green limbs of evergreens in William Land Park and surrounding City College seemed to reach out to scrape the bottom of the plane as I lined up with Runway 2/20.

"Flaps," Captain Mikey said. "Flaps smooth and steady."

I reached for the control lever on the floor and felt a jolt as the flaps positioned themselves under the wing, creating drag and slowing the descent.

"You're doing great. Just line her up and bring her down."

I understood the basic physics behind the landing of an aircraft, putting the plane into a stall a few inches above the ground. But comprehending the logic and being able to actually *do* it are not necessarily the same thing. The gray ribbon of concrete with the row of lights down either side, impossibly tiny at two thousand feet, seemed to rise up, ready to engulf the small plane.

"Take her down steady," Michael commanded.

I tried, I really did. But somehow I managed to flare out six feet or so above the runway. The wheels bounced on the cement and the landing gear screeched in protest.

"Throttle! Throttle!"

I pulled back on the throttle, the equivalent of stomping on the brakes in an automobile.

The plane seemed to be everywhere, skittering in a drunken path down the runway, bobbling all over the place, finally coming to a halt a few yards before the strip of concrete ended at the Bing Maloney Golf Course.

It wasn't exactly smooth and steady, and I was going to have to send my silk blouse to the dry cleaners before I wore it again, but what counted is that I managed to land the thing in one piece.

All that noise and jostling roused Richie from his stupor. He raised his head and looked around in dazed bewilderment, taking in the green field at the end of the runway, the ambulance, and the media vehicles racing in our direction. "Wha the — ?" he moaned.

"Welcome to Sacramento. Please remain seated until the captain turns off the Fasten Seat Belt sign."

I snatched the canvas tote bag, popped open the door, and stumbled from the plane. The bag slipped from my grasp and fell to the concrete, scattering cell phone, wallet, digital recorder, notepad, and scraps of paper. Who cared? I was back on terra firma. I probably would have collapsed, kissed the ground of dear Sacramento, had it not been for the mob scene that engulfed me with hugs, handshakes, cameras, and microphones. Captain Mikey, Glory Lou, Josh, Pete Kovacs.

Pete Kovacs?

"Aren't you supposed to be in Oroville?" I said as I flung myself into his arms.

"You think I'd stay up there after I heard on the radio what was going on? It was pedal to the metal the whole way back to Sacramento."

Captain Mikey and the fellows from the tower were all set to engage in that age-old tradition of tearing off the student's shirt and tacking it up on the bulletin board in the pilots' lounge to commemorate the first solo flight. No way was I going to allow them to strip me down to my skivvies, not with all the news cameras around. Sacrifice my best silk blouse, drenched armpits notwithstanding?

"Here guys, have your fun with this." I tossed them the purple Reginald Fessenden Royal Riding Gain Academy T-shirt.

I let the newspeople have their turn with me as soon as the ambulance sped off to deliver Richie to the emergency room. I noticed the petite figure and smooth black hair of Sapphire Ikeda in the throng, back at work already. Another attempt at keeping busy, I assumed, career as therapy.

"This is a fascinating story! I'd like to continue our interview back at the station," Sapphire said after the other reporters had begun to drift away.

"Love to, but I'm out of time. I go on the air at three."

"That's unfortunate. We were planning to use this as the lead on the five o'clock newscast. 'Local media celebrity pulls off dramatic landing at Executive Airport.' "

I turned to Josh and Glory Lou for guidance.

"TV? The lead on the five o'clock news? Go for it, girlfriend!" Glory Lou gave my arm a squeeze.

"No prob if you're late," Josh said. "I'll keep it under control. It wouldn't be the first time."

"You're on," I said to Sapphire.

I gave instructions to Josh about handling Janice Yount should I not arrive until after the three o'clock start of my show. "Just let her talk about how wonderful her recovery program is, and thank all of her generous donors. No hardball questions, and nothing — I repeat, nothing — about our trip to Footprints Lodge yesterday until I get there. Got it?"

"Got it." He stuffed the tote bag into my hands, pulled out a folded slip of paper from his pocket, and handed it to me. "Peg Waller asked me to pass this along."

I'd almost forgotten about leaving the note on the traffic coordinator's desk the previous evening. I studied the few lines of neat penmanship on the scrap of notepaper that Josh had just given me.

The bit of information just supplied by Peg Waller made it all too obvious who was behind the death of Travis Ikeda-Nyland.

"See you guys back at the station in a little while." I waved in the direction of Josh, Glory Lou, and Pete.

I followed Sapphire Ikeda to her station's van, a gleaming white vehicle with the logo emblazoned in blue, gold, and black on the side and satellite gear sticking from the roof. She helped herself into the driver's seat while I climbed in on the passenger side.

"I'm glad we're going to have a chance to talk," I said to Sapphire after she turned over the engine and began to steer the van off the apron and around the terminal building.

"So am I. This is going to be a terrific story."

"It's about Travis." I fumbled around to vocalize my next thought, unsure how to break it to her.

"Oh?" She signaled to make a right turn onto Freeport Boulevard.

"Why don't you make a stop at the cop shop before we go to the station. What I have to say needs to be shared with Detective Alvarado."

"I don't think that will be necessary."

I flinched at the sound of a male voice from the back of the van and turned to see Gareth Nyland hoisting himself up from the tangle of cables, cords, and duct tape.

"Stick with the plan," he said to Sapphire.

"Right." She pointed the van in a northerly direction, straight up Freeport Boulevard, past the shopping center where Dan Alvarado had his office.

"And you," he said to me. "Hand over the bag."

I hefted the canvas tote bag with its bright "Sharing the Pride" logo and passed it over the seat, giving Gareth my wallet, notebook, recorder, and cell phone.

What else could I do?

He had a gun pressing at the back of my head.

29

"Fine," I said. After all I'd endured today my emotions were numb, way past panic. If anything, I felt an overwhelming tsunami of annoyance. "Go ahead and shoot, mess up your pretty van. Ruin the new car smell. Right in front of all this traffic stuck at Freeport and Fruitridge."

"Don't tempt me." The cold circle of metal bore down against my skull.

"Tell me, what does the *I* stand for?"

"What *I*?"

"Gareth I. Nyland. Travis Ikeda-Nyland. G-I-N and T-I-N, Gin and Tin, your childhood nicknames. You were the anonymous friend who visited Travis last fall down at UCLA and invited him to go out clubbing. You knew it'd be too much temptation for a fragile kid like Travis. Why'd you do it, ruin his life?"

"You'd better watch it with your wild accusations."

"Humor me. What's the *I* stand for?"

"Ivar." Sapphire uttered the name through

lips set in a tense scarlet line. "Ivar Nyland founded the car dealership just after World War II. Gareth is named in honor of his grandfather."

"I'm having trouble understanding your involvement in this," I said to Sapphire. "I know Gareth's your nephew. But for god's sake, he killed your son."

"My son was killed in a random act of violence during a drug deal in McKinley Park." She turned the steering wheel to the left, putting the van onto Fruitridge Road.

"You can't possibly believe that, can you?"

"With all of my heart."

"All I can say is, you'd better hope Markitus Wilson never regains his memory and starts blabbing about what really happened that afternoon. Somehow I don't think you'll be able to buy his silence with a new car. For certain, not his Grandma Iris."

"Shut your pie hole." This from Gareth.

"No, keep talking," Sapphire said. "I want to hear what she has to say."

She tromped on the gas pedal with a chunky-heeled pump through the green light at the intersection with Land Park Drive. Part of me wanted to take Gareth's advice and keep my lips zipped. If he thought I possessed only parts of the puzzle and hadn't pieced together the big picture, he might let me go, maybe even give me back my bag, so I could hail a cab, make it to the station in time to finish the interview with Janice Yount. On the other hand, if I could convince Sapphire of the truth, the two of us might be able to overpower Gareth. I decided to bet my life on the mother.

"It's the old story, greed and jealousy," I said. "As long as Travis played the role of the goof-off party boy, Gareth's position as heir apparent to the Nyland automotive empire was secure. Then Travis surprises everyone by getting his act together. He stops drinking, knuckles down with his studies, starts making noise about becoming involved in the family business, comes up with a brilliant marketing plan."

"What does that prove?" Gareth said.

"You must have gone ballistic when you got wind of that marketing plan that Travis was planning to present to all the big shots at your company retreat. Here's this kid with some innovative, out-of-the-box concepts on how to sell cars, and you're still pushing that tired old 'Save With Ray' campaign."

"Hey, we moved a lot of units with those

commercials. But really, if I'd been so threatened by Travis's presentation like you say I was, why did I let you see it when you barged in last night?"

"Because you had no choice. You didn't find the CD-ROM. Sapphire did while she was cleaning out Travis's apartment. You had to pretend like you'd never seen it before."

"Is that true?" Sapphire said to Gareth. "Travis showed his presentation to you last fall, when he first put it together?"

"Who are you going to believe, your own family or some sleazy talk radio host?"

Sleazy? Now I was starting to build up a good steam of righteous anger. "How's this for sleazy: At first you thought you'd managed to sideline Travis for at least the season by tipping him into backsliding and earning himself a DUI and a trip to Footprints Lodge. But Travis sailed through the program, kept his sobriety pledge, attended AA meetings faithfully. That's when you realized, like it or not, Travis was going to be part of your future, your more-than-equal partner in the day-to-day operation of the Nyland Automotive Group once Ray and Bill go to that big year-end clearance sale in the sky. Unless you managed to take him out of the game permanently and quickly, before the rest of the management team got a hint as to how brilliant Ray Nyland's kid might be."

I paused for breath while Sapphire accelerated, propelling the van up the on-ramp to northbound Interstate 5.

"I don't know why I have to put up with this." Gareth raised his voice in response to the increased thunder of the engine and the surrounding traffic.

"Let her keep talking," Sapphire said. She cut across the far right lanes that would have shunted us off to the Business 80 loop and in the direction of her television station. Instead the van continued to zoom north on I-5. "How do you propose proving that Gareth pulled the trigger in McKinley Park?"

"He wants to set up a scenario that'll look like a drug deal that got out of hand. First he needs a patsy. I'm guessing he met Brenda Driscoll one night at Maury Flamm's skybox at Arco Arena. After all, the Greater Sacramento Automobile Dealers Association is one of Flamm's clients."

"Just great," Gareth said. "Now you're going to point the finger at every person who's ever been a guest in Maury Flamm's luxury suite. You're looking at a mighty big list of high-power suspects."

I ignored the outburst. "Gareth tempts Brenda with the possibility of appearing in a low-budget film, and asks her to recruit another member of the so-called cast. The part calls for a young African-American male, someone who could convincingly role-play the part of a two-bit drug dealer. She thinks of that janitor who's hanging around the dance studio every evening. Markitus Wilson."

"That's all very interesting, but how does that prove I killed my cousin?"

"Everything falls into place that Monday afternoon in McKinley Park. You arrange for Travis to meet you at the park. Maybe you even set out the bait that you're going to start filming one of his television commercials. Meanwhile, Driscoll and Wilson are on their marks, thinking they're rehearsing a scene involving a drug sale, a scene that climaxes with Wilson shooting the dealer. Played by Travis."

"Nobody's going to believe that. An amateur actor thinks an innocent bystander is another member of the cast and shoots him with what he thinks is a prop gun. Only it's the real thing, and this guy who's never touched a gun in his life manages to kill the innocent bystander with just one incredibly lucky shot. What a crock."

"I agree. And after you went to all that trouble."

"See?" He spoke to Sapphire. "I didn't have anything to do with killing my cousin. Even the sleazy talk radio host agrees."

"That's not quite what I'm saying." I didn't dare turn my head, not with that gun poking through my hair, but I did slide my eyes in Sapphire's direction. She kept her lips pressed together and her eyes focused on the heavy freeway traffic through the central city. Past the driver's side window, I caught a flashing glimpse of the Gold Rush–era brick buildings and imitation gaslights of Old Sacramento.

"Gareth held the real gun all along," I said. "When Markitus starting shooting blanks with the prop, Gareth pulled the trigger on the real thing. He figured in the confusion — before Markitus realized Travis wasn't just a good actor and it was real blood, not theatrical makeup, pouring from his chest — he'd take Markitus out as well. Was that part of the plan, Gareth?"

"What plan? The only plan is in your overactive imagination."

"Markitus had a lot more street smarts than you gave him credit for. He understood from the get-go that something was off. Way, way off. So he made a run for it. Tied up traffic for hours on Business 80 armed only with a prop gun. Lucky for you, he took that little dip in the American River. Otherwise, the cops could have tested his hands for gunshot residue and would have come up zero."

"Aren't you forgetting about Brenda Driscoll? If I'm this cold-blooded killer, wouldn't I have 'taken her out,' as you would put it, right there in McKinley Park when I had the chance?"

"You thought you could buy her silence with a new car. Tell me, does Vic Cortese always handle the nitty-gritty of these negotiations for you? Keeping you one step removed from the nasty business of bribery?"

"So Vic Cortese helped an aspiring actress fulfill her dream of owning a new car. What does that prove?"

"The more you thought about it, the more you realized Brenda was a liability as long as she stayed alive, new car or no new car. When you heard my interview with Iris Fontaine, you realized a nosy journalist like me would certainly track down Brenda and convince her to talk. So she had to be eliminated."

And it looked like my name was the next up on Gareth's hit list.

The van veered to the right at the Rich-ards Boulevard exit and hovered at the traffic signal at the foot of the off-ramp. I slid my hand down the side of the door, trying to remain as still as possible and not alert the man with the gun. I fumbled for the door latch.

"Don't even think about it," Gareth said.

The TV van plunged into the industrial depths of Richards Boulevard, past empty tomato canneries, abandoned railroad spurs, and nameless warehouses. This is the part of town to set up a business if you don't want to be easily found or have to deal with NIMBY neighbors. The California State Lottery has its headquarters in a converted warehouse, and the capital city's most noto-rious strip joint, Club Fantasy, makes its neon-splashed home on Richards Boule-vard.

Sapphire turned right onto one of the numbered streets, then left, then right again. She halted in front of an automatic gate and rolled down the window to punch in a series of numbers into the electronic lock. The iron gate swung back. The van crept past a wooden sign. "Stow It." I recog-nized the labyrinth of long, low buildings dotted with roll-up doors, the complex where most of the radio and television stations in the city, including my own, had storage space.

Where no one would think it odd to see a media van cruising the grounds.

And where the cacophony of the heavy metal bands that practiced here would drown out any screams I might make.

"You guys can't be serious," I said. "At least a half dozen people saw me get into this very same van with Sapphire Ikeda back at Executive Airport. They're expecting me back at the station any minute now. If I don't show up, who do you think will be the first person they'll call?"

"Shut up! Just shut up and let me do the thinking!" Gareth gave me a backhanded whack across the top of my head. With that verbal eruption and act of petty violence, I realized Gareth had slipped from the rational calculation of the cold-blooded killer into the frantic desperation of the hunted, and was infinitely more dangerous.

The van coasted to a stop halfway down a parallel row of walk-in storage lockers. "Now what?" Gareth bellowed.

Sapphire twisted in the driver's seat to face her nephew. I traced the glint of a tear making its way down one side of her face and felt a glimmer of hope. "Is it true?" she said in a choked whisper. "Is it true what she says?"

"For god's sake, we went over and over this last night. Travis was in the wrong place at the wrong time and was tragically killed in a random act of drug-related violence. The sooner we can put this all behind us, the better."

"Better for whom?" I said. "It sure as hell won't be better for Travis. Or his mother."

Sapphire wiped her face with the back of her hand and began to ease the van forward. "Gareth's right."

No!

"Family comes first."

"Pretty pathetic example of family values," I said.

"You have no idea what you're talking about," Sapphire said while Gareth continued to yell at me to shut up. "My parents had absolutely nothing when they were released from the relocation camp. They were dirt poor, worked an asparagus farm in the Delta their entire lives. I put myself through college on scholarships and part-time jobs. The Nylands paid for my mother's chemotherapy and stepped in to help when my father was going to lose his land and no one else would give him a loan. When my brother's dot-com went bankrupt, the

Nylands gave him a job. So don't talk to me about family values."

"He! Killed! Your! Son!" I pounded my fist against my thigh between each word.

"Did not!" Gareth howled.

"Where's the proof?" Sapphire said. "All I've heard is a lot of conjecture."

"How come my station's general sales manager came into the control room during the three o'clock hour the afternoon Travis was killed to pull a certain sponsor's spot and substitute another? Out went the clown urging us to 'Save With Ray' with that annoying jingle and the goofy bells and horns. In went twenty-five seconds of classical music, followed by a low-key announcement that this moment of serenity had been sponsored by the Nyland Automotive Group."

"What's the problem?" Gareth said. "It would have been in the worst possible taste to continue with the current advertising campaign, given the situation."

"Three o'clock? You already had a new commercial in the can and were driving it around to the radio stations at three o'clock the day Travis was killed. Yet the police didn't even release the name of the victim to the media until after six. His own mother didn't know until five."

"I was just starting dinner." Sapphire spoke as if she'd just been awakened from a deep sleep. "The five o'clock news was just coming on the television when the phone rang."

"Only one person would have the authority to make the switch — the marketing director of the Nyland Automotive Group. Normally I'm a big believer in planning ahead. But in this case, sorry, Gareth. Not one of your better executive decisions."

The van halted in front of a unit in a far corner of the complex. The roll-up door had already been raised, revealing an empty concrete cavern, roughly eight feet wide and twelve feet deep. Gareth unfastened the sliding side door of the van with a slam, leaped out, and before I could even react, opened the front passenger door and yanked me to the ground. He placed one arm across my neck and crushed me to his chest. With the gun still pointed to my head, he forced me to march to the driver's side, where Sapphire still sat.

"Out." Gareth had to holler to be heard above the ear-busting guitar riffs and drumbeats of the rock band rehearsing in one of the storage units in the next row.

Sapphire responded with a double-take registering pure shock.

"Sorry, auntie, but I know you too well. Your precious little Travis will always mean more to you than family loyalty. And now, thanks to your loud-mouthed friend, you know too much."

Betrayal began to mix with Sapphire's expression of surprise.

"Out, or you get to watch the sleazy talk radio host die."

Jeez, would he quit with the sleazy bit?

"So much for family values," I said as I watched Sapphire climb slowly from the van, teetering in chunky three-inch heels.

"Inside, both of you." He had the gun planted against Sapphire's skull while he continued to confine me against his chest, so close I could inhale the combined odors of male sweat, pine-scented soap, and the hamburger-with-onions that he must have consumed for lunch. For a flabby fellow who looked as if he spent most of his time behind a desk, he had an amazingly strong grip.

Gareth held the gun to Sapphire's head and forced her into the enclosure, dragging me along with him.

I had a sudden vision of the St. Valentine's Day Massacre. Was this his plan, to gun us down against the cement wall, just like Al Capone's henchmen taking out Bugs

Moran's bootleggers? Would they find my body and Sapphire's crumpled to the floor in a pool of blood?

He hurled the two of us against the wall and backed away a couple of feet. "Hands up," he commanded. Sapphire and I exchanged desperate looks while we hesitantly raised our arms. We could rush him, might possibly be able to disarm him. One of us, though, would most certainly end up taking a bullet.

Gareth continued to back away until he reached the roll-up door that made up the fourth wall of the storage unit. The winter sun crept close to the horizon, casting long shadows and turning Gareth into a bulky silhouette. He kept the gun trained on the two of us and put his free hand on the rope door pull. "Bye-bye ladies."

"You can't be serious," I yelled. At this point, my only hope was to distract him until I could think of an escape plan.

"I imagine you'll die of dehydration before you starve. Though maybe you'll get lucky and the temperature will drop below freezing one of these nights. I understand freezing to death is not an unpleasant way to go."

He apparently wasn't planning to shoot us. It was the best news I'd heard since I'd scrambled into Sapphire's van back at the airport.

"What happens when they finally find our bodies? How are they going to explain how two Sacramento media celebrities ended up locked in an empty storage unit?"

"Who cares? Both of your stations rent space out here. You needed to pick up some station coffee mugs. Sapphire wanted to put away the set for the holiday toy drive. You wandered into the wrong unit and accidentally got locked inside. So sad."

Gareth's plan had some merit, I was forced to admit. No bullets, no blood. Thanks to the racket created by the rock bands in the daytime, no one would hear us scream or pound on the door. As for the nighttime, well, there's no place quite so lonely as an industrial district after-hours. The nearest human life would be found a mile or so away inside Club Fantasy, where the bump and grind of the music and the whistles and catcalls of the patrons would drown out our loudest shouts for help.

Needless to say, Gareth had long ago confiscated my cell phone.

"My station will mount an all-out search when I don't turn up this afternoon. Sapphire's too, when she doesn't appear for the five o'clock newscast."

"Let them. How many days — or weeks — will pass before anyone thinks to look here?"

Gareth tugged on the rope. The roll-up door began to slowly descend with a screech of metal. "Keep those hands up, ladies, or I may change my mind and shoot both of you."

I could feel another layer of sweat flooding my armpits. I was still wearing the same outfit I'd donned this morning for the Sharing the Pride breakfast — the silk blouse, wool slacks, black leather jacket, and pumps. That cheap aluminum souvenir pin had kept its place in the top buttonhole of my blouse after all these hours.

Keeping my arms aloft like a good soldier, I dropped my chin to my blouse and felt the rough metallic edge of the pin. I pressed desperately, finally creating enough pressure. The tiny light popped on and began pulsating.

Gareth hesitated, the door halfway down.

One of two things was about to happen. Gareth would investigate the source of the strange little light. Or, he'd just start shooting.

I tensed myself for the sounds of gunfire.

Gareth uttered an oath and released his hold on the rope. The door began to slowly ascend, flooding the cement box with sunlight.

"My global positioning device," I said to Gareth. "Too late — it's already been activated. Even as we speak, it's sending out a signal straight to the PeeDee. They've undoubtedly already pinpointed my location. I'm sure a patrol car will be on its way any minute."

"Let me see that thing." Gareth stomped into the storage unit. He grabbed the front of my blouse, almost tearing the delicate fabric, and studied the shoddy piece of jewelry. He'd let his gun hand drop to his side and stood only inches away from me. Any second now, he'd see that he'd been fooled by a flimsy trinket, a geegaw suitable for a school carnival or the county fair.

I seized the moment and performed the classic knee-to-groin maneuver.

Gareth emitted a howl of pain and doubled over, clutching his privates. The gun clattered to the cement floor.

Mother was right. The old-fashioned strategies really are the best.

Sapphire reacted quickly. While I scooped up the gun, she removed one of her pumps and smashed the chunky heel across Gareth's nose, causing another yelp and a gush of blood. Gareth collapsed onto the floor, sending up a cloud of dust particles that danced in the waning sunlight.

"Keep him covered," I told Sapphire. She crouched over her nephew, the shoe clutched in both hands.

I kept one eye on the storage unit while I tore through the back of the van, searching for the item I knew I'd find without much trouble, almost as common as duct tape in any well-equipped media van.

Heavy-duty cable ties, for keeping miles of cords neat and untangled. Once the plastic tab is placed into the slot and tightened, a cable tie is impossible to separate without a knife or scissors.

They're hardly regulation handcuffs, but until the police arrived with the real thing, they did the job.

30

Of course, the cops wouldn't let me just head back to the station to meet my commitment to a little thing like a radio talk show, no matter how piteously I begged. But they couldn't stop me from using my cell phone. In between answering questions and making statements to the investigators, I managed to call in a series of reports to the on-air studio, where Glory Lou acted as fill-in host.

"Dr. Yount would like to speak with you off the air," Glory Lou said to me during a commercial break.

"I'll just bet she does. Put her on."

"I get the idea you have some sort of issue with Footprints," Janice Yount said into the phone.

"Spying on your clients? Involving them in a medical experiment under false pretenses?"

"It's easy for you to be sanctimonious. You have no idea what we're up against. The costs of running a residential treatment program like Footprints Lodge are enormous. Negative publicity could dry up most of our sources of donor support. Have you considered the consequences if we are forced to close?"

I paced in front of the police tape that stretched across the entrance to Stow It, the cell phone clutched to one ear. The fact is, there was little I could do to develop the story about the implants and the surveillance. The key piece of information was stored in the laptop that I'd stolen from Gavin Pruitt and then broken into with help from Andrew Stoller. In my own way, I'd behaved as unethically as Dr. Yount.

"Here's the deal," I said. "I won't go on the air with anything but positive news about the Footprints Institute. In return, you call a halt to the implant program. You get in touch with all of the clients who've received them, tell them the program has been discontinued, and offer them the chance to have the chip removed by a medical professional. At your expense, of course. You supply me with copies of signed statements from all of your clients attesting to that fact."

"And if I agree to your terms . . . ?"

"Then the story never airs. Unless I have even the slightest inkling you're engaging in more high-tech spying. Then all agreements are off."

I could hear the sounds of heavy breathing from the other end of the phone. "Deal," she said.

Josh pulled up in one of the station's news cars at around four-thirty and beckoned to me from the other side of the crime scene tape. I made a quick survey to make sure no men or women in blue were watching and ducked under the yellow-and-black barricade.

"I found something else you left behind when you spilled your bag all over the runway at the airport." Josh pressed a business card in my hand. Doyle Bollinger.

"He called for you at least three times this afternoon," Josh said. "His last words to me were that you'd better call by five or forget it."

I studied the name and logo in the dim light as if seeing the card for the first time. Then I slowly tore it into tiny bits, placed the scraps in Josh's hand, and folded his fingers over the remains of my big chance at Hollywood.

The cops finally let me go a little after five-thirty. I piled into the news car, too drained from everything I'd been through that day to even think about driving, and let Josh chauffeur me back to the station. I felt myself collapse into the passenger seat in sheer mental, physical, and emotional exhaustion.

"You're a good kid," I heard myself saying to Josh.

"Awww . . ."

"No, really." The red and white lights of a churning river of vehicles surrounded me as the news car merged onto Highway 160 at the peak of the evening commute. These past couple of weeks, I seemed to have attracted an unusually large number of young people with problems into my life: Travis, Chad MacKenzie, Camille, Corey Draper, Markitus Wilson, and poor Brenda Driscoll. That realization filled me with a giddy sense of gratitude toward the more-or-less normal college student sitting next to me.

The voice of Clarrisa St. Cyr spilled from the dashboard radio.

A week ago, I'd asked her to do a reading on me, to see if she could contact the departed spirit of the person on whom I concentrated. I had Travis in mind, but all that fraud of a psychic could conjure up was an image of a grandmother who had never existed.

Because everyone — at least, every rational person — knows you can't communicate with the dead.

She'd claimed to have seen the letters *B*, *N*, and *G*. And a dog, a little white dog with brown spots.

Then I got it. Travis as a boy, cradling a scrappy Jack Russell terrier in that memorial photo album Sapphire had put together.

And what was the dog's name?

Bingo!

About the Author

Joyce Krieg, like Shauna J., is a veteran broadcaster, both on and off the air. Krieg's many awards and honors include being named Professional of the Year by the Sacramento Public Relations Association and being inducted into the Valley Broadcast Legends for working in local radio for more than twenty years. She lives in Pacific Grove, California.